With a Kiss

By Kim Dare

With a Kiss
ISBN # 978-1-910081-27-3

Copyright © Kim Dare 2011

Published by Kim Dare
Edited by Chris Allen-Riley and Shannon Leeper
Cover Art by Kris Norris

First E-book Edition – October 2011
Second E-book Edition – August 2017

First Print Edition – November 2018

Chapter One

Liam didn't stop running when he reached the edge of the pavement. Stumbling off the curb, he raced headlong into the road.

Car horns blared. Headlights blazed around him. Holding up one hand to shield his eyes, Liam spun around, frantically searching for any way to escape the New Year's Eve chaos. He barely heard the angry shouts from the drivers as more and more cars squealed to a stop.

Squeezing between two car bonnets, Liam scrambled toward the opposite pavement. A dense crowd of people immediately closed in around him. The New Year's celebrations had brought everyone onto the streets. It was impossible to run now. All he could do was keep pushing forward, clawing his way a little closer to the hospital with each step he took.

Rain pelted down, soaking into Liam's jeans and plastering his thin white T-shirt to his skin. None of the New Year's revellers seemed to care about the downpour as they hurried toward the firework display due to start on the other side of town.

A group of a dozen men cheerfully forced their way through the crowd. They swarmed around Liam. He flinched away from raised fists and beer bottles as drunken hand gestures swung wildly toward him.

A terrified attempt to back away from one man sent him crashing into another. Twisting around, Liam held up his hands, desperate to pacify. "I'm sorry," he babbled, stumbling away from them all as quickly as he could. "I'm so sorry, I…"

He looked frantically over his shoulder. The crowd

behind him thinned out just enough for him to make his escape. Spinning away from the gang of men, Liam took his chance, turned tail and ran.

The wind whipped at his face as he dodged between the laughing groups of men and women, all of them ready to celebrate and all of them heading in the opposite direction to him. Lifting a hand, Liam swiped at the raindrops running down his face and into his eyes, but he didn't dare stop.

He couldn't stop. He couldn't turn around and calmly follow the crowd toward the firework display.

The hospital and Marcus—those were the only two things he could think about now—the only things that offered him any chance of keeping his sanity through the New Year's Eve celebrations and on into January the first.

Finally, the huge grey building came into view on the opposite side of the road. Liam raced toward it, forcing his shaking legs to keep moving when they threatened to collapse.

Brakes squealed once more. Another set of drivers cursed. Liam didn't even look over his shoulder. His trainers pounded against the tarmac as he threw himself toward the hospital entrance with every scrap of energy he had left.

A security guard stood just to the left of the door. He straightened up and reached for his radio when he saw a mad man hurtling toward him, but Liam had too much momentum to come to a sudden stop. Arms flailing, shoes skidding through the puddles, he finally brought himself to a halt just a few feet from the guard.

The man's eyes narrowed slightly, bushy grey eyebrows almost meeting beneath his water-proof cap. A moment passed, and a slight smile touched his lips. He pressed the button on his radio once more. "Scratch that, Tony. False alarm."

Another man's voice crackled through the radio, too low for Liam to be able to make out the words.

"You're eager tonight, Liam," Mr Clark said, slipping

back into his usual jovial manner as easily as another man might flip a switch.

Liam tried to force a smile. The taste of blood flooded his mouth. He automatically lifted his fingers to his split lip, as he saw the guard's frown return.

"Ran faster than my feet could keep up with, Mr Clark," Liam mumbled.

Mr Clark nodded, but he didn't put any noticeable effort into pretending he really believed that.

Liam dropped his gaze. Edging around the guard, he backed into the hospital. Hunching his shoulders and keeping his head down, he rushed along the deserted corridors, following the path that had become second nature to him over the last few months.

Water pooled around his feet as an elevator carried him up to the third floor. Closing his eyes, he wrapped his arms around his torso. The cold was sinking into him now that he had stopped moving. A shiver danced along his spine as he prayed for the lift to travel faster.

He was just about able to keep on forcing air into his lungs, but he couldn't make his breaths follow anything like a steady rhythm. Panic clawed through his insides, sending more and more adrenaline pumping through his veins until he trembled with it.

Finally, the elevator chimed its arrival at his destination. The doors slid slowly open. The moment there was enough room for Liam to squeeze through the gap between them, Liam hurried out of the lift and along the corridor.

Sister Pritchard's head jerked up as Liam's sodden trainers squeaked against the dull grey flooring. A frown flitted across her forehead as she glanced at the watch pinned to her uniform.

When he reached the nurses' station, that was set halfway down the corridor, Liam looked from Sister Pritchard to the door leading into the private room at the end of the hall and back again.

"Please?" he whispered.

She ran an assessing eye over Liam, taking in every detail as she silently debated the fate of a visitor who seemed completely incapable of abiding by proper visiting hours. Liam held his breath, his grip on his own arms turning white knuckled as he dug his fingertips into his biceps.

Finally, the sister nodded. Relief swept through Liam, damn near washing away the last tiny bit of strength he had left. Somehow, he managed to walk the rest of the way along the corridor.

Reaching out, he wrapped numb fingers around the door handle. In that moment, it was almost impossible for him not to think back to the first time he'd visited that room.

* * * * *

Six months earlier…

"I just talk to him?" Liam looked from the woman behind him, to the sleeping form in the hospital bed and back again.

"That's the general idea," she said, lifting her attention from her clipboard for a moment and glaring at him as if he'd just made a very improper suggestion toward her. "It is what you volunteered to do after all!"

Liam turned back to the slumbering man. "I know, I just…" Well, for one thing, he'd assumed that when he agreed to spend one afternoon a week visiting lonely hospital patients, he'd be talking to someone who was able to talk back.

"If there's a problem," the hospital administrator began, each word more clipped and impatient than the last.

Liam shook his head. "No, it's fine."

One curt nod, and the woman strode away, pulling the door to the private room closed behind her.

4

For several long seconds, Liam stood in the middle of the highly polished floor without the least idea what to do with himself. Pushing his hands deeper into his pockets, he rocked back on his heels and studied the comatose patient.

"Just talk to him," Liam murmured. The words sounded far too loud in the otherwise hushed room. The only other noise that broke the silence was the beep of a heart monitor.

Taking a deep breath, Liam took a step forward, determined to make the best of the situation. "Hi. My name's Liam Bates. I'm a volunteer visitor with the hospital. Do you mind if I sit down?"

To Liam's complete lack of surprise, the coma patient made no response. Pulling up a chair, Liam perched uncomfortably on the edge of the bright red plastic. Hell, he didn't even know what to call the guy. Standing up, Liam peeked out through the small glass aperture in the door. The nurses' station he'd walked past a few minutes before was deserted.

Liam turned back to the room's only other occupant. His attention fell on a wire container hanging from the footboard of the hospital bed, then on the paperwork within it. "I'm...um...just going to look in your records for your name," he said as he crept forward and picked up the file. "Don't worry. I'm won't read any of the confidential stuff or anything. I just want to know what to call you."

The file was well over two inches thick. Liam frowned as he carefully flicked open the cover to examine the first page.

"Marcus Corrigan," he read aloud, before dutifully closing the bulging file and returning it to its proper place without snooping further.

"It's um...it's a nice name," Liam hazarded as he sat down again. "It suits you." It might have been a bloody stupid thing to say, but at least it was true. A handsome name for a very handsome man...

Against all logic, the guy didn't actually appear ill. It looked like he was simply sleeping, as if he might open his eyes at any moment. Pushing that idea away, Liam took the opportunity to study the man's features without any fear that he might be caught.

Long black hair framed his face, standing out in stark contrast to the crisp white hospital pillowcase, but someone had obviously shaved him recently. There wasn't the slightest hint of stubble along his jaw. High cheek bones and an aquiline nose gave the man an almost aristocratic appearance, but his lips were pink and full, just begging to be kissed.

Liam cleared his throat as heat rushed to his cheeks. He was checking out the coma patient. That was just wrong—on so many levels.

"So, um...I guess I'd best tell you a bit about myself, since it seems like we're going to be spending quite a bit of time together." He leaned back in his chair, trying to look casual, confident, and completely at ease, but it was no use. He soon leaned forward again, resting his elbows on his knees as he knotted his fingers together.

For a full minute, Liam stared down at his intertwined knuckles. "I guess there's not really much to say. I'm kind of boring."

He glanced up at the sleeping patient through his lashes. Marcus... Mr Corrigan... No, Liam finally decided. There was no need to be stand-offish. It was much better to call him Marcus.

Marcus didn't look bored. There was no expression whatsoever on his face.

Liam chuckled slightly to himself. "Well, at least I don't have to worry about you falling asleep on me." He took another deep breath. "Okay, let's try this again. I'm Liam Bates. Twenty-eight years old. I used to work just across the road from here. I waited tables in the cafe opposite the hospital for about three years, but now that we've moved in together, Ralph doesn't like me to..."

Liam's eyes opened very wide as he mentally cursed himself. The last thing he needed in his life right then was some homophobic jerk who…

His thoughts slowly faded away as he blinked at Marcus's sleeping form.

There wasn't going to be any visible reaction to anything he said. Liam looked over his shoulder. No one else was in earshot.

"I guess it really doesn't matter if you know I'm gay, does it? It's not like you're going to make a complaint or ask for a different visitor." Liam pushed a hand through his hair, disordering the mousey brown strands. "You know, it's lucky you probably can't hear a word I'm saying, because I'm making a complete balls-up of this visitor thing, aren't I?"

Rising from the chair again, Liam strode across to the window. It practically filled the wall on that side of the room, from waist height all the way up to the ceiling. He looked out over the gardens surrounding the hospital. It was a nice view. It was a pity the patient wasn't in any condition to admire it.

"Anyway, like I was saying, Ralph asked me to hand in my notice at the cafe. He's got a good job. And he's right, there's no need for me to wait tables for a pittance. I just…"

Liam frowned. Turning his back on the view, he leaned against the window sill and pushed all those silly thoughts out of his head. "I should be counting my blessings, right?" he said. "A rich boyfriend who wants to spoil me is a good thing!" Liam forced a smile, but maintaining it for even a few seconds made his face ache.

Marcus made no comment.

"And he's a good guy too," Liam pressed on. "He doesn't screw around on me or anything like that. And he's working on his temper, so—" He froze with his hand halfway to his right cheek as the door swung open.

A young, red-headed nurse backed into the room, pulling a trolley full of medications and dressings along after her.

"Hi."

The nurse twirled around, knocking over several of the medicine bottles on her trolley as she backed away. Her eyes went to Marcus for a moment, before swinging wildly toward Liam. "Bloody hell—for a moment I thought he'd actually woken up!" Leaning back against the bland cream paintwork next to the door, she patted her chest as if trying to still a racing heart.

"Sorry, I'm one of the volunteer visitors," Liam began to explain.

The nurse waved him into silence. "Not your fault. Our Mr Corrigan here has always given me the heebeegeebees. There's something about vampires that just makes me want to cover my neck whenever I'm around them," she added, the Irish note in her accent softening as she pulled herself together.

"Vampires...?" Liam echoed.

The nurse finally seemed to recover enough to step away from the wall without fainting. "They didn't tell you? Well now, isn't that typical? They're supposed to, you know?" she added, as she turned the trolley around and pushed it closer to Marcus's bed.

The routine was obviously well established. While her hands moved on automatic, the nurse's words continued to flow without pause. "Regulations state that everyone who has any contact with a patient has to be informed of their species. Unless the patient is human of course—no one minds humans."

"He's a..." Liam stared at Marcus as if he was seeing him for the first time.

Of course he knew all about vampires, who didn't? And, yes, he had always been aware in a very general sort of way that he probably spoke to a dozen people who needed to drink blood every day, but that wasn't the same as actually knowing the man he stood next to had fangs.

Liam watched in silence as the nurse—Sophie Roberts,

according to the hospital ID clipped to her uniform—fussed around, taking down the empty IV hanging from the metal stand next to Marcus's bed and replacing it with a bag of blood.

A bag of...

"Is that blood?" Liam took a step back, pressing his backside against the window ledge, as if the stuff might leap out of the bag and attack him.

The nurse looked over her shoulder. "It is indeed. Animal blood rather than human, of course—bovine to be exact."

"Oh..."

"Can't let the poor little parasite starve to death while he's too ill to be any danger to anyone, can we?" Nurse Roberts asked. She picked up a metal bowl from the trolley and placed it on Marcus's bed.

Lurking uncertainly on the other side of the room, Liam watched her deftly remove a bandage from the vampire's hand and toss it in the bowl. Blood stained that part of the fabric that had been wrapped around the top most part of Marcus's index finger.

Quickly cleaning the wound, the nurse replaced the dressing. Her every movement made it clear she wanted to have as little physical contact with Marcus as possible.

Within a minute, she'd bustled back out of the room, once more leaving Liam on his own with the sleeping man...with the sleeping vampire. Stepping forward, Liam took great care to make no sound, to keep all his movements calm and controlled, as if he might rouse the vampire to attack if he weren't very careful.

He lowered himself into his chair with the same intense attention to detail, not quite able to drag his eyes away from the bag of blood hanging above him. Animal blood, he reminded himself. It was nothing to be scared of. But at the same time it became almost impossible to stop his eyes following the intravenous line down to where the needle disappeared into Marcus's arm.

Liam glanced at Marcus's face for a moment, then back to the blood supply draining steadily into his vein. Heat rushed to his cheeks.

"Sorry. I..." Liam cleared his throat. "I guess I didn't handle that very well, did I? I'm not usually so... I mean, I don't have any problem with vampires. You're just like us, only you need to drink blood occasionally, right?"

Marcus said nothing.

Liam ran his hand down his face. Damn, but it was a good thing the guy was completely oblivious to his presence. Any conscious man would have probably given him one hell of a back hander. Liam's hand automatically strayed toward his cheek. The bruise was gone now. It had barely even been worth mentioning from the start, but it had completely faded away now, and...

"The nurse made it sound like you've been here a while," Liam blurted out, desperate for any topic of conversation that would distract him from a day he'd much rather forget. "Is this something that often happens to vampires?" He frowned slightly. "No. Stupid thing to say. That's like people thinking any time a gay man is ill, it has to be HIV. Although—"

Liam cleared his throat, only just keeping back a really bad joke about fang shaped condoms and safe biting. He shook his head at himself, but at the same time, his lips quirked into a small smile. "I have a really bad sense of humour," he confessed, dropping his voice to a whisper, as if sharing a secret with a good friend.

His expression faltered as it occurred to him that he was probably speaking to the one and only person on the planet who really could be trusted to keep any and all secrets someone shared with him.

Marcus Corrigan wasn't going to rush off to Ralph, carrying tales. Liam was safe there.

"So, um, where was I?" he tried again, finally able to

relax into his chair a little. "I was going to tell you about me, right?"

* * * * *

Liam closed the door leading into the private room behind him and leaned back against it. He thought about shutting his eyes in an effort to hide a little bit more thoroughly from the world, but the sight before him was far too beautiful to waste.

Marcus lay exactly as he always did, right in the centre of his hospital bed, his long black hair trailing over his pillow.

Liam took one more deep breath and let it out very slowly. There was something amazingly reassuring about entering a room and knowing exactly how the man in there was going to react to his presence, something gloriously safe about knowing that the man in front of him would never lash out in his direction, no matter how badly he screwed up.

"Hi, Marcus." Liam whispered the words so quietly he could barely even hear them himself. Clearing his throat, he looked up at the bright florescent lights set into the ceiling and tried to summon up the will to make another attempt at it.

It was no use. Speaking wasn't in him right then. He wasn't sure he even had the strength to take another breath. Adrenaline ebbed away rapidly, allowing Liam's pain to flow back into his body and make itself felt in every joint and sinew.

His frantic dash across the city had inflicted its own blows, apparently aimed at all those places where Ralph's fists hadn't landed that night. Very slowly, Liam bent his knees and let himself slide down the door, until he sat, curled into a tight ball on the hard floor.

Folding his arms on top of his drawn up knees, he rested his forehead against his damp forearms. For a long time, he just sat. Unable to think, unable to move, Liam merely existed.

11

Time passed. Liam had no idea how long he remained on the floor just inside Marcus's door, but, eventually, some tiny part of his mind that was a little more ready to face the world than the rest of his psyche, began to focus on the steady beeps emanating from one of the machines by Marcus's bed.

Liam slowly lifted his head. For a few seconds, everything remained a blur. Blinking his eyes, Liam swiped at the drops of rain lingering on his lashes with the back of his hand.

The beeps continued, one every second, one for every beat of Marcus's heart, just as they had ever since Liam first met him. The News Year's Eve festivities hadn't made any difference to Marcus. The vampire hadn't gone out drinking with friends from work; he hadn't come home spoiling for a fight.

Liam swallowed rapidly. There was something incredibly pathetic about sitting alongside a man in a coma and being jealous of his life. Pulling himself to his feet, Liam slowly crossed the room until he stood next to Marcus's bed.

"Have you had a good day?" he asked.

No answer was forthcoming, but Liam was already used to filling in Marcus's side of their chats.

"Sarah was on duty today, wasn't she? Did she tell you her plans for tonight?" Liam managed a small smile for the picture that formed in his head. "I bet they were wild!" He couldn't imagine the stunning blonde nurse from the day shift doing anything that *wasn't* wild.

Gradually, Liam felt even that mild trace of a cheerful expression fade from his face.

"You've probably guessed that my plans didn't exactly go the way I hoped they would," he mumbled, as he fidgeted with the edge of Marcus's bed sheet.

Whoever had washed Marcus's hair that day had left one dark lock trailing across his forehead. Liam reached out and stroked it back from the vampire's face without even thinking about the gesture.

Marcus was the type of man who would want to look his best at all times. Sighing quietly to himself, Liam stepped away from the bed and paced over to the window. "It's stopped raining," he said, before glancing at his watch. "And it's three minutes to twelve. The weather men were right for once. It's cleared up just in time for the firework display. That's good…"

Rubbing at his bare arms, trying to warm them up, Liam couldn't help but wonder if Ralph had gone to one of the displays on his own, after Liam had run out on him. A shiver traced its way down Liam's spine. He'd have hell to pay for that when he went home.

Crossing the room, Liam peeked through the little window in the door leading out into the corridor. No one was within view. Ralph hadn't guessed where he'd fled to and come after him.

Liam ran his hand down his face. Blood from his cut lip smeared on his fingers. He absentmindedly wiped it on his wet jeans. He was just being stupid now. Ralph hadn't followed him to the hospital in all the time they'd been together. He wasn't going to start now.

Liam glanced at his watch again. Pinning a smile to his lips, he made his way back to Marcus's bed and picked up the ear phones attached to the hospital radio system. Putting one ear bud in Marcus's ear, he slipped its companion into his own ear.

They were only just in time. The chimes on Big Ben were already counting down the last moments of the year. Under his breath, Liam counted down the seconds along with them, his eyes never leaving the sleeping vampire's face. "Three…Two…One…"

Marcus didn't join in. He didn't smile, or wish Liam a happy New Year as the noisy celebrations were relayed to them over the radio. He didn't turn his head when the first firework whistled into the air not far away and pretty colours exploded in the night sky outside the window either.

"Happy New Year, Marcus."

Liam's brain, pounded by both fists and panic, packed its bags and slipped away for an impromptu holiday.

It was good luck to welcome the New Year in with a kiss, and God knew that Liam needed all the luck he could get. Unable to think of a single reason why it was a bad idea to do so, Liam leaned down and pressed his lips very chastely against Marcus's mouth.

A frown spread across Liam's forehead as he straightened up. Against all logic, he was almost sure he'd felt Marcus's tongue brush against the cut on his lower lip as they kissed.

Chapter Two

Blood.

For the first time in three years, the taste of it danced on Marcus Corrigan's tongue as an impossibly soft mouth brushed against his lips. It was only the tiniest drop, but it was real, human blood, and it was enough.

The droplet sparked frantic messages that raced through Marcus's veins faster than sound, or light, or even thoughts could travel. There was blood to be had. It was his for the taking. The call to arms bounced off nerve endings and ricocheted through Marcus's joints, reactivating muscles that had lain dormant for so many long, painful months.

Marcus's tongue slipped out to taste the kiss — his first voluntary movement since he'd been admitted to the hospital. His taste buds brushed against a cut on the boy's lower lip.

The bastard had hit him again.

If Marcus hadn't been sure of it before, the split in Liam's skin confirmed all his worst fears.

A shocked little noise caressed Marcus's mouth. Liam jerked away from him.

No! That couldn't be allowed to happen.

It was far from the first time Marcus's brain had demanded that his limbs reach out and catch hold of the boy. The only difference that night was that his body actually seemed willing to obey those orders.

Marcus's fingers twitched. His hand slowly rose from the bed sheet. He fumbled blindly at empty air until he finally found Liam's arm. He wrapped his fingers around the boy's wrist — his thumb and forefinger meeting easily on the other side.

"What the — ?"

Panic filled Liam's voice. He tugged at Marcus's hold on him, but mere human strength was no competition for a vampire's grip.

Little by little, Marcus managed to remember exactly how a man went about prying open his eyelids. Harsh white light stabbed at his senses, vicious as a knife.

Growling his displeasure, Marcus squinted up at Liam, desperate to catch his first glimpse of the man he'd been picturing in his mind's eye for months. All he could make out was a blur. He forced his eyes to open completely. Pure survival instinct kicked in then, and made him lift both his hands to shield his eyes from the light.

Liam's wrist slipped from Marcus's grip. A shadowy outline backed away from the side of his bed.

With depth charges still exploding through re-activating joints and nerve endings, Marcus didn't have energy to waste on complex thought processes. All he could do was react the way nature intended a vampire to react when his prey was trying to escape.

The scent of Liam's blood insisted Marcus play his part in the chase. After all the time he'd spent unable to do anything but listen to his visitor babble away at his bedside, he'd be damned if he'd let him withdraw now. Other muscles finally sprang into action.

Barely aware of wires and leads being yanked and torn from his body, Marcus threw himself out of the bed. Pain shot through his feet as his soles hit the floor. Tendons screamed in agony. Joints exploded as if a sledge hammer were being brought down on each one in turn.

Liam stumbled backward. Marcus's fingers brushed against the boy's T-shirt only for the thin material to slip from his grasp as Liam jerked away.

Gradually, the world swam into focus. Marcus saw a clear image of Liam for the first time, and he saw the way the boy was scrabbling at the handle of the door leading out of the room too. A clumsy step brought Marcus within arm's reach of him.

Catching hold of Liam's shoulder, Marcus jerked him away from the door.

And, as suddenly as Marcus's ability to stand had returned to him, it vanished again. His knees buckled. His muscles battled to keep him upright, but it was a war they were always destined to lose.

Gravity dragged Marcus unstoppably toward the floor. He instinctively tightened his grip on Liam. The boy looked over his shoulder. His eyes opened very wide as their gazes met. Twisting around as if in slow motion, he opened his arms to catch Marcus, as if he really believed there was any way in hell he'd be able to support a man twice his size.

The room spun around them both, walls rising rapidly on all sides as the floor rushed up to greet their flailing limbs. Marcus landed hard on the cold ground. Pain flared in his shoulder and quickly spread through his entire body. Liam tumbled down half next to Marcus and half on top of him.

With what little strength he had left, Marcus tightened his grip on Liam's T-shirt—determined to maintain his hold on the boy, even if he couldn't keep his own balance.

Liam's body was pressed against Marcus's bare chest. His hands were resting neatly on Marcus's shoulders. That was all fine. But Liam's eyes were full of panic. Not fine.

"Safe," Marcus tried to say, but his throat howled in agony as he tried to force words through it.

Liam didn't seem to understand the word. His gaze travelled rapidly over Marcus's face as if he was desperately trying to get a read on him and work out how to protect himself.

"You're safe," Marcus tried again. His vocal cords still weren't his to command. His voice didn't sound anything like he remembered it. There was no strength to it, no certainty. A frown creased Marcus's forehead.

Dropping his gaze to Liam's throat, he saw the boy's

Adam's apple bob as he tried to swallow down his nerves. His jugular pulsed right next to it.

Blood. Fresh and delicious, and right there. All he'd have to do was pull Liam's neck down a few inches and he could take all he wanted from him. Liam wouldn't be able to stop him. Predatory instincts howled inside Marcus, but he shoved them away.

"Safe. Understand?" he pushed. That was important. Liam wanted to feel safe. If all his babbling had told Marcus anything at all, it was that Liam wanted to feel safe more than anything else in the world.

Liam didn't answer. He wasn't even looking at Marcus. All his attention was on the door leading out into the hospital corridor.

Marcus frowned as a loud banging sound registered in his senses for the first time. He followed Liam's gaze up to the door. Someone was hammering on the other side of it, trying to force it open. It jerked against Marcus's bare skin, hitting into his shoulder over and over again, but whoever was trying to get in wasn't strong enough to move him.

Liam pushed at Marcus's chest, trying to get up and scramble away from him.

"No." Marcus lost all interest in the door. Tugging at Liam's sodden T-shirt, Marcus pulled him back down.

Their eyes met. "Please don't tell them."

Marcus's frown deepened as he fought to make sense of the words.

"Please don't tell them that I kissed you," Liam whispered, urgently. "I... They'll... I'm sorry, I know I shouldn't have..."

Marcus somehow managed to summon the energy to lift his free hand and press his fingers clumsily against Liam's mouth. "Not mad," he forced out. His voice was still thin and raspy, but it was finally starting to sound a little more like he remembered it being three years ago.

"You're not?" Liam's eyes opened very wide as if he'd

never heard anything so shocking in his life.

Marcus's lips curved into a smile. He didn't even need to order them to do that. The muscles remembered how to form the expression entirely on their own.

The boy really was charming. Perhaps not as pretty as Marcus had pictured him, but he was just as easily shocked as Marcus had known he'd be, and his blood still called to Marcus as strongly as ever.

Liam looked up at the door again.

"They won't hurt you," Marcus promised, quietly impressed with himself for managing to say something that sounded suspiciously like a whole sentence.

He stroked his fingertips over the cut on Liam's lip. The scent of the blood made Marcus's teeth ache and his veins plead with him to feed. A bruise was forming on Liam's temple too. His blood was pooling just beneath his skin— what a criminal waste.

"I think you're freaking out some of the nurses," Liam said.

Marcus didn't bother to offer any comment on that. Who gave a damn about the bloody nurses?

Liam nibbled on his bottom lip, right next to the split. "I...I'd like to get up now, if you don't mind?" he asked, cautiously.

Getting up... Marcus mentally cursed—the boy might as well have asked him to leap from the roof of the hospital and fly. He had no idea how the hell he could accomplish such a complicated manoeuvre as getting up, until he'd had a proper feeding.

"Maybe I could help you back to your bed?" Liam offered. "And we could let the nurses in?"

Marcus's shoulders tried to tense at a mere human thinking that he couldn't get up on his own, but the energy wasn't there. It wouldn't be there until he'd fed, and the nurses would be able to supply him with blood until Liam could offer his freely.

Marcus reluctantly nodded his willingness to grant Liam's request. "You should be checked over," he said, his attention once more straying back to Liam's bloody lip. Yes, the boy needed to be checked over and cleaned up, before Marcus gave in to the temptation to feed from him no matter what Liam's views on that were.

"Me?" Liam asked, as he pulled himself up into a kneeling position at Marcus's side.

"Bastard hit you again."

All the colour drained out of the boy's face. "You...?"

"Heard every word," Marcus finished for him.

Liam pulled away, scrabbling backward on the floor as if *Marcus* was the man who knocked him to the ground, and kicked him while he was down, every damn time he had a drink.

"I... You... I..." Liam sat on the floor at the foot of the hospital bed, wide-eyed, with his hair dripping wet.

Marcus brushed a hand against his own chest. He was damp now too.

"I'm sorry," Liam whispered. A shiver ran through him. He was soaked through to the skin.

Marcus lifted a hand and held it out toward the boy. "You offered to help me back to my bed."

Just as Marcus suspected, the reminder brought Liam hurrying back to his side, just like the good little sub he was so blatantly cut out to be.

It should have been the other way around. Marcus should have been the one supporting the younger, weaker man. He knew that, in a part of his soul that went even deeper than his desire for blood. He was the one who should have all the strength, who should be offering to help and heal his new submissive. The fact that their roles were reversed was enough to send a wave of familiar anger coursing through him.

Vampires weren't designed to be helpless. They were designed to feed.

As Liam pulled him awkwardly to his feet, Marcus reached out and put his hand on the door, keeping it closed in the face of the hospital staff a little while longer. His gaze homed in on Liam's neck. Everything would be so simple, so easy, if he took just a little from the boy.

Marcus could almost taste Liam's blood filling his mouth. It was so easy to imagine the hot sweet liquid caressing his throat as he swallowed it down. Every cell in his body ached, crying out for the energy and the pleasure that blood would bring with it.

Lifting his gaze to meet Liam's eyes, Marcus swallowed rapidly.

Liam blinked and seemed to refocus in on the world around them. He dropped his gaze but remained close, allowing their bodies to brush against each other. As scared as he obviously was, Liam's desire to help and serve another man won out. He slid his arm cautiously around Marcus's naked body.

Marcus somehow found the strength to lift his arm and allow the boy into his space. Liam took hold of the wrist resting on his shoulder, as he turned within Marcus's embrace.

The moment Marcus stepped away from the door, all hell broke loose. A few more stumbling steps forward under Liam's guidance and Marcus was able to half sit, half collapse onto the hospital bed. His head was spinning. His stomach turned over from the supreme effort of sitting upright without anything to support him.

Catching hold of Liam's hand to stop his retreat, Marcus saw the panic in his eyes as noise and confusion filled the room.

Marcus raised his other hand. "Enough!"

The word brought blessed silence down around them. Marcus dropped that hand and turned his head to look at each member of the crowd packed into his room in turn. They were all staring at him with the same dumbfounded expression in their eyes, as if they'd never seen a vampire wake up before.

As much as he longed to chase them all out, Marcus pushed that desire down. "One doctor and one nurse can stay. The rest of you, leave."

There was much frantic whispering by the door. Every word of it would have been loud enough for Marcus's vampiric senses to pick up, if he'd actually given a damn about anything they were saying. As it was, he didn't bother.

Finally, two people separated themselves from the rest of the group.

The doctor — a Dr Blackhill according to his name tag — turned to face Liam as the others left. "If you'd like to wait outside while we examine Mr Corrigan," he began.

"He stays here."

The doctor looked from Marcus to Liam and back again. Squaring his shoulders, he tilted his chin up. "If you don't release him, then security —"

"Won't be any more of a match for a vampire than any other human," Marcus cut in.

The doctor faltered. His body language retreated. His hands rose in a conciliatory little gesture. "If you need to feed then we can arrange for —"

"I don't want you to get me a blood whore. I want you to check his injuries and make sure he's not seriously hurt. If you're not capable of that, go and find a doctor who is."

The room fell silent. Marcus didn't have to turn his head to see how quickly Liam's anxiety levels were skyrocketing. He could practically feel the panic emanating from him.

A nurse stepped forward.

Marcus glanced at her name tag. Jenny Trent. Her expression was wary, but her movements had a determination about them. She had a confidence that the others who entered the room with her had lacked. "Hi, Liam."

"Hi."

Marcus watched her run an assessing gaze over Liam

before turning her attention back to him.

"He needs dry clothes. I'm going to open the door and ask one of the other nurses to fetch him some clean scrubs and a towel."

Yes, dry clothes. He should have thought of that. Marcus nodded his permission to the nurse.

Rather than rushing to do his bidding, she looked at the floor by the bed. "Your IV fell out. I'll ask for another bag of blood to be—"

"Human," Marcus said.

Jenny opened her lips to speak, but the doctor got there first. "It's hospital policy not to waste our limited human blood supply on—"

"Would you rather I feed from you?" Marcus cut in.

"What! Who do you think you're—?" the doctor began to bluster.

"I am going to feed in the next few minutes," Marcus said. "It will be on human blood. From a bag or from your neck, I don't care which."

*

The room fell eerily silent. Still standing right next to Marcus, Liam was suddenly acutely aware of every beat of his own heart. Rumour had it that vampires could hear a human pulse from miles away, that they could home in on whoever they wanted to feed on and...

Liam closed his eyes and did his damnedest to remain calm. There was nothing to be afraid of. It wasn't exactly the first day he'd wondered if he wouldn't be better off dead. Perhaps it would be easier if Marcus did feed from him. It was supposed to be a pleasant way to go.

He was vaguely aware of Jenny going to the door and speaking to someone on the other side of it, but Liam couldn't make his mind focus well enough to pay attention to details. It was as if the whole world was full of cotton wool. The air was dense and fluffy. Movements had to be slow. Thoughts were even slower, as they too fought their way through the soft white fog.

Liam remained next to Marcus, but he wasn't really present in any meaningful sense of the word. Marcus was awake. He'd heard every syllable. Liam wasn't ready to deal with a third bombshell.

"The hospital has rules for a reason!"

Every muscle in Liam's body tensed as the doctor's yelling suddenly pushed its way into his mind. He flinched away from Dr Blackhill, knowing what kind of pain angry voices usually led to.

Turning his head, he looked instinctively toward Marcus.

The vampire sat calmly on the edge of his bed, apparently unconcerned by the fact he was still stark bollock naked.

Anger burned in Marcus's eyes. It was impossible to imagine that the fact he was in hospital made him any less dangerous. Just because he could barely stand, that didn't make him any less bloodthirsty. Hell, after three years, he had to be more desperate to feed than ever.

Liam stared at the pure fury in Marcus's expression for several long seconds, unable to move, unable to think, as trapped as any rabbit in the headlights could ever have been.

Marcus's attention was all on Dr Blackhill, until, without any warning, it swung around to Liam. The vampire's eyebrows drew closer together. His expression mellowed slightly. "Everything's fine, Liam. This is nothing you need to worry about."

Liam found himself nodding, even though he wasn't entirely sure what he was agreeing with. "Can I...can I help you properly back into bed?" he asked, cautiously.

Their gazes met. Marcus seemed to think about it for a long time before he gave a curt nod. Liam wasn't really sure how to help him. It seemed like he did little more than fuss around the edges of the bed, straightening the blankets, but Marcus let out what sounded suspiciously like a relieved little sigh as he lay back. Liam knew he'd been right to ask then. Marcus was exhausted.

As he rested his head back against the pillow and closed his eyes, Marcus was instantly transformed back into the man that Liam had become so familiar with over the last few months. Without thinking about it, Liam pushed Marcus's hair back from his face, the same way he had so many times in the past.

It was all Liam could do not to leap away from the bed when Marcus opened his eyes again.

Liam's hand went to his own mouth. His lips still tingled from the kiss.

The sound of the door opening behind him made Liam glance over his shoulder. He saw a set of scrubs and a bag of blood being handed to Jenny. Just a moment later, the scrubs were placed in his hands.

"You know where the en-suite is," Jenny said.

Liam wasn't sure why he felt as if he had to look to Marcus for permission to leave the room, but he didn't take a single step until Marcus had nodded to him.

As he closed the door in the far corner of the room, Liam dropped his head forward and rested his temple against the woodwork.

He'd heard it all. Marcus had actually been listening to him the whole time. Liam closed his eyes very tightly and ignored the way his head throbbed in response. A shiver ran down his back and called him back to more immediate concerns.

Quickly stripping off his wet clothes, Liam picked up a towel and rubbed vigorously at his skin, trying to warm himself up, as much as dry himself off. Skirting around sore spots as much as possible, he hurriedly finished up with the towel and pulled the scrubs on.

His ribs called him an idiot for rushing. The sense of

foreboding he felt at leaving Marcus all alone with people who were practically strangers to him, didn't care what his ribs had to say.

As soon as he was covered, Liam stepped back into the hospital room. Everyone promptly stopped talking. Liam looked from one face to another and finally to the hook on the stand alongside Marcus's bed, where the new IV of human blood should have been hanging.

Nothing.

Liam frowned slightly. There had definitely been a bag of blood delivered. He lowered his gaze and spotted an empty IV bag on the floor near the side of Marcus's bed.

Stepping forward, Liam picked it up. The bag was empty, but it was definitely the one that had contained human blood. It now harboured two puncture marks, about an inch and a half apart. Something had sliced cleanly through the toughened plastic. There wasn't even a residue of blood remaining. It had been…drained…completely…dry…

Liam's thoughts slowed down until they moved like treacle being poured from a great height. Doing his best not to let anyone see the way his hands shook, Liam walked across to the medical waste bin in the corner of the room and dropped the empty bag into it as if it were just another bit of litter.

"Isn't there something you should be doing?"

Liam looked across to Marcus, but the vampire wasn't talking to him.

"I told you he needed to be checked out. Don't just stand there," Marcus snapped at the doctor.

Dr Blackwell turned to Liam. His expression was completely blank, but Liam had heard enough gossip to know Dr Blackwell by reputation. He had no interest in treating anyone who wouldn't get his name into a medical journal.

Examining a vampire who'd just came out of a coma was exactly his kind of thing. Dealing with a few scrapes and bruises would be a waste of his time and skill.

"What happened?" Dr Blackwell asked, his boredom barely concealed by a thin veneer of professionalism.

Liam looked in every possible direction bar the doctor's face. Shrugging slightly, he wrapped his arms around his body. Even with the dry clothes, he was still chilled down to the bone.

"I didn't do anything. He just woke up," Liam mumbled.

"And that was when he hit you?" Dr Blackwell asked.

Shocked into looking the doctor in the eye, Liam opened and closed his mouth several times, but no words emerged.

"No," Jenny said, from his left. "The bruises were from before you got to the hospital, right?"

Liam turned to her, but he still couldn't make words happen.

"Honey, you only ever come here outside regular visiting hours when he's been drinking," Jenny said, very softly.

Feeling the heat rush to his cheeks, Liam dropped his gaze to the floor and let it stay there.

A moment passed. Dr Blackwell cleared his throat. "Let's see what damage has been done."

It was, well, it was the kind of examination a doctor gave someone who'd been beaten up by his boyfriend. Liam knew the routine well enough. He had all the pat answers lined up in his head and went through them on rote, trying not to care that Marcus was on the other side of the room and could hear every word he said.

Liam closed his eyes for a moment. It was pointless for him to try to keep secrets now. Marcus had heard it all—every stupid confession, every pathetic little admission. Liam's eyes were still closed and he was still cursing himself for being so stupid, when the exam came to an end and Dr Blackwell stepped away.

"Well?" Marcus demanded.

Liam blinked open his eyes.

Dr Blackwell peered down his nose at him. "Nothing serious. His ribs are bruised, not broken. His lip and his other bruising will heal on its own. The only treatment is rest..." His words slowly faded away.

Marcus didn't say a word, but Liam felt the temperature in the room drop. He obviously wasn't impressed with the doctor's answer.

"But I suppose I could prescribe some painkillers and some anti-inflammatories," Dr Blackwell added quickly. "They'll keep him more comfortable while the injuries heal."

Marcus turned to Liam. "Come here." His voice was so different compared with when he spoke to the doctor; it could easily have been mistaken for coming from a different person.

It never occurred to Liam to try to disobey. He stepped forward.

"I'm fine," he whispered. "I really don't need anything. If I wasn't so clumsy then..."

Marcus pressed his fingertips lightly against Liam's mouth to silence him. "You can both go now," he informed the doctor and nurse, never once breaking eye contact with Liam.

When the door had closed behind them, Marcus dropped his hand back to the bed. "It's far too late for lies."

Liam swallowed rapidly, but didn't try to speak. He stared down at where Marcus's hand rested on the sheet. Every line of Marcus's body seemed different now that he was awake. It was impossible for Liam to put his finger on what the difference was, but ever since he'd fed —

"Look at me, Liam."

Liam found himself closing his eyes instead.

"You're not going back to his house tonight."

Liam's gaze snapped up to meet Marcus's as shock made him open his eyes. "I should..."

Marcus shook his head and Liam's ability to speak evaporated.

"You'll stay here tonight."

It sounded so much like a statement of fact, Liam had no idea how to contradict it. He glanced at the chair by the side of the bed. Even the uncomfortable moulded plastic looked tempting.

"Ralph can be dealt with in the morning," Marcus said.

Liam glanced back towards Marcus. Ralph probably wouldn't even notice he was gone. And he'd have hell to pay when he saw Ralph next, anyway. The chances of him staying at the hospital displeasing Ralph even more were low.

"I want you to stay."

Liam met Marcus's eyes.

Marcus wanted him there. As soon as that fact registered inside Liam's head, everything else seemed far less important. He nodded and took a step back toward the chair.

Marcus's hand was instantly wrapped around Liam's wrist. "Where are you going?"

Liam waved his free hand toward the chair. "I... Do you mind if I sit down?" Suddenly it was obvious that he should have asked before taking such a liberty. Heat rushed to his cheeks at being caught out on such bad manners on top of everything else.

"You can't sleep on that. You'll lie here, next to me."

"What?" Liam automatically tried to take a step back, but the grip around his wrist didn't yield in the slightest.

"You'll sleep next to me," Marcus repeated.

Liam looked at the bed Marcus lay in as if he'd never seen it before. There was no logical reason why he should agree to do any such thing, except that he wanted to. Liam looked at Marcus's grip on his wrist. It was strong, but it was careful, too. His grip didn't hurt, it just wrapped around him, making him feel strangely safe and protected.

"What would the doctors and nurses think?" Liam said.

Marcus paused for a moment. Liam was sure that Marcus checked whatever his first response would have been, but when he finally spoke, Liam couldn't have been more surprised.

"They'll probably assume that, after so long trapped in my sleep, I was reluctant to sleep alone tonight."

Liam met Marcus's eyes. There wasn't even a hint of emotion on his face, but Liam was sure that meant nothing. He'd always known that Marcus would be good at hiding his pain if he ever woke up.

"I..." Liam nodded. "Okay." There was no way he could say anything else.

Marcus carefully shifted himself across to the far side of the narrow hospital bed.

Well aware that he should be putting up far more of a protest, Liam somehow found it impossible to bring the words to his lips. The idea of hiding away in the hospital all night appealed. Hell, as much as he should hate to admit it, the idea of curling up with Marcus appealed too.

Blushing a little at his complete lack of coordination, Liam carefully climbed onto the free side of the bed. The mattress was warm where Marcus had lain.

Marcus's arm looped around Liam's shoulders. Liam knew that was just to make the best use of the limited room, but it still felt like Marcus was keeping him safe and encouraging him to curl more comfortably into his side.

The vampire's body was wonderfully hot against Liam's chilled frame, and when Marcus pulled his blanket up around Liam's shoulders, a snug little cocoon formed around them. Resting his head carefully on Marcus's shoulder, Liam did his best not to take up too much room, not to jostle Marcus.

Closing his eyes for a second, Liam tried to focus on timing his breaths so they didn't compete with the rise and fall of Marcus's ribs, but settled neatly into time with them.

There was no way he'd actually be able to sleep though. The bed was too small, he was pressed too tightly against a man he barely knew, and he never had slept during those nights after Ralph had been out drinking.

No, Liam told himself, as he subconsciously snuggled a little bit more comfortably into Marcus's embrace. He wouldn't sleep. He'd just close his eyes for a few moments…

Chapter Three

Marcus stared up at the bland white ceiling above the hospital bed, unable to move a muscle. It would be too big a risk to even twitch. Liam needed his sleep. Marcus glanced down as Liam stirred only to snuggle in against him once more.

A soft, contented little noise escaped from the back of Liam's throat as his arm slid a little farther around Marcus's torso. The gentle caress went straight to Marcus's cock. Risk or no risk, there was no way he could stop his shaft from rising in response to the boy's squirming.

Three years of being unable to react to any stimulus only made his cock more eager to show off its newly regained ability to harden. Six months of fantasising about the boy who'd just climbed into his bed wasn't quite the equivalent of a cold shower either.

Marcus barely held back an irritable growl. It wasn't natural for a vampire to sleep with a human this way. His whole body screamed that humans were prey. They were for sucking and screwing. A bag of blood was no substitute for a vein.

If there was any justice in the world, he'd already have had his cock buried in Liam's arse and his fangs penetrating his neck. Blood would be flowing into his mouth, hot, metallic, and full of the pleasure Liam gained from having his new master screw him hard into the mattress.

Marcus closed his eyes for a moment, but quickly opened them again. Even with Liam wrapped around him, it felt far too much like he'd never be able to lift his lids again if he allowed them to fall. He instinctively tightened his hold on the boy, as if a sweet little sub could somehow protect him from the darkness he'd been trapped in for so long.

Rolling his eyes at himself, Marcus found himself absentmindedly rubbing his thumb against the bandage wrapped around his index finger. Moving carefully so as not to disturb Liam, Marcus brought his hand to his mouth and caught hold of the edge of the dressing with his teeth. It only took seconds for him to have the damn thing off and tossed aside.

Still lying almost flat on the bed, he held his hand above his face so he could study his finger properly. A bright white scar extended from the crease inside the top knuckle, over the flesh of the fingertip, continuing almost all the way over to the top of the fingernail.

Marcus stared at the mark, as if he could somehow make it disappear if he glared at it hard enough. It remained as vivid as ever. Nothing would get rid of it now. It would be there for the rest of Marcus's life, and for far, far longer than Theo Wallace would live.

Ice cold fury burned in the centre of Marcus's chest, right beneath where Liam rested his head. The boy whimpered slightly as if he could somehow sense Marcus's displeasure.

Marcus frowned. He patted Liam vaguely on the shoulder. "Hush. You're fine."

That seemed to do the trick. Marcus made a mental note of Liam's response for future reference. If he was going to keep the boy permanently, he'd have to learn how humans needed their masters to treat them.

Looking for a distraction from his anger, Marcus turned his head very slightly and looked toward the visitor's chair. It was a cheap plastic thing that looked as uncomfortable as hell. There was no way Liam should have spent so many hours sitting on it. His arse was probably still sore.

Marcus only just managed to stop himself sliding his hand down from where it rested on the small of Liam's back to check.

Eager to remind himself why that would be a bad idea, Marcus made a concerted effort to make his mind travel back to Liam's first return visit to his room.

* * * * *

"Hi."

Marcus mentally sighed. So he had come back — the boy from the previous week. What the hell was his name?

"Um...I'm Liam Bates. I stopped by last week. How are you feeling?"

Even after years spent unable to move a muscle, Marcus still tried to lift an eyebrow at the question. How the hell was he supposed to feel, trapped in this damn bed, surrounded by idiots?

"I'm doing okay," Liam went on. "I brought a magazine. I thought you might like to hear a bit about what's going on in the world. Just in case you wake up. That could come in useful, right?"

There was no way Marcus would have ever managed to keep back a sarcastic response if he'd had even the tiniest bit of control over his vocal cords. As it was, he had little choice but to allow the boy to go on uninterrupted.

A rustle of glossy pages informed him that the boy was getting ready to read. Liam cleared his throat.

Marcus refocused his attention on the slight hum of the electrical motors in the monitors alongside his bed. The constant buzz had been annoying for the first year or so, but it had its uses. It came in very handy when he wanted to tune out voices he had no interest in hearing.

The radio that played on the nurses' desk reported the news every damn hour on the dot. He didn't need to hear it all over again. It would be far better for him to devote the time to his favourite hobby — that of deciding what he was going to do with Theo Wallace when he finally woke up.

Before Liam had so rudely interrupted him, Marcus had been deep in thought, trying to work out, not for the first time, if it would be better to hang the little prick out in the open where everyone would be able to see what happened to any man who was stupid enough to lash out at him without making sure he finished him off completely, or if it would be more satisfying to watch him squirm in private, when there would be nothing to distract Marcus from every detail of Theo's agony.

"She's getting married again!"

The vision of a gloomy little cellar, decorated only with a strong hook hanging from a beam, a length of rope and the object of Marcus's revenge, shattered.

He turned his attention back to Liam.

"It says here that she'll be getting married later this month at a secret location. A private ceremony with only a few select guests... And they've got exclusive access!"

Without the slightest idea who the boy was talking about or why he should care, and lacking any way of posing those questions, Marcus had little choice but to simply wait until the boy dropped the woman's name into the conversation.

"Listen to this," Liam ordered. "Sandra Smithson has told them that..."

Marcus would have given anything for the ability to roll his eyes right then. Sandra bloody Smithson. In that moment, any good opinion he'd ever had of Liam crashed straight down. Once it hit rock bottom, it kept going, drilling its way toward the core of the earth at granite-shattering speed.

It had been bad enough when he'd had to listen to some silly teenage nursing student babble on about the latest no talent bimbo to do the rounds of all the reality shows and skin mags, but, in a strange way, he'd expected something a little better from Liam. For some reason, he'd actually assumed that there was some kind of intelligence hidden away behind those stammering attempts to speak.

Without further ado, Marcus turned his attention back to the hum of medical machinery and waited impatiently for Liam's voice to fade from his notice.

"Dress designed by… Raised on a rough estate in… Rose to fame after… Talented football player fiancé…"

Signals rushed from Marcus's brain to the muscles on his forehead, ordering them to frown. Nothing happened on his brow, but that wasn't what surprised Marcus. The boy's voice was unshakeable. It wasn't that he had an appalling accent like that silly old fool who they'd sent to visit him the year before. Liam's voice was actually rather nice—soft, but still masculine. But there was also something about it that cut through Marcus's usual defences against the banality of average humanity.

"Three bridesmaids… His bachelor party is going to be held in… Flowers from…"

Words rolled over Marcus and he found himself entirely unable to escape from them. The enthusiasm in the boy's voice was strangely captivating, even if the words weren't. Marcus could easily imagine him poring over the magazine, his eyes darting over the page, taking in every detail.

He was probably pretty, Marcus decided. He sounded pretty. From what Marcus remembered from the previous week's babbling, he was living with some sort of sugar daddy.

No doubt about it, then. If there was a rich guy paying for the pleasure of keeping him around, he'd be cute and pretty. Big blue eyes, floppy blond hair, a tight arse and flirtatious mannerisms—Marcus had known a lot of men like that over the years. He'd have smiled at the memory if he could have.

"Two children from his previous marriage… Her ex-husband… Do you remember him? He was in all the magazines a few months ago. He had a drug habit. He went into rehab for a while, but he relapsed almost as soon as he came out."

The boy sounded so heartbroken. As if it could really matter to him what a man that he had never met, and probably never would meet, was idiotic enough to inject into his body.

The sympathy sounded genuine enough, but, of course, any gold-digger would be a really good actor — they'd have to be in order to get the most out of their lover. And that's what it was always about. That was probably why Liam was visiting him too. Visiting a wealthy hospital patient had probably sounded like a good way of injecting himself into the good graces of someone who'd leave him something in his will and —

"Do you think they'll be happy together?"

Marcus didn't give a damn if they were or not. But he was sure that Liam would be able to make him very happy, if he wasn't stuck in that damn hospital bed. Soft pink lips wrapped around his cock, big soulful eyes staring up at him as Marcus put his hand on the back of Liam's head and guided him to take his shaft deeper into his mouth, into his throat.

Yes, Marcus would be very happy with that. And, no doubt, he'd be happy enough to pay for the privilege too. A nice simple business arrangement, a willing mouth to suck his cock, and a willing neck to feed from.

"I think they'll be happy," Liam decided.

Finally, the tell-tale increase of foot traffic in the corridor outside informed Marcus that visiting time was almost over. Liam seemed to notice it too. Clothing rustled as he, no doubt, checked his watch the way all the visitors did around that time. "I guess I'd better get going. Ralph will expect me to be there when he gets home. And you're probably bored to death with me rambling on anyway…"

The chair squeaked against the floor as Liam got up. "I'll be back next week," Liam promised. "I'll bring that exclusive the magazine promised."

Marcus mentally cursed. That was all he needed, another day full of tittle-tattle and stupid celebrity gossip. Yes, Marcus mentally muttered. That was going to be something special to look forward to…

* * * * *

Shaking his head, Marcus made a concerted effort to pull himself out of the memory before it took hold completely, and he found himself trapped in a coma all over again.

It had seemed so real. He frowned up at the ceiling. There was pleasure to be had in being able to control the muscles in his brow well enough to do that. Any kind of voluntary movement was something to be cherished now.

The reason for the expression, however, diluted the bliss he should have felt. How the hell had he been stupid enough to think that Liam had been after a single penny of anyone's money?

Focusing very hard on the boy lying by his side, Marcus took stock as best he could. Liam's breaths were slow and even. That seemed to be a good thing. His heartbeat was no longer racing. Marcus was reasonably sure that was also a positive sign among humans. He appeared to be relaxed and at peace, knowing that he was safe with his master.

Or his soon-to-be master, at least. Even if Liam didn't know that was what Marcus would soon be to him, Marcus had no doubt about it. A naturally submissive human. A naturally dominant vampire. The boy would be his within a day.

Marcus smiled slightly as Liam squirmed a little and pressed himself closer to his side once more. Reaching out, Marcus summoned up the coordination to pull the blanket a little more firmly around Liam's shoulders.

"You know he has a boyfriend?"

Marcus jerked his head up and turned his head to glare at the nurse in the doorway. She was tall, with long brown hair, plaited back at the nape of her neck. Jenny Trent, his memory supplied—the vaguely sensible nurse from earlier that night. She had a bag of human blood in her hand.

"Yes," he said, taking care to keep his voice soft for Liam's benefit. "I am aware of that."

Jenny stepped forward until she stood behind Liam's chair. Resting her fingers on the back of it, she studied both Marcus and his sleeping boy very carefully.

"I fail to see what business it is of yours," Marcus added.

Jenny didn't seem the least bit intimidated by the snap in his words. "You know how many times he's visited you?"

"I do," Marcus confirmed.

"Well, you're not the only one who's got to know him over the last few months," Jenny said. "He's a good guy."

"Yes, he is," Marcus agreed—the kind of human who would make him a very suitable submissive.

"He's got a crush on you," Jenny said. "Some of the nurses laugh about it."

"You don't," Marcus said, with complete confidence. He'd made a point of listening to any conversations where Liam's name was mentioned.

Jenny's eyes narrowed for a moment, then she shook her head as if dismissing the subject as unimportant. "If you heard the nurses talking, you must have heard at least some of what he said to you. You seem reasonably intelligent. Even if he didn't tell you what kind of bastard his boyfriend is, I'll assume you were able to put together the pieces on your own."

Reasonably intelligent? Marcus ground his teeth together. The nerve of a human, talking to a vampire that way. "Yes," he bit out, keeping any other response back for Liam's benefit.

"So you know you'd have to be a real arsehole to use him up and throw him away as if he was nothing more than a snack," Jenny said. She met Marcus's gaze and held it, her expression calm and serious.

Every muscle in Marcus's body tensed. Primitive instincts rose up inside him. He wanted nothing more than to tear out the woman's throat for even suggesting anyone would treat Liam that way.

Liam shifted uncomfortably in his sleep, as if sensing Marcus's anger. A confused little whimper left his lips as he turned his face into Marcus's chest.

Marcus clumsily stroked the boy's shoulder in that way that had worked so well before. "I heard every word he's ever said to me," he forced out, as evenly as he could.

Jenny didn't appear impressed. "Before I worked here, I was a nurse at one of your blood banks. I saw the way the donor boys and girls were treated, and heard enough to know that blood whores are treated even worse. I know all the sayings vampires have about being at the top of the food chain for a reason—and I know the comparisons that you make between humans and livestock. We're little more than cattle to you."

Marcus didn't deny any of it.

"Liam deserves better than that," the nurse said. "If you don't know how to provide him with better than that, leave him alone." As she spoke, she made her way toward the hook the IVs were hung from. She nodded toward it. "Do you want this one intravenous or oral?"

Marcus clenched his jaw so tightly, his teeth ached, and not just out of the desire for blood. He turned his arm so his vein was accessible, and let that be his answer.

The nurse had the needle in his vein in seconds. Marcus stared straight ahead, ignoring her the same way he had always ignored humans who he had no interest in feeding from.

Jenny studied him in silence for several seconds as the blood made its way down the line. "If you don't intend to treat him any better than his current boyfriend, let him walk away in the morning. He doesn't need another selfish arsehole in his life." Turning on her heel, she walked out of the room without giving him time to say anything in response.

Anyone would be better than Ralph. Marcus growled softly under his breath as he thought about the man and what he'd put Liam through.

As soon as his strength returned, Marcus was going to pay a very interesting visit to that man. He was going to show Ralph exactly how it felt to be smaller and weaker than another person, how it felt to be trapped and not have any chance of escape. Marcus smiled slightly. He wasn't usually one to condone wasting food, but, in Ralph's case, he was more than willing to make an exception.

Sometimes meat was so rotten all anyone could do was dispose of it and make sure it didn't contaminate anything else.

Marcus looked down at Liam for a moment. As the boy slumbered against his chest, it was hard to imagine that anyone could ever want to do anything other than protect and cherish him.

It was strange to think back to a time when he hadn't wanted to be the one to do that. Marcus took a deep breath. He might not know how to look after a human, but he was bloody well going to learn.

As determined as he was to never sleep again, when his anger drained away, it was impossible for him to keep his eyes open. For the first time in three years, he slid into real slumber.

* * * * *

"It says here that they flew in one of the best chefs in the country to cater for the wedding party. There's a picture of the meal. It looks so amazing!"

Marcus let his mind wander around the boy's words, picking up on the interesting ones while all the boring details of that silly woman's wedding floated straight past him.

He was quite willing to bet that Liam tasted fantastic. Without anything to go on but the sound of his voice, Marcus still had no doubt the boy would taste wonderfully sweet.

Marcus's teeth ached with the need to feed—just as they had for more than two years—but not just from anyone. The need was specific now. He wanted to feed from Liam. Just one drop of the boy's blood... It would be worth selling his soul, if vampires even had souls, to get a taste of him.

He could make a better banquet of Liam than any chef could from paltry human food. A picture sprung up in Marcus's mind of the boy stretched out on a fine white tablecloth, wrists and ankles bound, candlelight flickering over his skin. Liam's cock would be hard and flushed with blood, rising up from his body, begging for his touch. He'd be desperate, aching to come after being kept chaste and frustrated for weeks on end. Yes, Marcus could see it all so clearly.

A faint tingling sensation danced down Marcus's spine, heading for his cock. Of course, nothing actually happened when the sensation reached his shaft. Movement was as impossible there as it was in every other part of his body. There was no chance of relief for him—just as there would be no way that Liam would be able to come.

The boy wouldn't be able to move far, bound to a vampire's dining table like that. He'd only be able to squirm— just enough to show off a hot young body and make his chains rattle a little.

It had been so long since Marcus had heard a submissive's chains sing for him. But Liam would sing beautifully, with chains and whimpers, and no doubt with pleasure-filled screams when the time came. As far as Marcus could work out, the guy didn't have a clue how much of a natural submissive he was, but it wouldn't take long to bring him up to speed on that fact. In Marcus's experience, most humans caught on quickly once they were in chains and on the verge of climaxing without permission.

The door leading into Marcus's hospital room squeaked as it was pushed open. Liam fell silent. Within the confines of his own mind, Marcus cursed. It wasn't as if he enjoyed listening to the boy babble, but that was still no excuse for people to keep interrupting him for no good reason.

"Hello, Liam." That was the anti-vampire nurse. Marcus added an extra curse to those scrolling through his head. The less time she spent around his boy, the better. Untrained humans were far too impressionable. It wouldn't do for Liam to be picking up those sorts of habits.

"Hi." Liam's voice had moved away from the chair by the side of Marcus's bed. He was over by the window now. He'd moved away from her. She'd called him by name and he hadn't done the same. Marcus mentally nodded his approval.

"Can you pass me the packet from the trolley?"

Tell her to do her own damn job, Liam, Marcus ordered. It wasn't really fair to blame him for disobeying his master when there was no way he could have heard the mental command, but Marcus still wished Liam had more sense than to give in to the obvious ploy to bring him across the room and get closer to him.

"Bloody hell — what happened to your eye?"

"Nothing!"

For the first time since she'd come to work at the hospital, Marcus actually wanted that particular nurse to speak. As blind as he had been for more than two years, he needed her to say out loud exactly what was wrong with Liam's eye.

"I walked into —"

"Someone's fist," the nurse finished for him.

"No. I was trying to fix the hinges on one of the cabinets in the kitchen. It swung back and…"

And Liam was a bloody awful liar. While Marcus lay helpless, his brain whirled faster and faster. Mugging? Homophobic bastards?

"It's nothing," Liam said.

"According to who?" the nurse asked.

"According to me." Liam was back over by the window now. Marcus could so easily picture him backing away in his mind's eye. "Can we just drop this?"

"What's his name?" the nurse pushed.

"Who?"

"In my experience, when a man lets another guy get away with hitting him, it's more than a one-night stand. I'm guessing you know his name."

The words punched Marcus in the stomach. Unable to move, there was no way he could defend himself. He just had to take it.

"I..." Liam whispered.

"There are places you can go, places you can get help," the nurse cut in, when it had to be obvious to her, as well as to Marcus, that Liam wasn't going to get any further than that one word. "There are shelters specifically for gay men who—"

"I'm not..." Liam began, but even without being able to see the boy, Marcus knew that Liam had already realised that there was no point denying it.

"Would you assume I was getting beaten up by my girlfriend if I was straight?" Liam demanded, now sounding as if he was as far across the room as he could get.

"Yes. That happens more often than you'd think. You can be straight, gay, or into whatever the hell rocks your boat. I'd think the same about anyone who reacted to my questions the way you just did." The nurse's tone of voice was matter of fact. "I worked in accident and emergency for years. I've seen hundreds of people go home with partners who they know damn well are going to give them another hammering the moment the front door closes behind them."

Marcus would have held his breath as he waited for Liam's answer, but he couldn't even do that. His chest continued to rise and fall with the same rhythm as it had maintained ever since his downfall.

"It's not like that..."

"It never is," the nurse muttered.

Marcus felt a sharp scrape across the inside of his elbow as another bag of animal blood was hung beside his bed. Pain immediately swept through his veins as the poor substitute for human blood made its way through his body.

Fighting back a wave of nausea, Marcus kept all his attention on Liam.

The boy hadn't said anything about a black eye.

He'd sat there for all that time babbling on about weddings, worrying about the happiness of a woman he'd never meet, telling Marcus a million different things he had no interest in hearing, and it hadn't occurred to him to mention something Marcus would have actually wanted to know.

The nurse finally left them alone again. Silence fell over the room. Marcus waited for the boy to speak up, but he didn't. Marcus sensed Liam cross the room to sit on the chair by the side of the bed, but the boy still didn't say a single word.

Marcus desperately tried to open his eyes, to lift an arm to reach out to Liam, to move muscles that hadn't been his to control for over two years and —

* * * * *

Bright light blinded Marcus as his eyelids fluttered open. It took him several panic-filled seconds to completely believe that he was actually able to open his eyes. It had been the God-awful memory of that oh-so-informative third visit by Liam that had been the nightmare. The memory of waking up and finally being able to reach out to Liam hadn't been a dream after all.

Marcus took a deep breath and let the relief sink into his brain, but he refused to give himself any longer than that.

Blinking his eyes very rapidly in an effort to focus, Marcus extended his arm across the narrow hospital bed, wondering how the hell the boy could have managed to move so far away from him without falling off the thin, uncomfortable mattress.

Marcus turned his head. The rest of the tiny bed was empty. Levering himself awkwardly up onto one elbow, Marcus pushed his hair back from his face with his other hand. He peered over the side of the bed, then into every corner of the room and through the open door into the en-suite.

He was gone. Liam was gone.

Marcus tried to sit up, only to collapse back. He looked at the bag of blood on the stand by his bed. It was empty. His veins weren't much better. He could almost feel his arteries collapsing in on themselves.

Reaching up to the headboard, for the first time since he arrived in the hospital, Marcus pressed the buzzer and summoned one of the nurses.

Chapter Four

Liam carefully unlocked and pushed open the front door to 21 Oak Drive. Straining his hearing, he lurked on the doorstep, trying to work out if Ralph was in the house. Even though it felt as if several lifetimes had passed since Liam had run to the hospital, it was still only New Year's Day. Ralph wouldn't be at work. But maybe he could have gone to a friend's house or, more likely, to a pub?

No sound came from inside the placid looking semi-detached house, but it still seemed like finding that Ralph had gone out was too much to hope for. Taking a deep breath, Liam finally stepped inside. Closing the door softly behind him, he crept along the hallway. An old floorboard creaked beneath his foot. Liam froze, closing his eyes, waiting for the angry words that he was sure would fill the air. Nothing. Liam began to breathe again.

Opening his eyes, he moved forward once more, until he was able to peer past the open living room door.

A fist full of panic caught Liam around the throat, threatening to choke the air out of him. It was an entire minute before Liam was able to take in the fact Ralph was asleep. Liam managed to pull a little oxygen into his lungs as panic eased its grip on him.

Ralph lay sprawled out on the sofa, one arm thrown over his eyes to block out the light pouring in through the big bay window. His other hand still gripped a bottle of whiskey. There didn't appear to be much liquid left in it. Liam studied Ralph's shirt, just above where the bottle lay against his chest. There was no tell-tale whiskey stain. It had been silly to hope that most of the alcohol was simply spilt.

"Asleep," Liam whispered to himself. Ralph was

asleep, and Liam was safe, for now at least. Ralph probably didn't even know he'd been away all night. There was no reason why he should suspect that Liam had only crept home after dawn.

Liam fiddled nervously with the hem on his T-shirt. He was wearing exactly the same as he'd been wearing when he left. The fabric was still damp around the edges, but there was no evidence to suggest that he'd spent the night in borrowed scrubs, that he'd slept in another man's arms.

Taking a deep breath, Liam forced his mind back to the present. Whatever insanity had overtaken his little bit of the world last night, it was done with now. Marcus was awake. No doubt he had a life to get back to. There would probably be a family waiting for him, maybe even a wife...

Dropping his gaze, Liam stared at the broken glass scattered across the carpet. He had no reason to think Marcus was actually interested in someone like him. Hell, Marcus probably wasn't even gay. The only reason he hadn't beaten the hell out of him for that kiss was because he was grateful for being woken up. Then, he'd just wanted someone who was familiar to hang around for a little while, that was all.

And, Liam swallowed rapidly—he had his own life to get back to as well. Maybe if he stopped spending so much time focused on some stupid stranger in a hospital bed, he'd be able to keep Ralph happier.

Liam looked slowly around the room. Ralph obviously hadn't been impressed by the way he'd run out on him the night before. Liam nudged one of the larger shards of glass, which had once formed the top of a coffee table, with his toe. Everything that he'd arranged so neatly on the mantelpiece above the fire now lay broken on the carpet to one side of it.

That was a good thing, Liam told himself. Ralph had let his anger out elsewhere. If it already was out of his system, then maybe they could just pretend this had never happened and everything would be okay.

Liam silently made his way across the room and picked

up a photo frame. The glass was cracked, but the simple silver frame was still fine. A picture of him and Ralph stared up at Liam. They were both smiling. They looked so bloody happy together. Liam carefully set it back in its rightful place on the mantelpiece.

"You really outdid yourself last night."

Liam spun around to face the sofa. Ralph peered back at him, his eyes bloodshot, his hair disordered. He was sitting up now, wide awake and already glowering his displeasure with life. And he was between Liam and the door.

Swallowing down his nerves, Liam struggled to find the right words to calm Ralph's anger. He failed completely. There wasn't a single syllable inside his head; fear had dissolved them all. He had no choice but to remain silent.

Ralph rubbed at his jaw line, scratching the two day's growth of stubble that created a dark shadow across the lower half of his face. "You should know better than to wind me up that way," he bit out.

"I'm sorry," Liam whispered, staring down at his trainers. He couldn't help but wonder at what point the mornings after the nights when Ralph lashed out at him, had become about him apologising to Ralph rather than Ralph begging for his forgiveness.

"Clean this shit up. Place is like a bloody pigsty. If you can't earn a decent wage, the least you can do is keep the house in order." Ralph stomped out of the room.

Unable to make his limbs work, Liam remained exactly where he was, as still as any easy target, until he heard the shower start up in the en-suite directly above him. The pattering of water gave control of Liam's body back to him.

Making his way through to the kitchen, he picked up a dustpan and brush and set about sweeping the glass from the living room floor before someone got hurt. Kneeling on the rug at the edge of the debris, he slowly settled into his task, and a little of the tension seeped from his muscles.

He was fine. Ralph was fine—and he'd sobered up

overnight, too. There would be no repeat performance this morning. It wouldn't be the same as things had been with Marcus, but—

Liam shook his head. Desperately trying to refocus his attention on the task at hand, he pushed the memory of the previous night away as hard as he could, just in case Ralph might have somehow acquired the ability to read his mind while he slept off his latest binge.

Piece by piece, the living room resumed its usual appearance. The system Liam had developed for repairing the damage from an outburst saw him in good stead. By the time Ralph walked back in and retook his habitual seat on the sofa, Liam was on the final repairs.

Ralph made no comment on any of it as he opened his first beer of the day.

Liam's mind raced as he carefully reset the time on the mantle clock, trying to work-out if speaking up and asking if Ralph had enjoyed the previous night would be counted as snooping, or if not asking would show an unacceptable lack of interest, trying to calculate which failure would annoy Ralph less that day.

Once the clock was back in its place, the living room was as perfect as it could get until the coffee table was replaced. Liam continued to fuss and adjust little details though, straightening photo frames and ornaments, putting off the moment when he had to turn his attention back to Ralph.

A sudden loud ringing filled the room. Liam jumped, dropping the cushion he had been shaking into shape, but it was only the phone. The handset rested on the side table right next to where Ralph sat. Liam hurried across to it, desperate to answer it before the ringing pissed Ralph off.

He was only a step away when Ralph finally decided to pick up the handset and put it to his ear.

Liam heard a woman speaking on the other end of the line. He knew far better than to ask who it was, or to stay within what Ralph might consider to be eavesdropping range.

Pacing nervously into the kitchen, Liam crossed to the sink and filled the kettle with water. Setting it to boil, he leaned back against the cabinet and ran his hand over his face.

As soon as he closed his eyes, the image of Marcus raced into the front of his brain, demanding that he not just remember the vampire's appearance, but that his body replay every single sensation that being with him had provided.

As he stood in the kitchen and listened to the kettle begin to boil, Liam was almost willing to swear that he could feel Marcus's arms wrap around him. He leaned back against the edge of the work surface a little more firmly, as if the vampire's body really was right there within his reach.

The scent of Marcus, the warmth of his skin, the slow, gentle rhythm of his voice coupled with the steady beat of his heart while Liam rested his head on Marcus's chest. It was all right there, as if he could simply reach out and take it.

He smiled slightly at the memory, knowing it was more than half false, but willing to cherish it, regardless. A shiver ran down his spine as he blinked open his eyes and stared down at the old wooden floorboards beneath his feet.

It was nothing like the stark grey hospital flooring. Liam wrapped his arms around his torso. The space around him smelled like spilt beer rather than cleaning agents. There were no beeps and hums from machines nearby, no half audible conversations floating in from the nurses' station. All he could hear was the distant sound of Ralph chatting to someone on the phone and…

Liam's thoughts slowly congealed as he realised that he was wrong. There were no words seeping through from the other room. Frozen in place, he strained his hearing, desperately trying to work out where Ralph was, where he might have moved to while Liam wasn't paying attention.

Upstairs to crash out? Through the front door and out for the rest of the day? It was impossible to tell. All Liam knew for sure was that Ralph wasn't close enough to be heard.

Then, just when Liam was about to breathe a sigh of relief, a sharp little sound made its way across the room to him — a clink of glass against granite.

It ripped through Liam's senses like a gunshot.

He slowly dragged his gaze up the cabinet door directly opposite him. An empty beer bottle rested on the counter. Fingers were still wrapped around the neck of the bottle. Fighting for each inch of progress he made, Liam forced his gaze up Ralph's arm until he finally met his eyes.

"Have a good night last night, Liam?"

Run!

The same voice that had screamed inside his head the previous night screeched through Liam's brain, demanding that he flee while he still had the chance. Liam took half a step forward, but Ralph was once more between him and the door.

There was no way he'd be able to dodge him. Ralph wasn't drunk enough this time. His reactions would be too quick. But that didn't really matter, because every one of Liam's joints was gradually turning to lead as the reality of the situation sank in.

Unable to move or speak, Liam could barely even focus on the words hitting the air. Frowning slightly, he peered at Ralph's lips as Ralph moved closer and closer. With his eyes locked on Ralph's face, Liam could almost believe there were no footsteps being taken. Ralph seemed to float, disembodied in front of him.

"Anything you want to tell me?"

Liam managed to shake his head.

"Who were you with last night?" Ralph's loomed over him, the scent of fresh beer and stale whiskey surrounding him like a thick cloud of smog.

Liam opened his mouth. He closed it again without saying a word.

Without warning, the back of Ralph's hand slammed into Liam's cheekbone, sending him tumbling toward the kitchen floor. Fingernails clawing against the floorboards, he scrambled up and skirted around Ralph, running for the hallway door.

He was almost there when a painful grip clamped around his wrist and spun him around. Nothing could have been more different than the way Marcus had held him the previous night. Ralph's fingers bit painfully into the inside of Liam's wrist, threatening to burst the veins beneath the skin, as Ralph stepped past him.

Dragging Liam along in his wake, Ralph headed for the living room. Stumbling, forced to stagger bent forward and off balance by Ralph's grip on him, Liam caught hold of the doorframe as he was hauled into the room. His fingers clawed at the paintwork, but Ralph was far too strong for him. Liam tumbled, only just missing the metal remains of the coffee table.

Suddenly, Liam had words. They fell from his lips so quickly he could barely make sense of them himself. Words like "please" and "sorry". Even while he had no idea what he was begging for, he couldn't quite stop them from pouring out — not even when he knew they wouldn't do any good.

"Did you really think I wouldn't find out, you stupid little slut?"

Ralph lunged forward and caught hold of Liam's shirt when he would have fallen, half keeping Liam on his feet and half choking him with the garment.

"I didn't," Liam babbled. "I was at the hospital, I—"

"You were visiting your sleepy little pal?" Ralph demanded, jerking Liam forward, so they were almost nose to nose.

Liam nodded rapidly.

"And when exactly did you plan to tell me he's woken up?"

The world spun as Liam tumbled back onto the smaller of the room's two sofas. Scrabbling at the cushions, he tried to pull himself to his feet, but he was too late. Ralph was right there in front of him, looming over him, his massive form blocking any route toward the door.

"Did you beg him too, Liam?" Ralph taunted. "Did you beg him for his cock? Plead with him to fuck you harder?"

Liam shook his head. He glanced over his shoulder, but the sofa was set right back against the wall. There was no escape, no way to retreat any farther. Holding up his hands, Liam cringed into the cushions.

"I'm going to make sure you never want to look at another man again!"

Physical escape impossible, all Liam could do was close his eyes and pretend he was somewhere else, pretend he was somewhere safe — maybe even in the hospital at Marcus's side. Yes. As the first real blow for the day fell against his skin, that was where Liam's mind went.

* * * *

"You'd never do anything like that, would you?" Liam asked the sleeping form.

He was about to return his gaze to the magazine lying open on his lap, when he hesitated.

"You're a good man, I can tell," he whispered to the vampire. Liam looked down at his fingernails as he toyed with the edge of a magazine page. "I know you're going to laugh, but I often think about the day when you'll wake up."

He risked a glance at Marcus. His sleeping form showed no signs of humour.

Liam leaned forward a little in his chair. His words became more confident.

"I imagine that you'll open your eyes, turn your head toward me, and tell me to shut the hell up, because you're trying to sleep. But you'd be smiling as you said it, so I'd know you weren't really angry."

Liam smiled too, but the expression soon faded away. "I know you've got a life to get back to. You've probably got a family and everything. I wouldn't expect you to let me keep hanging around you or anything, I just..."

He sighed as he leaned back in his chair.

"It would be selfish of me to want you to stay like this forever, just so I could keep visiting you, wouldn't it?"

Marcus said nothing. There was no reprimand, no sarcasm, no slap.

Liam scraped up another smile as he turned to the next page in the magazine. Perhaps, if he just enjoyed the time Marcus could spend with him, that wasn't as evil as wanting more.

* * * * *

Marcus turned his head toward the door leading into his hospital room. If that was another damn doctor coming to try and poke at him, he wasn't sure he had enough control to resist tearing their jugular out—not to feed, just to make a point.

"Jenson!" At last, a human he could rely on to show at least a modicum of common sense!

Marcus frowned as his butler of over thirty-five years stood in the doorway and gawped at him as if he'd never set eyes on a vampire before. "Jenson!" he snapped.

Several seconds passed before, with a slight shake of his head, Jenson seemed to refocus on the world before him. He stepped into Marcus's hospital room, his movements as neat and precise as they had ever been.

"I need you to find a man for me," Marcus said.

Jenson blinked in that slow, butlery way he had—the one that implied that he had seen and heard everything in his years of service and wasn't about to let his profession down by appearing shocked at anything his current employer could throw at him. "Certainly, sir. Do you have any particular requirements in mind? Hair colour, build, blood-type...?"

"Don't be a fool, man!" Marcus snapped.

"My apologies, sir." Jenson gave a little half bow. "It

seems your sudden awakening has gone quite to my head."

About to speak again, Marcus paused and considered the man standing in front of him more carefully. It would have been easy to say that Jenson hadn't changed in the slightest over the last three years, but it wouldn't have been entirely true.

There was more than a little extra grey in Jenson's hair. There were some extra lines around his eyes too, and they didn't hint at years of laughter.

Jenson cleared his throat. "Your affairs have all been taken care of in your… absence, sir. I hope you will find they are to your satisfaction, and —"

"Jenson," Marcus cut in, impatiently.

"Yes, sir?"

"I have no doubt that my bank balances are all flourishing and there isn't a speck of dust in any property I own. I know how well you'll have served me while I wasn't available to give specific orders. I haven't once doubted it. Now, I would appreciate it if you would stop fussing and obey the order I am trying to give you right now!"

"Certainly, sir. You wish me to locate a specific gentleman for you?"

Marcus nodded, leaning back against the pillows piled high behind him as his energy waned. "His name is Liam Bates. He's twenty-eight years old. Short, light-brown hair, brown eyes. Submissive as hell, although he hasn't got a clue about that, and if you so much as mention the word in his presence I'll see that you're hanged for it."

"Understood, sir," Jenson said.

Marcus relaxed slightly. Yes, completely unshockable, and not the least bit intimidated by his employer's species. It had always been reassuringly difficult to scare the man who'd practically raised him, who'd known him back before his fangs had developed.

"He was a volunteer visitor at the hospital. Someone somewhere must have contact details for him. If not, try

asking about him in all the cafes close to the hospital. He said he used to work in one of them."

"Mr Bates is a human gentleman, sir?" Jenson asked, taking a notebook out of his pocket and jotting down several lines of information.

Marcus nodded. "Yes, human."

Jenson looked up at him for a moment, a question in his eyes.

"Yes, he's gay too, although probably not openly so everywhere. Don't out him."

"I wouldn't dream of it, sir. And when I find Mr Bates?"

"Bring him here," Marcus said.

"And would you like that done politely or impolitely, sir?"

"Politely," Marcus specified. "Very politely. No one is to lay a hand on him. No one may even raise his voice to him. Just find him and bring him here."

"Very good, sir." The notebook disappeared into a pocket. "I'll attend to it at once."

Marcus nodded his approval. There was something very wonderful about a perfectly trained vampire's butler. No task too big, too small, or too bizarre.

Jenson once more folded his hands neatly behind his back. He seemed about to turn and leave the room, when he paused.

Marcus had rarely seen the man hesitate in all the time he'd known him. He frowned, not liking the sight at all.

"May I just say, sir, that —"

"I heard everything you said to me while I was asleep," Marcus cut in quickly. "You have nothing to explain." He remembered Jenson's words very clearly. His recollection of the pain in his butler's voice when he'd explained that, while there was no way for him to be of service to his employer at his bedside, he'd be transferring his attention to managing Marcus's affairs until such time as Marcus was able to turn his mind to them once more, was perfect.

"Thank you, sir," Jenson said, dropping his gaze for a moment as he turned away.

"One more thing," Marcus called out, as he managed to drag his mind away from his own worries for a moment. "Mrs Jenson?"

"A picture of health, sir. If you don't mind me saying so, sir, she's already started putting your townhouse in order, in anticipation of your release from hospital."

Marcus nodded, just once. "I look forward to seeing her again."

"Good of you to say, sir." Jenson stepped out and silently closed the door behind him, sealing Marcus alone in the hospital room once more.

Marcus closed his eyes for a moment. When he opened them, he half expected to see Liam sitting there next to his bed, head no doubt bowed over some trashy magazine.

Marcus's fingers clenched around the blankets at his side. Not knowing where the boy was seemed so unnatural. To be awake and to have as little power as he had when he'd slumbered through those years, to be so exhausted that he felt the hands of sleep pulling him down, dragging him back into the hell he'd only recently escaped.

He forced open his eyes, making a point of not looking at the empty chair by the side of his bed. His mental picture of the room hadn't been too inaccurate, apart from the colours.

The machinery had been switched off now, but it was all where his audio map of the room had led him to expect. The various warm and cool drafts he'd felt brushing against his skin had informed him where the windows, doors, and heaters were.

The curtain around the bed was pushed back, but he'd known where the rail would be just from the noise the nurses had made when they pulled it open and closed each day. Marcus turned his head and glanced through the glass panel in the door, looking out into the corridor.

He'd been wrong about how the nurses would look. That was somewhat annoying to discover. Their voices had been quite deceiving. The pretty little redhead had the clipped tones of a far more matronly lady. He'd never guessed that the woman with such a huge collection of dirty jokes would have looked like such a sweet, innocent grandmother either. And as for Liam…

Marcus turned his attention back to the ceiling. The Liam in his mind had been very different.

The fact the boy's hair wasn't the golden blond it had been in his mental image, or that he wasn't anywhere near as pretty as Marcus might have imagined him to be, was neither here nor there. The fact that chocolate brown eyes peered up at him rather than big blue ones couldn't have mattered less. He'd been prepared to be wrong about such insignificant details.

But Marcus hadn't been ready for the fear he'd seen in Liam's eyes. He hadn't prepared himself for the way the boy flinched away from him in something akin to terror in those first few moments after he'd woken up.

Marcus swallowed down the bitter taste in the back of his throat. His mental picture of Liam had been so comfortable in his leather bondage, so confident while he knelt at his master's feet and…

He shook his head. It wasn't the time for that. Maybe one day. No. *Certainly* one day. But not today. Today, he simply had to find Liam and bring the boy back where he belonged.

Shifting his position slightly, Marcus tried to make himself more comfortable. Even that minor exertion exhausted him. A glance at the bag that had contained blood, but which was now hanging empty on the stand by his bedside, and he pressed the buzzer for a nurse.

His teeth ached for a real feed, but Marcus pushed away the idea. He'd waited this long, he could wait for Liam's return.

Chapter Five

Intense light shone against Liam's eyelids. Pink and red blurs filled his world. Frowning, he tried to turn his head and close his eyes tighter to escape the brightness.

A wave of agony rolled through him. Liam immediately stilled, fighting down nausea. Trying to move again was out of the question.

"Liam? Are you with us?"

The voice was right on the edge of his hearing. It seemed to come from a long way away.

Was he with who? He didn't know. Liam tried to focus, tried to make his thoughts travel through the thick wadding that filled his brain. He'd been...thinking about Marcus. He remembered that much. He'd been thinking really hard about Marcus and the way it had felt when Marcus wrapped his arms around him and held him close in the tiny hospital bed.

He'd been thinking about how wonderful it would have felt to have been able to snuggle in closer and take deep breaths full of Marcus's scent, to be allowed to tilt his head back and offer up his lips to be kissed.

"I was..." he mumbled.

Liam lifted a hand and rubbed at his face in an effort to clear the sleep and fog from his view of the world. Pain exploded in his eye. There was only one thing he knew of that could lead to that kind of throbbing agony.

Yes... He remembered now. Pain. There had been a lot of pain. Even as the memory brushed against the edges of his conscious mind, Liam gasped, his body somehow hoping that enough oxygen would allow fight or flight to be more successful this time.

"Liam?"

Blinking, Liam looked up. A man swam into focus in front of him. White coat. Stethoscope. Doctor.

"The runner at the top of the stairs," Liam whispered, his words slurring despite all his best efforts. "I... My lace came undone, it got caught in the loose runner. I must have fallen. I don't really remember much..."

The doctor didn't even blink. His lips narrowed into a thin disapproving line as he made a note on his chart. "This particular *fall* has left you with some pretty serious injuries."

Liam nodded his head very slightly. "My ribs," he whispered.

"Yes," the doctor said, staring at another page in the file. "For the third time, apparently."

"Broken?" Liam asked.

"Cracked. Four of them," the doctor said. "Those stairs kicked you pretty hard. Their shoe imprint is quite noticeable. Luckily, you seem to have escaped without any internal bleeding."

Liam kept his eyes on the back of the file. It wasn't quite as thick as the file that hung on the bottom of Marcus's bed, but more pages had been added every time he turned up at the hospital. It probably wouldn't be long before his file overtook Marcus's now that the vampire was awake.

"There's also a nasty concussion we want to keep an eye on."

Liam once more nodded his understanding.

"Now that you're responsive, I'll need to examine you for—"

"No!"

The doctor had barely taken a step forward before Liam had his back pressed hard against the sloping frame of the hospital bed. His ribs screamed in pain. His head felt as if it were being split open. Other injuries quickly made themselves known. His wrist caught fire. A sharp stabbing pain sliced up through his rear.

There was no way he could let anyone lay a hand on him.

The doctor hesitated for a moment, a touch of sympathy joining the impatience in his eyes. "I'll make everything as painless as I can, Liam, but this needs to be done."

Liam nodded his understanding, but there was no way in hell he could make his heart stop racing or release his painfully tight grip on the bedding.

As the doctor cautiously approached him once more, Liam stared down at his knuckles. He focused as hard as he could on the cramp that spread through his hand and up his arm. That was the only thing he allowed into his mind.

Everything else was happening to someone else, someone who was a long way away, someone who wasn't even a little bit scared of having another man's hands on him, someone who wasn't reminded of an even more painful touch with every movement. It was someone else who was being moved so that intimate parts of his body could be examined, someone else who was finally rearranged again so he lay on his back again.

"You can relax now." The words must have been spoken to that other man. Liam did his best not to eavesdrop on a conversation that couldn't possibly have anything to do with him. There was no way in hell anyone could be stupid enough to order him to relax—to think he was capable of obeying such an order.

"Liam."

A hand came to rest on a shoulder. It shook him very gently. One brain cell at a time, Liam turned his attention away from the hand he'd been staring at for the last fifteen minutes.

Yes, he remembered now, that was his hand. And that was his shoulder that someone was shaking, wasn't it?

He looked up, into the doctor's eyes.

"Do you have any questions?"

Liam cleared his throat before he attempted to speak, but the words still came out in a thin rasping sound. "Which hospital am I at, please?"

"St. Luke's," the doctor said. "Does it matter?"

Yes, it mattered. Liam could barely stop himself from looking over his shoulder, as if some fluke might have led him to be sharing a room with Marcus. But, of course, he wasn't. Marcus was probably long gone by now.

"I..." Liam swallowed down the lump in his throat and tried again. "When may I leave?"

The doctor peered at him over the top of his glasses. "We're still waiting for a few test results to come back. Even if we weren't, you're in no condition to go anywhere. I'm putting you under observation for twenty-four hours minimum."

Liam looked down. He was just as trapped there as he had been back in Ralph's house. It didn't look like there were steel bars on the doors and windows, but there might as well have been.

Turning his back on the door as the doctor finally left his bedside, Liam tried to curl into as small a ball as his injuries allowed, and pulled the blankets tight around his shoulders. It was all he could do not to give in to the temptation to tug them up even further, all the way over his head, as if he were a little kid who could escape the monster who'd shared his bed as easily as he'd evaded those he'd thought might live beneath it.

* * * * *

"Liam?"

Liam tried to open his eyes. One side of his face was still a mass of pain, but somehow he managed to pry both lids up.

A nurse stared down at him, barely disguised horror in her eyes. The rest of her expression was cheerful and reassuring, but that didn't quite conceal how she really felt. Even while his vision remained blurred, Liam recognised her. She didn't belong in this part of the hospital at all—she should have been up with Marcus. "Jenny?"

The nurse crouched down by the side of the bed so he didn't have to tilt his head in order to see her properly. "How are you feeling?" she asked.

"I'm fine," Liam murmured, but he couldn't make the words sound convincing. "Can I go home now? I…"

She made any other words pointless when she shook her head. Liam didn't have enough strength to fight about it.

"I do have a nice surprise for you, though," Jenny said, with an even brighter smile.

Liam frowned slightly. He'd been to the hospital lots of times since he'd moved in with Ralph. There had never been surprises involved before. He wasn't at all sure he was capable of dealing with another shock to his system.

"Someone has come all the way down here, especially to visit you."

The words turned the world slow and sticky. The air around Liam congealed. There was no oxygen. A vacuum pulled every molecule of it from his lungs. In slow motion, he managed to shake his head.

That movement woke up other muscles. His shoulders came to life. His arms pushed against the bedding, trying to scramble away from the idea.

He couldn't be there. Ralph never came to the hospital. In all the times he'd sent Liam to one hospital or another, he'd never once come to visit. He just tossed him in a taxi and paid off the driver. That was the way things were supposed to be.

Twisting his head, Liam looked around the room for any sort of escape route, but there was only the door leading into the hallway, and that was the door that Ralph was going to walk through at any second and…

Liam pressed himself back against the pillows, hard enough to send waves of pain rebounding through him, up through the cleft between his buttocks and into every other part of his body. Footsteps sounded in the hallway. Something squeaked against the freshly mopped floor.

A wheelchair came into view, a blanket tucked neatly around the legs of whoever was sitting in it. Liam dragged his gaze up to the person's face.

Marcus...

Liam tried to turn his head toward Jenny, but his eyes remained fixed on Marcus's face.

"No!" Finally, he managed to look across at Jenny, his eyes pleading. "No, Jenny, I...I don't want to see him. Please, tell him to—"

"Liam?"

It was too late. The strong, deep voice already emanated from inside the room. Liam turned away from it as quickly as he was able, painfully rolling his body toward the window and turning his face into the pillow.

The cotton was soft, yet it scraped against his injured face like sandpaper.

Another squeak of rubber wheels against the lino floor sent a second wave of panic through Liam. No. He might have been able to take the rest, but the idea of this sort of pain invading his one refuge, of Marcus seeing him like that—that would make it real. It would make it inescapable and—

"Leave us."

"Liam?" Jenny asked.

Turning his face more firmly into the pillow, Liam tried to hide from her too. As tears flooded his eyes, gentle fingers stroked through his hair. A moment later, he felt something touch his hand. Hard plastic gradually wormed its way beneath his palm. "Just press the button if you want me. I'll be right outside. Okay?"

A moment later, the door into the tiny room clicked closed. Marcus was still there. Even while he refused to look in the vampire's direction, Liam could feel his presence. The room wasn't quite the haven Liam remembered Marcus's room being before Marcus woke up, but an unexpected calmness slowly seemed to settle over the space as the seconds passed.

No one said a word. Liam frowned into his pillow. Unease quickly began to bubble inside him. Marcus remaining silent because he was sleeping was one thing. Marcus being silent when he seemed to have put so much effort into coming to talk to him, hinted that all wasn't as well with Marcus as Liam desperately wanted it to be.

Very slowly, he forced his eyes open and turned his face away from the pillow. The world remained blurry for a few seconds. As it cleared, Liam saw Marcus sitting directly in front of him, studying him very seriously.

Liam closed his eyes again, knowing what Marcus must see when he looked at him and hating the whole world for it.

Something brushed against Liam's hand once more, but it wasn't plastic this time. Marcus slid his hand into Liam's, just as Liam had held Marcus's hand so many times over the last few months — on those occasions when he'd needed gentle contact and hadn't thought that Marcus would either know or care that their fingers were wound together.

"I'm sorry," Liam whispered.

"Hush." The word was gently spoken, but that didn't make it sound any the less like an order. Liam had no doubt that Marcus expected it to be obeyed. "You have nothing to be sorry for — except not waking me before you left."

Liam pried his eyes open once more. Marcus's hand was bigger than Liam's, his fingers were longer and they wrapped around Liam's hand perfectly, completely encasing it and protecting it from the world.

Liam didn't try to make any sort of excuse for anything else. There didn't seem to be any hope that Marcus would take any notice of it if he did. Liam had the distinct impression that Marcus wasn't the type of man to accept excuses under any circumstances.

Silence descended. It remained until Liam couldn't

stand it anymore. "It...it's good you're feeling well enough to get out of bed," he whispered.

Marcus lifted his free hand and moved it very slowly toward Liam's face. There was no threat in the gesture—probably because Marcus seemed to be working very hard to ensure that was the case. His fingertips carded through Liam's hair, brushing it back off his face.

Liam almost smiled at the gentleness, until he realised that Marcus was merely trying to get a better view so he could assess the damage more easily.

"How much pain are you in?"

Liam shook his head and ignored the way the gesture made his head ache all the more. "I'm fine, I just—"

Marcus's fingertip came to rest against Liam's mouth, silencing him. It pressed against a part of his bottom lip that wasn't split, but that still didn't make the touch entirely painless. Somehow, Liam managed not to flinch.

If he pulled back, he had the horrible feeling that Marcus might take his hand away, that Marcus would never want to touch him again. Liam couldn't let that happen. He needed Marcus's touch far too badly to risk losing it.

"Vampires and humans are different," Marcus said, his expression very serious. "Vampires are stronger, more resilient. We don't feel pain the same way humans do. Even so, I'm not a fool, Liam. You're not fine."

Liam swallowed rapidly, unable to look Marcus in the eye when he spoke to him like that. It brought back far too many memories, not of his time with Ralph, but of a life before that, of those times when he'd been caught being naughty as a child. His eyes turned watery at the memory. If his parents could see him now...

"Try to answer my question again," Marcus ordered. "How much pain are you in?"

Liam turned his attention back to Marcus's hand. When he'd been really little, his mother had held his hand when he'd been sick. That had made him feel better too. He found himself tightening his hold on Marcus's fingers, scared that Marcus might try to take them away.

He was completely incapable of lying. "A lot," he whispered. He was in a lot of pain. "The doctor said they can't give me anything too strong because they don't want to mask any indications of a concussion and..."

Marcus shook his head, freeing Liam from the responsibility of finding more words to add to the end of the sentence. The vampire was silent for a few moments. He stared down at Liam's hand, his expression emotionless.

He was obviously deep in thought. Liam didn't interrupt.

Several seconds slipped passed. Liam risked another glance at Marcus's face. Marcus wasn't staring at his hand anymore; he was staring at his neck. Liam had never seen such an intense expression.

No!

Without thinking, he snatched his hand out of Marcus's hold and covered his neck.

No!

Something inside Liam screamed the word so loudly, it drowned out any other thoughts in his head. No, he didn't want a vampire's teeth inside him. He didn't want any part of any man inside him ever again.

Liam closed his eyes very tightly, cowering away from Marcus until his back hit into the cot-like railing on the far side of the hospital bed. Tucking his head down, Liam protected his neck as best he could. He curled into a ball as his whole body started to shake.

Sweat broke out on his skin. His breathing sped up. Liam's heart raced faster and faster. His ribs screamed. Half the muscles in his body seemed to moan in pain, but all he could do was try to force himself into as small a space as possible.

"No..."

Liam could barely gather enough breath to do more

than whisper the word, but that made no difference to how loud the screams were in his head, how real Ralph's hands felt against him. Pain burned inside him, and it was almost impossible to believe that Ralph wasn't right there, his body pressed against Liam's back, and his cock forcing its way inside him.

"No…" It was half a protest, half a sob.

"Liam." Something came to rest on his shoulder. "Liam."

Liam tried to twist away, but whatever it was still lay on his shoulder, impossible to shake off. Whimpering into his blanket, Liam gave in and stopped trying to escape.

"You're safe. No one can hurt you now."

The hand on his shoulder slowly warmed the skin beneath it. No pain followed. Liam shuddered as he frowned into the darkness behind his eyelids.

He heard something behind him and whimpered.

The hand didn't move. "Liam's going to be fine," the person in front of him repeated.

They sounded so confident, it was impossible to dismiss their words entirely. The idea that nothing would ever be fine again suddenly had competition inside Liam's mind.

Another noise behind him made Liam uncurl slightly.

"It's okay, she's gone. It's just you and me now."

The hand on Liam's shoulder didn't move. It just lay there, reminding him that Marcus was still sitting alongside his bed. Very gradually, Liam's panic began to drain away.

He uncurled far enough to lift his head a little. He opened his eyes. Marcus's expression was still impossible to read.

Keeping his left hand where it was, Marcus extended his right hand toward Liam, palm open and upraised as if to prove there was nothing in his grip.

He brushed clumsily at the skin beneath Liam's eyes with his thumb. He obviously wasn't used to wiping away another man's tears. There was no reason why he should be.

Slowly, Marcus resolved into the same person who had lain in the bed Liam had visited. There was nothing to fear from him. Liam uncurled a little more and stopped trying to cover his neck.

He brushed away the tears himself, ashamed of their presence. Both of Marcus's hands retreated in response.

"I'm sorry."

Marcus said nothing for several long seconds.

Working entirely on instinct, Liam shuffled closer to him, wanting Marcus's hand to return to his shoulder, needing Marcus's touch in a way he'd never needed anything before.

"I can ease your pain," Marcus finally said. "If that's what you want."

Liam frowned slightly, staring at Marcus through watery eyes, unable to make any sense of his words.

"You know what I am," Marcus said, with that same great care. "Vampires would have died out a long time ago if the humans that we fed from felt pain — or if they didn't heal quickly. My bite could ease some of your pain and help you heal — but having me feed from you right now... If you're not ready for that..."

Liam stared at Marcus's interlinked fingers as Marcus rested his elbows on the arms of his wheelchair. Marcus's hand had felt so good in his. He'd felt safer than he had in as long as he could remember.

If Marcus wanted his blood in exchange for that then... Liam took a deep breath. It wouldn't be so bad. It wouldn't be anything like what happened with Ralph. Teeth weren't the same as...

Liam closed his eyes for a moment. When he opened them, he knew he wasn't going to refuse Marcus anything he wanted. But, as more of the vampire's words forced their way through the fog of pain and sank properly into his mind, Liam began to frown. "No." He looked up and met Marcus's eyes with all the determination he could muster. "Not if you'll feel my pain when you…"

Marcus shook his head, and Liam's will to speak faded away. "That's not the way it works."

*

After three years trapped in a hospital bed, Marcus had thought he understood everything there was to know about feeling helpless. He'd been wrong. Wide awake and out of his bed, all he could do was sit there and watch the emotions flicker through Liam's eyes.

Knowing exactly how to help the boy, but not being able to do so without Liam's permission, made every muscle in Marcus's body tense. But at the same time, to demand the right to help him, to take away the choice to accept or refuse his offer — it would have made him no better than that bastard, Ralph, or whatever people who didn't know he was a complete bastard referred to him as.

An acrid taste flooded Marcus's mouth, reminding him how bitter an experience being awake and back in the real world could be, but he took care to keep his expression completely impassive.

No pressure, no judgment, just complete acceptance of whatever it was that Liam needed from him. If that was a feeding, fine. If it was for Marcus not to feed from him, that had to be fine, too. As those thoughts circled around and around in Marcus's mind, he lost track of who exactly he was trying to convince.

As unnatural as it felt, as unvampire-like as it felt, Marcus remained perfectly still and waited with more patience than he'd ever known he possessed.

Finally, Liam met his eyes. Their gazes only locked for a second, but that was all the time Marcus needed in order to realise that Liam had made his decision. Reaching out to him, he took Liam's hand in his once more, taking great care not to accidently crush the fragile bones as his anxiety doubled over and over again.

For a fully grown vampire to be nervous about a feeding…

Marcus knew he should have been ashamed of himself. It was pathetic. But at the same time, this wasn't just any feeding. And that wasn't merely because this was his first feeding in three very, very long years. Liam wasn't some anonymous body in a human leather bar. The boy wasn't just looking to get whipped and screwed and bitten.

"It has to be a vein?" Liam asked, very softly.

Marcus nodded, forcing his mind to simplify the whole task down to its most basic components. "Yes."

"My neck?" Liam's free hand went up to his jugular.

Marcus's mouth watered at the prospect, but he forced himself to shake his head. "Any vein. Your wrist would be fine."

Liam's eyes immediately went to the hold Marcus had on his hand. Marcus didn't follow his gaze; he kept all his attention on the boy's face. Liam seemed to relax somewhat as he realised Marcus wasn't going to jump on his bed and pin him to the mattress as he bit.

"There's a natural anaesthetic in the bite which will ease your pain," Marcus explained again. "And it will release endorphins that will help you feel calmer too."

Liam swallowed. His teeth nibbled at an un-split portion of his bottom lip as he seemed to give the whole matter careful thought. Then, very slowly, he took his hand from Marcus's hold.

Holding back his disappointment, determined that Liam should see no hint of how much it hurt him to know that Liam was too traumatised to accept the only help he could give him, Marcus leaned back a fraction in his chair, letting the canvas behind him support his weight, allowing his muscles to relax.

In that same slow way, Liam turned over the hand Marcus had been holding and offered it back to Marcus, palm up—vein up.

For an incredibly long time, Marcus sat like a fool, while Liam offered him everything he wanted. When he finally reached out to him, Marcus's movements were even slower than Liam's had been.

Marcus ran his thumb very gently over the spot where he could see Liam's vein pulsating. "You're certain?" he asked.

Liam nodded. "As long as you're sure it won't hurt you," he whispered.

Marcus shook his head. "You don't need to worry yourself about my well-being. Leave that to me, okay?"

Liam didn't nod the way he usually did when anyone asked him to do something. Until then, that particular response had seemed to be as instinctive as his habit of agreeing with everyone, but there was something in Liam that wasn't willing to accede to that request. He wasn't willing to not care about someone—not even someone who'd never given him the slightest reason to give a damn about him.

"If you say stop, I will." It was the first time Marcus ever remembered saying such a thing—the first time it had ever occurred to him that a man he was feeding from might change his mind and want him to stop.

Liam did nod his acceptance of that point, a jerky little bob of the head, but he didn't seem as reassured as Marcus had hoped he would. Helpless to do anything else to ease Liam's fears now, Marcus didn't give him any extra time to get even more nervous about it. He bowed his head over the offered wrist.

It took all the strength Marcus had been aware he possessed, and more, to make sure he didn't kiss the skin before he let his teeth scrape across the pale surface.

He had permission to *bite*, not to make the feeding about anything other than that.

For the first time in three years, Marcus's teeth sliced cleanly through human skin. The first drop of blood exploded on his tongue, setting fire to every taste bud it touched. It was ambrosia after so long spent barely surviving on a meagre diet of animal blood. Marcus's veins quickly accepted Liam's offering without the slightest hint of discomfort.

Marcus longed to simply let his eyes drift closed and savour it, but he kept his gaze up and his attention on Liam's face, searching for any hint that Liam had changed his mind, that this wasn't what he wanted.

For a moment, the only expression on Liam's face was shock. His hand tightened into a fist. Then, very slowly, his expression changed. A touch of something that looked suspiciously like serenity crept across Liam's features. His hand unfurled, offering his open palm to Marcus once more.

At the same time, the taste in Marcus's mouth changed. Yes, it was human blood and it was exactly what he had longed for. To a sadist it would have no doubt tasted like the most exquisite vintage. To Marcus, it quickly turned sour.

He was almost willing to swear that he could taste each blow that had landed on Liam's skin, that he could sense the way each bruise had formed, and the way each nerve ending had relayed its distress through Liam's body.

Within moments, all Marcus could taste was Liam's pain and fear. He swallowed it down regardless; his body in frantic need of the blood, his soul desperate to do whatever it took to ease Liam's anguish.

Above his bowed head, Marcus heard Liam's breaths even out, as if they were no longer inhibited by his damaged ribs and his lungs were now able to work however they wished.

Marcus ran his tongue over the wounds penetrating Liam's vein. Blood still seeped steadily into his mouth. Liam had plenty to spare. He wouldn't miss what his lover was—

Marcus mentally shook his head at himself. What his *friend* was taking from him. That was important. Liam needed a friend. He didn't need a vampire metaphorically humping his leg.

Marcus could be a friend to a human in need. He wasn't sure exactly how someone went about being such a thing, but if humans could manage it, he was quite sure that he could, too. Vampires weren't top of the food chain because they were incapable of being better than humans were at any given task.

Gradually, Liam's scent changed. Marcus's senses immediately homed in on the alteration. There was no fear in the air now, just desire, just sex.

Chapter Six

The scent of Liam's arousal filled Marcus's senses as he took a series of deep breaths. It rushed to Marcus's cock just as fast as his newly improved blood supply. Within seconds Marcus was painfully hard, his cock straining against the inside of the pyjama bottoms that Jenson had somehow summoned up when he'd finally realised that Marcus fully intended to visit his located submissive, trousers or no trousers.

Marcus's eyes dropped closed for a moment. He'd imagined the scenario so often—Liam stretched out languidly in a bed, the boy's blood on his tongue, and the scent of their mutual desire hanging in the air.

If it weren't for one little detail, it would have been perfect. Marcus pried his eyes open. The lingering taste of pain and fear in Liam's blood killed his fantasy completely.

In his daydreams, there had only been pleasure. There had also been a never-ending supply of blood that could be swallowed down without harming anyone. He'd taken enough to ease the boy's pain now. He couldn't in good conscience take more.

Withdrawing his teeth from the wounds, Marcus ran his tongue over them, gently encouraging them to heal. Within seconds, the bite was closed. As he pulled away, Marcus quickly inspected Liam's wrist. Every trace of blood, any vestige of a scar, anything, in short, that could upset Liam, needed to have disappeared, before he could risk lifting his head further and allowing the boy a clear view of the skin covering the vein.

As Marcus drew back a little more, his shadow moved

off Liam's wrist. Strong overhead lighting poured down on his skin, but Marcus's assessment had been accurate. There wasn't any hint that a feeding had taken place. Even after all this time, Marcus still had the knack. But there was no time to smile in triumph.

Looking up, Marcus focused in on Liam's face. The boy's eyes were closed, his teeth were biting down on his bottom lip hard enough to turn the skin beneath his teeth white.

Marcus took another deep breath, assessing Liam's scent. There was no fear in the air now, but there was desire, so much desire, and it wasn't all Marcus's own. Yet the blush staining Liam's cheeks didn't appear to be entirely caused either by pleasure or by the sudden relief from pain. A frown crept across Marcus's brow.

"Liam?" Marcus leaned forward and stroked Liam's cheek with his knuckle. "Liam, open your eyes, look at me."

A lifetime passed before Liam did as Marcus commanded.

"I know it's just a reaction to the bite, to the pain fading away so quickly. I'm not going to think it means anything else, and I'm not going to think it gives me any rights that I don't have," Marcus said, as gently as he knew how. Right then, that didn't seem to be anything like gently enough.

Liam swallowed rapidly, his Adam's apple bobbing as he made a blatant attempt to keep his emotions under control. "I'm sorry—"

"You have nothing to be sorry for," Marcus cut in, firmly. "Nothing at all."

Liam nodded as if he believed him, but his eyes proclaimed that to be a lie, so did the blush still darkening his cheeks.

Scrambling for anything he could say which might make Liam feel better, Marcus blurted out the first thing that came into his mind. "The bite has the same effect on vampires."

Liam lowered his eyes. For once, that didn't seem to have anything to do with embarrassment or submission. His gaze hit Marcus's crotch. The next moment Liam's attention was back on Marcus's face, and it didn't waver from there again.

Marcus scrolled through every curse he knew. The last thing Liam needed was some fool waving a hard-on in his direction.

"I'm a grown man, Liam. I learned a long time ago that, if a man ignores an erection for long enough, it will go away on its own, no matter what a teenage vampire might think."

A burst of surprised laughter escaped from Liam. He lifted one hand to cover his mouth, but his other hand didn't move to hold his ribs. They were obviously causing him far less pain. The anaesthetic in the bite was working.

Marcus smiled as he swallowed once more, trying to rid his senses of the bitter aftertaste the boy's agony had left in his mouth.

Liam smiled back. It was a tentative expression, but Marcus was willing to take whatever he could get.

"How do you feel now?" he asked.

Liam parted his lips to answer, only to stop himself short. He frowned slightly. "Better," he finally whispered, confusion hanging on each syllable. "I feel a lot better. Thank you."

Marcus waved away his gratitude with an idle gesture, almost all his attention still devoted to watching Liam's movements and assessing the extent of his remaining injuries. "That's good," he finally said. "It should let you rest more comfortably for a little while at least."

"And you're okay?" Liam asked.

Marcus nodded. Okay—that was probably one word for it. More accurately, it felt like someone had taken a tin opener to the top of his head and all his thoughts were floating out through the top of his skull.

Human blood... He was as giddy now as he had been

as a teenager, taking his first ever feeding.

It wasn't quite what he'd expected his first new feeding to be like when he finally woke up. There was far less leather in the room for one thing. And, while there was a bed, a hospital contraption wasn't quite what he'd had in mind.

Marcus smiled slightly. The only similarity was that the man he'd hoped for really was there.

"What are you thinking?" Liam whispered.

Marcus focused in on the boy with only a little difficulty. "I'm thinking that it's been a very long time since I tasted human blood," he said, honestly.

Liam dropped his gaze for a moment. "You missed it?"

"Every minute of every day."

"The animal blood—"

Marcus shook his head, a sharp, angry little gesture he was incapable of keeping back.

Every muscle in Liam's body tensed, as if he expected the sky to fall down upon him, or perhaps the earth to tremble and huge fissures to open up beneath him, ready to take him straight down into the deepest hell imaginable, just because he'd said the wrong thing.

"Animal blood isn't the same," Marcus explained, taking care to keep his voice level and unemotional. "Neither is a transfusion. It will keep a vampire alive in an emergency, but it's like having stinging nettles injected into your blood stream."

Instant sympathy flooded Liam's eyes.

"You don't taste at all like nettles," Marcus reassured.

That raised a smile.

Marcus prayed that the boy wouldn't ask him what he actually tasted like. He'd hate to have to lie to him.

"The bite, it's supposed to make a guy..." Liam dropped his gaze toward the tent in his hospital gown. His teeth nibbled against his bottom lip—if the split there caused him any discomfort, he gave no indication of it.

"It can't force unnatural feelings on someone," Marcus

said, carefully. "All that bull about vampires binding humans to them is nothing more than Hollywood's stupidity."

Liam serenely nodded his understanding. Marcus was reasonably sure he'd have done the same if he'd told him that he was bound to him for the rest of his life. The endorphins from a feeding were a wonderful thing.

Liam's eyes were drooping as if he could hardly keep them open. Marcus felt much the same way. His body seemed to have realised that if it wasn't going to be allowed to have sex, sleep was its next best option.

"I should leave you to get some sleep," Marcus said, hiding his reluctance as best he could.

"No!"

Marcus paused in the act of taking his hand away from the side of the bed as Liam caught hold of his sleeve.

"I'm sorry," Liam said a moment later, snatching his hand back.

Reaching out, Marcus carefully took Liam's hand in his and guided it forward to rest on his arm just as it had a moment before. The only difference this time was that he covered the boy's fingers with his own palm, making sure that Liam was left in no doubt that his hand was very welcome there. "No?"

"I don't want you to go," Liam blurted out.

"Then I'll stay," Marcus said, easily. His back cursed him for an idiot. There was no way in hell he was going to be able to sit upright much longer. Even with Liam's blood giving him strength, his muscles simply weren't used to it. It would take time to build up their stamina again. Adrenaline was only going to take him so far.

"I'm not afraid of you."

That was the bite talking. While it couldn't make a man feel something that was against his nature, it wasn't exactly unknown for it to loosen a guy's tongue a little.

"That's good," Marcus said, doing his damnedest not to offer the slightest nudge to make Liam open up even more.

There was obviously a reason he'd never bothered to develop a conscience before. Trying to be a good guy sucked, and not in the way his canines thrived on.

"We could… This bed's the same size as the one in your room," Liam whispered.

Marcus nodded as he caught up with what Liam was trying to offer him, what Liam was trying to ask him for. Yes. His back needed him to be able to lie down. For some more mysterious reason, his arms seemed to need his permission to wrap around Liam's body just as badly. "With one proviso," Marcus said, seriously. "You don't leave while I'm asleep."

Liam opened his mouth, but Marcus spoke up again before he had a chance to say a single word. "I don't want you to apologise. I don't want you to feel guilty. I simply want your word that it won't happen again."

Liam stared down at the cheap hospital blanket for several long seconds.

"You can leave whenever you wish. I won't try to stop you," Marcus promised, even though it went against everything his instincts demanded. "But I want to know before you walk out of this room."

One little nod.

Marcus breathed a little easier. If the bite had encouraged Liam to trust him, then it seemed to be having the same effect on Marcus. And, as a reward, he now had the pleasure of sleeping chastely next to the man he'd been fantasising about having sex with for the last six months.

He was slowly starting to understand exactly why vampires had a habit of using blood sources and throwing them away without ever getting attached. Getting to know someone, realising that they deserved to be treated with kindness, made things far more complicated.

Liam edged closer to the farthest side of the bed.

"The other side."

Liam blinked at him.

"I'll sleep on that side, between you and the door,"

Marcus said, without really thinking about it.

Liam looked down. "I meant it when I promised I wouldn't leave without—"

"No," Marcus corrected. "So I'll be between you and anyone who enters the room."

Liam glanced up at him, then down, as if he didn't understand why anyone would want to do that. As if it had never occurred to him that someone willing to stand strong between him and anything that might hurt him was exactly what he needed.

* * * * *

Warmth and comfort completely surrounded Liam. He squirmed slightly, relishing the sensation. Whatever was wrapped around him, tightened its hold in response. That was even better. Liam smiled sleepily as he turned his face into his pillow.

No. It wasn't a pillow. It was harder than that. Liam frowned slightly as he tried to work out what it was. An arm. His head was resting on someone's arm. That was it.

Ralph!

Every muscle in Liam's body tensed.

"Hush." The word was murmured in Liam's ear—as gentle and as non-threatening as it could possibly be.

That was strange. Even when everything had been good between them, Ralph had never spoken to him in that soft tone of voice. Whenever he woke up, Ralph had always been pissed off, and almost inevitably sporting morning wood.

Liam's stomach turned over at the possibility. If he said no, Ralph would just get even more pissed off with him. But the idea of saying yes…

"It's early, try to go back to sleep," that same voice whispered to him.

Marcus. Slowly, memories started to present

themselves for Liam's consideration. As the vampire's body moved against Liam's back, wrapping itself around him more comfortably, Liam felt the hard length of an erection press against his buttocks.

Opening his mouth to speak, Liam found his mind completely empty of words. Sleep, he'd said. Marcus didn't seem to be in any rush to demand that Liam take care of his hard-on for him. All Liam had to do was stay calm and —

All his very sensible thoughts failed him as he opened his eyes.

"What the hell?" Liam tried to jerk away from the figure sitting in the chair alongside the bed. There was nowhere for him to go, Marcus was right behind him. Except, suddenly, Marcus wasn't behind Liam, he was above him. Before Liam knew what was happening, Marcus had rolled over him and half-pinned him to the bed. He let out a low snarling growl at the intruder.

Liam stared up at Marcus, wide-eyed. But, as quickly as he had transformed into someone Liam had never set eyes on before, the vampire morphed back into a calm, gentle figure and rolled them back into their original positions.

"Liam meet Jenson, Jenson this is Liam."

"A pleasure to meet you, sir," the man rose from his seat and half-bowed in Liam's direction.

All Liam could do was stare. There wasn't anything particularly scary about the guy. He was dressed in a very non-terrifying business suit and looked to be in his late fifties, with greying hair and pale blue eyes.

"I..." Liam shook his head in an effort to clear it. He looked to Marcus for help.

"Just say hello back," Marcus ordered.

"Hi," Liam managed to mumble.

The older man, Jenson, Marcus had called him, gave another one of those strange little half-bows.

Liam looked over his shoulder at Marcus once more.

"Jenson works for me," Marcus said, a trace of sleep

still in his voice. "He's my butler."

He might as well have declared the guy to be his astronaut. Liam would have had about the same chance of wrapping his mind around that.

"Butler," he repeated, blankly.

"He's been looking after my affairs while I've been...unavailable."

Liam nodded, as if that explained everything. Dropping his gaze to the bed they shared, reminded Liam exactly where he was. A blush rushed to his cheeks. He automatically reached out to pull the blanket up so he could hide behind it as much as possible.

"I took the liberty of obtaining replacement garments that you may find suitable, sir."

It took Liam a full minute to realise that Jenson was talking to him. "I...I probably won't be able to pay you back straight away," he blurted out. He doubted Ralph would be in any mood to offer any hand-outs any time soon.

Liam shuffled away from Marcus a little, wondering how the hell he was going to make sure Ralph never found out about any of this. His mind whirled faster and faster. Ralph was going to be angry, but...

He closed his eyes. "When I get home, maybe I could ask Ralph if—"

"Liam." A hand came to rest on Liam's cheek and demanded that he turn and face Marcus properly. "You're not going back to him."

"I—"

"It's not open for debate," Marcus cut in. "You can't go back to him again, not this time. You see that, don't you?"

Liam stared down at the blanket between them.

"Jenson, give us a few minutes."

Liam was vaguely aware of the butler leaving the room, but he didn't look up.

"Liam?" Marcus asked.

"I..." He had no idea what to say.

"Are you in love with him?"

Liam shook his head, taking the opportunity to rub his cheek against Marcus's hand at the same time. Any love he might have felt for Ralph had died a long time ago, but that didn't mean he could just walk away.

"Does he have some sort of hold over you?"

Liam frowned slightly. He risked a glance up at Marcus's face. "I don't..."

"Is there some way he could make things difficult for you if you left him?" Marcus translated.

Liam shrugged. As if things wouldn't be difficult enough once he was out on the streets without a penny to his name.

"Take some time to think about it," Marcus ordered.

Marcus fell silent then, and Liam couldn't help but obey. Life without Ralph. Not having to worry every time he heard the front door open, not having to watch how much whiskey Ralph had poured down his own throat just in case fists were about to fly.

Life without a front door between him and the world...

Liam closed his eyes for a moment. Not this time. Marcus was right. He couldn't go back to him this time. "I'll be fine," he whispered.

The words didn't come out strong and confident, the way he'd intended. They sounded more like a child whispering in the dark—a child who was too young to have any real faith that the darkness around him would eventually pass and the sun would come up.

"Yes, you will." Marcus sounded like someone who knew all about the dawn.

Liam glanced up at him once more. Marcus's lips were curved into a slight smile. Liam smiled back at him, only to wince as the cut on his lip pulled at the skin around it.

"How are you feeling?"

Liam pressed his fingers to his lips. There wasn't any blood. That was good. "I'm fine."

"The bite is wearing off." It wasn't a question; Liam didn't bother to try to lie in response. Trying not to wince, he sat up and turned away, letting his feet dangle over the edge of the bed.

His head swam. It wasn't the same as he usually felt the first morning after a beating. It felt far more like he'd already had several days to heal, but it was still painful to move off the bed. A breeze caressed his back. Liam frowned as he reached behind him. The back of the hospital gown he'd been given didn't quite meet. How could he have forgotten something like that!

He was flashing his bare arse at Marcus. Liam spun around. There wasn't a window in the room, just the one door, and it was on the other side of Marcus. Liam took a step back, then another. Metal and plastic clattered to the floor as he reversed into the bedside cabinet.

Water cascaded onto his bare feet as the jug on the cabinet tipped over and the contents splashed off the edge of the melamine surface.

Liam jerked back again, crashing into a flimsy plastic chair.

"Liam!"

He turned back to Marcus, just in time to see the vampire reach out toward him. Liam's attention focused in on Marcus's hand. It wasn't shaped into a fist, but it didn't need to be to give him the back-hander he deserved.

"Liam, you're okay."

A click from the door had Liam turning his head toward it. The other guy, the butler—Jenson, stood in the doorway.

"Everything's fine, Jenson. Close the door on your way out."

The door clicked closed. They were once more left alone in the room.

"Look up, Liam. Look me in the eye."

Liam stared down at his wet feet.

"If I have to get up and make you do as I say then…"

Liam knew what would come next. Knew he probably deserved the imminent beating for acting like such a complete idiot.

"…Then there'll be two very dizzy men standing in the middle of the room. I'd rather we didn't end up in a tangled heap on the floor again, if we can avoid it."

The words shocked Liam into looking up and meeting Marcus's eyes. When Marcus smiled at him, Liam managed a half-smile back.

"Jenson said he brought some clothes for you." Marcus waved a hand toward a bag placed in the corner of the room. "They're probably in there."

Liam sidled along to the bag, careful to keep the open back of his gown to the wall, and tentatively undid the zip. There seemed to be at least half a dozen sets of clothes in there, everything from jeans and T-shirts to pyjamas.

"If you'll feel more comfortable dressed, put something on," Marcus ordered.

The temptation was too great, the idea that Marcus could catch sight of any of the injuries that might be glimpsed through the gap in the back of the gown too horrifying.

Making sure he stayed facing Marcus, Liam pulled out a pair of pyjama bottoms and tugged them on underneath the gown. The world was a far better place once his arse was covered up. It lulled him into a false sense of security. Liam pulled the gown off and tossed it aside, thinking of nothing other than how wonderful it was to be rid of it.

An indrawn breath from the other side of the room caught Liam's attention; he looked down at his own body. Bruises had blossomed overnight. Liam ran his fingers very gently over the vivid purples and blacks.

Each mark was a memory. He only just stopped himself flinching from each blow all over again.

"Grab a T-shirt and come here."

Liam found himself doing as Marcus said without even

a moment's hesitation. Marcus took the T-shirt from Liam as he reached the edge of the bed, and tried to help him into it. He didn't seem to have a lot of experience with assisting anyone getting dressed. Liam was pretty sure that, injured or not, he could have done a quicker job by himself, but Marcus looked so pleased with his efforts when Liam's face finally appeared over the top of the cotton, those kinds of facts became irrelevant.

"Thanks."

Marcus nodded his satisfaction as he straightened up the T-shirt a little more. Tapping the bed, Marcus called him to sit on the mattress next to him.

"I should..." Liam waved toward the mess of water on the floor.

Marcus shook his head. "It's not going anywhere."

Liam looked over his shoulder. The puddle wasn't spreading. It didn't seem to be hurting anything.

"Come back to bed."

There was only so much determination that could be directed toward mopping a floor, Liam gave in and climbed stiffly into the bed.

"The bite helped before it started to wear off?"

Liam nodded as he lay down and rested his head on Marcus's shoulder once more.

He looked down at his wrist. There wasn't a mark on it.

"It's up to you," Marcus whispered to him.

Liam didn't even think about it before he found himself offering the vampire his wrist once more.

Marcus cradled it gently in his hand as he brought it to his lips. The angle was different this time. Liam could see what was actually happening. He saw the flash of teeth before Marcus's fangs sliced into his skin.

A gasp escaped from Liam's mouth as he felt Marcus's lips caress the skin around the bite. Marcus lapped against the wounds, driving little peaks of sensation into Liam's body as he encouraged the blood to seep more quickly into his mouth.

Unable to feel afraid, Liam simply closed his eyes and rested his head against Marcus's chest. Marcus wrapped other arm around Liam's shoulders in return, gathering him safe and close as the pain slowly drained from Liam's body.

Within what felt like moments, lack of pain had turned into real pleasure. Whatever blood wasn't flowing out through Liam's wrist raced straight to his cock. He hardened, and there was no way to hide that fact while he was pressed tightly against Marcus's side.

Liam tried to keep control of his body, but he couldn't quite stop his hips from rocking in a way that caused his cock to rub against Marcus's hip.

Whimpering gently, Liam turned his face into Marcus shoulder. Biting down on his bottom lip, he kept his mouth shut, trying not to moan, trying not to writhe.

He couldn't remember the last time he'd felt pleasure like it. Part of him was sure he never had. Once upon a time, sex with Ralph had been something he had looked forward to, but it had never been like this.

Images flashed through Liam's mind, full of naked skin, muscles and long dark hair. Marcus looming over him, pinning him down against black silken sheets. Flickering lights surrounding them, highlighting high cheekbones and serious eyes.

Teeth flashed. The scent of blood filled the air, but for the first time Liam could remember, the smell of it didn't scare him, it didn't come with a wave of pain and nausea, it brought with it pleasure and the need to feel another man's skin against his own. Being trapped by Marcus didn't feel scary, it felt safe.

While his mind was far, far away, in a world where there was no need for hospitals to exist, Liam felt his wrist being moved away from Marcus's mouth and guided down to rest on Marcus's chest. Liam shook his head as he arched his body, pressing himself more firmly against Marcus's side.

"More?" he asked, completely incapable of keeping the

word back.

"Hush. Just rest."

He shook his head, desperate to keep the same warm, contented feeling forever.

"It'll do you more harm than good if I take any more from you now. We need to pace ourselves so you'll be able to get more anaesthetic when you need it."

With just one last whimper of protest, Liam did as he was told. He closed his eyes and just let himself float on a little cloud of pretty pink bliss.

A gentle knock on the door half-roused Liam from his pleasant stupor. The butler guy was back. Liam peered at him through arousal-addled eyes.

He was vaguely aware of the butler moving around the room. It took him a few seconds to realise that Jenson was cleaning up the mess he'd made. Liam tried to get up.

Marcus's arm around his shoulder killed that idea in its tracks. "You need to rest after a feeding."

"But..."

"No buts," Marcus corrected.

Liam tried to look over his shoulder. Marcus's hand came to rest on the back of his head. The vampire clumsily patted his hair while he kept him exactly where he wanted him.

Marcus wanted Liam curled up against him. The thought damn near took Liam's breath away. Even after Marcus had drunk his fill, he still wanted him there. Marcus wanted him. Liam smiled into Marcus's shoulder.

He couldn't see what Jenson was doing. That meant it didn't really matter. Liam let the clouds float back into his mind and block out any rays of worry. He didn't chase them away until the butler left the room.

"Do you have any questions?" Marcus asked, as he seemed to realise that Liam was back with him.

"You woke up because I kissed you?" Liam blurted out, as he lifted a hand and rubbed at his uninjured eye with his knuckles.

"Yes."

Liam nodded, quite content to accept that as perfectly logical while the pleasure from the feeding still danced inside his veins.

"Anything else?" Marcus asked.

"Why did you fall asleep?" Liam asked, as he peered up at the vampire.

"Last night?" Marcus asked, smiling slightly, as if he thought Liam was being silly but was in a good enough mood to find that amusing rather than annoying. "Because I was tired. My body needed time to absorb the blood I took from you when I fed."

Liam shook his head. "No. I meant before, when you were in a coma?"

Marcus tensed.

As easily as that, every bit of happiness vanished from Liam's world. Panic rushed into him, chasing away all the pleasure that he'd found in Marcus's arms. Liam lifted his head slightly. Marcus was angry with him. He'd learned to spot all the signs of the man he was with being pissed off with him. His survival had pretty much depended on it.

"It's a long story," Marcus said. "I'll tell you another time."

Liam nodded very quickly. The boat they were on didn't need to be rocked. It was already out at sea with waves tilting it and Liam didn't need to look overboard to know that there were sharks circling in the water around them.

No. Liam didn't need to know anything at all. Pulling away from Marcus, he sat up. Marcus didn't try to stop him. Liam turned so he sat on the bed facing Marcus, and pulled his knees up in front of him.

Marcus's hair was spread out across the pillow. Liam's fingers itched with the desire to reach out and touch it, but he wrapped his arms around his legs instead. There was no need to go out of his way to invite Marcus's anger. He was pretty sure he'd end up pissing him off easily enough even when he did his best. It was his one talent. He was really good at making guys want to swing for him.

As Marcus frowned, Liam forced a smile, hoping he might somehow be able to salvage the moment. As if everything really could be as easy as that, Marcus smiled back.

A tap on the door caught both their attention.

"Come in," Marcus called.

It was the butler again. "Your continued absence from your room seems to be causing quite a disturbance on the third floor, sir. When it is convenient, perhaps you would like to formally check out of the hospital?"

Marcus sat up with a sigh. "I'll see to it now." He seemed to move more easily than he had the day before, but he still allowed Jenson to help him into the wheelchair.

"You know where my room is," Marcus reminded Liam. "I'll talk to your doctor about releasing you today, but you're not to leave the hospital without speaking to me."

Liam nodded.

Marcus waited, apparently not completely satisfied by that.

"I won't leave," Liam promised.

One nod of acceptance, and Marcus allowed Jenson to wheel him out of the room, leaving Liam all alone.

Chapter Seven

"May I inquire if Mr Bates will require assistance to pack his bags?"

Marcus tore his gaze away from the scene beyond the hospital window. It wasn't quite as he'd imagined the view to be, and it certainly didn't overlook anything fascinating, but being able to stand up and look out of the window was still a novelty. "No," Marcus said. "He doesn't have anything to pack. Only those things you brought to the hospital for him."

"Very good, sir." Jenson picked up Marcus's own bag and turned toward the door.

Marcus remained by the window for a few extra seconds. It was strange that, after all the time he'd spent longing to get out of the room, now that he was finally about to be released from the hospital, his will to make his way to the door had faded to almost nothing.

"I'm sure Mr Bates will be looking forward to being discharged today, too," Jenson observed.

"Yes," Marcus agreed. Although probably not quite as much as Marcus was looking forward to being able to take the boy back to his own house. "His injuries are beginning to heal well." The physical ones, at least. He was sure that none of the doctors had any idea how deep Liam's psychological wounds went.

Marcus's hand clenched into a fist at his side. The thin line of the scar on his index finger throbbed under the increased pressure and did nothing to improve his mood.

"Your feedings can take most of the credit for that, I believe," Jenson said.

"You really haven't changed at all," Marcus muttered,

watching a young couple walk arm in arm along the other side of the street. "I can still hear the disapproval in your voice, as if I were seven years old and sneaking into Mrs Jenson's kitchen."

"Yes, sir. And I expect my disapproval will have as little effect now as it did then," Jenson observed.

Marcus smiled slightly as he refocused and considered their reflections in the window pane rather than the view beyond it. "Vampires aren't designed to be nice, or obedient. We're designed to own submissives, not become them."

"Yes, sir."

His tone of voice might have sounded polite to anyone else, but Marcus knew better. Jenson might as well have slapped him across the back of the head and told him to stop acting like a spoiled little brat. Turning around, Marcus leaned back against the window sill, folded his arms across his chest and raised one eyebrow at his butler.

"Mr Bates is somewhat different to the other…gentlemen you have brought home over the years," Jenson mentioned.

"A fact I am well aware of." Marcus was far better at hiding his emotions than any human could be. No hint of how he really felt about Liam leaked into his words.

"Perhaps—"

But Marcus had already heard enough. "You're forgetting the difference between us, Jenson," he bit out, as he stepped away from the window and strode across the room. "You work for me, not the other way around."

The butler didn't blink, didn't back down.

"You might not have changed over the last three years," Marcus said. "But I have." Or, at least, he hoped he had. If he hadn't, Liam was in trouble.

Fuelled by his first ever taste of righteous indignation, Marcus marched out of the door and along the corridor. He was vaguely aware of nurses turning to stare at him, but he paid no attention to that.

He kept moving, determined to keep up his momentum. Leaving the room had been far easier last time. Pushed along in the chair by Jenson, he hadn't needed to maintain the will to place one foot in front of the other again and again. He'd been too focused on his need to ensure Liam's safety to worry about how open and exposed the corridors seemed to be, how vulnerable he suddenly felt, without that damn hospital room surrounding him.

Reciting mental curses, half aimed at Theo and half at Ralph, Marcus continued to stubbornly stride forward. It seemed to require more and more effort to keep going as he made his way first to the elevators, then along the corridors toward Liam's room.

A rush of relief swept through Marcus when he saw the boy was still there. Liam sat on his bed, silently staring at the far wall of the room.

"Ready to go?" Marcus asked.

Liam nodded, not turning to face him.

"My car is waiting out front."

Liam nodded once more. He still didn't turn around.

Marcus stepped forward. About to put his hand on Liam's shoulder, he stopped himself short. It was one thing for Liam to invite contact, quite another for Marcus to reach out to him when he'd received no such invitation.

He dropped his hand back to his side. "Liam?"

Finally, the boy looked toward him. Pushing his hands into the pockets of the jeans Jenson had procured for him, Liam tilted his head back and smiled up at Marcus. The smile didn't appear to trouble the half-healed split lip. It didn't reach his eyes, either.

"Ready as I'll ever be," he said, with just as little sincerity.

Marcus merely nodded as if he believed every word and stepped back to let Liam precede him from the room. Now wasn't the time to confront him. The only thing Marcus had room for in his head was the necessity of getting them both out of the hospital and on their way to his house. Once that was accomplished, he'd deal with everything else, not before.

Another elevator ride gave Marcus a brief respite from the uncomfortable openness of the hospital corridors, but their ride in it was both short-lived and completed in stony silence. Liam was apparently fascinated by the numbers above the sliding doors. Marcus could barely hold back the desire to reach out, press the emergency button and bring them to halt, just so he could remain in the comfortably enclosed space for a little while longer.

It was only the realisation that he needed to be strong for Liam that convinced Marcus to step out of the elevator when it reached the ground floor of the hospital and to keep moving forward as they made their way into the main lobby of the building.

The air in the high, light space was crammed so full of scents and sounds, there didn't seemed to be any room left for oxygen. Images bombarded Marcus from all sides. He tensed. A weight suddenly seemed to be pressing down on his chest, threatening to squeeze what little breath he could find out of his lungs.

A baby cried somewhere. Marcus looked around the waiting area, but saw no screaming child. For all he knew, the baby could have been halfway across the hospital. He no longer had any way of controlling his heightened awareness of his surroundings. Barely used to a few hours of very mild stimulus a day, his vampiric senses suddenly picked up everything. His head spun as his brain tried to process it all at once and quickly overloaded.

Coins rattled in a vending machine. An ambulance's siren wailed. Pens scratched against appointment forms. Computer keys rattled behind the receptionist's station. Patients chatted. Magazine pages were turned. And Marcus had no way of knowing which sounds were important, which tiny details he should concentrate his senses on, which implied a threat—which might be made by another vampire.

"Are you okay?"

The question was jumbled in with all the other sounds, but something about it tugged at Marcus's consciousness. There was something important about that particular type of sound. Marcus's gaze travelled quickly around the room, trying to home in on where the question came from. Finally, his gaze came to rest on a pair of worried brown eyes.

Liam. Yes, the question was asked in Liam's voice—that was what made it important. Marcus frowned as he concentrated on pushing all the other sounds away so he'd be able to make sense of the boy's words.

"Yes," Marcus managed to say. "I'm fine. Why do you ask?" Had he made a fool of himself? Marcus looked down. Nothing seemed to be out of place. He was standing quite calmly in the lobby. He wasn't grabbing his head and curling into a tiny little ball in the middle of a crowd of horrified onlookers. Everything was fine.

"You stopped."

Marcus blinked down at Liam. The boy's hands were still in his pockets. They remained there as Liam shuffled his trainer-clad feet.

"Stopped?" Marcus asked.

Liam swallowed. As Marcus focused in on the boy, he could hear even that tiny little noise.

Stopped. What had he stopped doing? Marcus scrabbled for an answer while somehow managing to maintain a calm expression. What had he been doing?

Walking. Damn! Marcus stared down at his feet as if he had never seen them before. Brightly polished leather shoes stared back at him. His feet weren't moving. A moment passed. Finally, Marcus managed to kick his limbs into action. He strode forward, acutely aware of Liam casting worried glances up at him as he silently fell into step beside him.

Marcus kept going, one step at a time, until the wide automatic doors leading to the outside world slid open. He forced himself to step out into the open air. A light, fresh breeze caressed his skin, almost taking his breath away. Inhaling deeply, Marcus tried to savour his first breath of true freedom in three years, but it was impossible to like anything about being out in the open.

His attention went straight to the sleek black limo on the other side of the road. As he watched, Jenson exited the front driver's side door, and opened the back door in anticipation of their arrival. There was a familiarity to the car that called to Marcus. His feet didn't need to be cajoled into stepping forward then, any more than he'd have needed to be coaxed into swimming toward a life raft.

Marcus soon stood next to the car, eager to slide inside and cocoon himself away from the overpowering sense of space and light. Liam had followed along behind him obediently enough until then, but he stopped short when Marcus stepped back to let the boy reach safety first.

Liam stared down at his own shoes for a long time.

Marcus followed his gaze, but failed to see anything unusual about the trainers Jenson had brought to the hospital to replace the blood-stained ones Liam had been wearing when he arrived.

"Thanks for the clothes and everything," Liam suddenly said.

"It's nothing," Marcus replied, only just convincing himself not to ask why the hell they couldn't exchange these niceties inside the damn car.

The breeze blew against his neck. It felt like it might take his skin off.

Liam nibbled at his bottom lip. "I..." He closed his eyes again. "Will I see you again? I mean..." He looked past Marcus, to the trees that edged the car park.

Marcus never took his eyes off the boy's face. "Liam?"

"Yeah, of course, you're right." Liam swallowed. "I guess we move in really different circles, don't we?" He tried to chuckle and failed miserably.

"What are you talking about?" Marcus asked, as patiently as he could.

"I'm really screwing up this goodbye, aren't I?"

The boy wasn't a quitter; that was for certain. He tried to laugh yet again. He was no more successful this time than he had been the last.

"Goodbye?" Marcus echoed, blankly.

Liam looked along the road leading away from the hospital and dug his hands even deeper into his pockets. "I should get going."

"You're coming with me," Marcus corrected.

Liam glanced briefly at him before turning his attention back to the road. "I don't really need a lift. It's not far. I can walk it."

"Where?"

Liam blinked at him. "Pardon?"

"Where do you intend to go?" Marcus asked, as calmly as he could while anger flooded through his veins. "We spoke about this. You can't go back to him again."

Liam dropped his gaze for a moment. "I get that. I'll just…um, stay with friends for a few days or something—"

"You'll stay with me." Marcus didn't make it a question. There was no doubt in his mind about what was going to happen next.

Liam glanced up at him, before quickly shaking his head. "I…"

Marcus reached out and carefully placed his palm on Liam's cheek, stilling the gesture. "You'll come home with me, to my house."

Liam tried to shake his head again, his eyes fixed firmly on his shoes once more.

Panic spiked inside Marcus. He scrambled for something, anything he could say that might change the boy's mind. "You'll be given your own room. No one will expect anything of you in return for putting a roof over your head. Not even your blood." Marcus's stomach turned over at the idea of it being denied to him, but he knew if it came down to it, he'd deal with the refusal.

Liam's cheek pressed against Marcus's hand as he tried to shake his head once more.

"You need more time to heal, somewhere comfortable to rest," Marcus reminded him.

"You don't have to do that," Liam began.

"You didn't have to visit me, to sit at the bedside of a man who couldn't even talk back, but you did."

A touch of warmth blossomed under Marcus's palm.

"I can—" Liam cleared his throat as the blush spread across his cheeks. "I can be useful, help out and stuff. Maybe I could pay for my keep that way?"

"I don't doubt it," Marcus said. Whatever it took to get Liam into the car was fine with him.

Liam looked from him to the car and back again. "Maybe just for a day or two," he whispered. "If you really don't mind."

Marcus smiled and nodded toward the car door Jenson still held open for them. It was only then that Liam seemed to remember the butler was there. He dropped his gaze as he scrambled into the car, even more colour rushing to his cheeks.

* * * * *

All of Liam's vague intentions regarding sofa surfing for a few days had faltered when Marcus insisted that he stay with him. A man like Marcus obviously wasn't going to live in the kind of house where guests stayed on the sofa in a sleeping bag. But, Liam hadn't really wrapped his head around just how bloody huge Marcus's place would probably be until the limo turned into the long drive leading up to his house. Inside, it seemed even bigger.

"My bedroom is here," Marcus said, pointing to one of several, heavy, oak doors that lined an upstairs hallway.

Liam glanced at it, but said nothing as he trailed along behind Marcus. He should probably have guessed how rich Marcus was the moment he set eyes on the butler. Liam mentally cursed himself for being such an idiot. If he'd needed any further proof that a man like Marcus couldn't have any use for a guy like him, he had it now.

"This will be your room." Marcus pushed open the door leading into the room next to his own bedroom. It swung back to reveal a space that was easily bigger than the flat Liam had lived in before he met Ralph. Rich tapestry curtains hung at the windows. A huge mahogany bed dominated the room, but Liam wasn't in any condition to take in any further details — not while Marcus stood next to him.

Reaching just inside the door, Marcus unhooked something from the wall. Turning back to Liam, he held out a key.

Liam stared at it as if he'd never seen a bit of metal shaped like that before.

"No one will enter your room without your permission." Marcus proffered the key toward him again.

Liam glanced up at Marcus as he took it. His nerves peaked and his fingers curled so tightly around the key, the edges of it bit into his palm. "Thank you."

"There are clothes in the wardrobe — you should find that they all fit. The door on the left leads through to an en-suite. If there's anything else you want, just mention it to Jenson, and he'll see to it. I've yet to come up with any task he's incapable of fulfilling."

"You didn't have to do all this," Liam blurted out, tilting his head back to look up at Marcus once more. "I mean..." He cleared his throat. "Thank you. I won't get in your way, I'll just..."

Marcus turned away, obviously not the least bit interested in listening to him babble now he was freed from his coma and had a chance to escape. Liam dropped his gaze to the richly patterned hall carpet wondering how many times

Marcus had longed to be able to leap out of his hospital bed and run away from his stupid ramblings.

"Do you feel up to a brief tour now, or would you prefer to rest a while first?" Marcus asked.

Liam lifted his gaze. Marcus was standing just a yard or two down the hall from him. He hadn't run away after all. Liam's desperation to remain close to Marcus for as long as it was permitted saved him from standing there like an idiot while waiting for his brain to kick into action.

"I'm fine." The bite from that morning still made his injuries irrelevant. "If you don't mind, a tour would be great." Liam stepped forward, more than ready to follow wherever the vampire led.

The house was big and old. Marcus spoke about the history of it very casually as they walked through the huge rooms on the ground floor. Priest holes. Roundheads. Shell-shocked soldiers. It seemed like the whole world had passed through there at one time or another.

Liam had no doubt that when he finally laid his head down on one of the huge feather pillows that decorated his bed that night, his dreams would be full of adventure and intrigue. It would certainly make a pleasant change from the dreams he'd had in Ralph's house. That building had been new. There had been no history to take his mind off present pain.

Several hours later, after he'd switched off the elaborate brass light by the side of his bed, Liam closed his eyes. The house was very quiet compared to Ralph's house in the suburbs. There were no close neighbours here. He wouldn't have to worry that the people next door might hear his lover's temper flare and anger him even further by summoning the police to their house.

Liam shook his head as he turned over and tried to nudge his pillow into a more comfortable shape. Adventure and intrigue—that was what he wanted to dream about. Not Ralph, and not Marcus, either.

He was not going to fall for the vampire. And he wasn't going to think about what might have happened between them if Marcus had decided that his guest wasn't going to be allowed to have a bed all to himself.

Liam closed his eyes a little tighter and pulled the blankets more firmly around his shoulders. No, it was best all-around that Marcus had nothing more than a temporary interest in his blood, and no interest at all in any other part of his body.

* * * * *

Hands wrapped around Liam's wrists, pinning them painfully down on either side of his head. The world closed in around him, crushing him, suffocating him. A loud cracking sound filled the air as his ribs gave way beneath the onslaught.

Pain swarmed through him, like a million fire ants racing through a newly formed colony. Liam scrabbled at the faceless form above him, trying desperately to get free. His feet kicked out, only to find themselves tightly bound by something he couldn't see, couldn't escape.

Liam had to get free. He had to. He had to…to get to the hospital. Yes. He'd be safe there. Even through the pain and the fear, part of him knew that just as surely as it knew Ralph really was going to kill him this time.

Pain flared through Liam's cheek. Hands closed around his throat. He tried to scream, but no words emerged. He didn't even have enough breath to beg for mercy. Tossing his head back, Liam summoned every ounce of energy at his disposal and screamed.

The sound had barely faded from the air, when it was drowned out by the splintering of wood from the other side of Ralph's living room.

* * * * *

Liam jerked into a sitting position, arms flailing as he was thrown unceremoniously out of his dream and came crashing back down into the here and now. For several long seconds, he had no clear memory of what particular reality he was living in.

The room was dark. It only took him a second to realise that he was far away from any room in Ralph's home. Knowledge of where he actually was came far more slowly. The only thing Liam could make out in his unfamiliar surroundings was a faint outline of light where a door used to be.

He wasn't in Ralph's house, but that didn't mean Ralph couldn't be there. Ralph knew about Marcus. Ralph knew Marcus was awake. It didn't take too great a panic-fuelled mental jump to realise that meant Ralph could have found out where Marcus lived.

Scrabbling for the bedside table, desperately trying to find a lamp he only vaguely remembered the location of, Liam finally managed to press the switch on the side of it with trembling fingers. Warm, yellow light spread through the room, mellowed by an old fashioned glass lampshade.

A shadow in the middle of the room moved and grew, gradually forming the figure of a man.

Unable to breathe, Liam couldn't even convince his heart to take another beat. Pressing himself back against the headboard, he tried to work out how small his chances of making it to the door were. The figure was between him and the splintered remains of the only entrance and exit. The fact the key still rested on his bedside table was no help to Liam.

The figure moved again. Ralph completely failed to look up at Liam. Instead, Marcus pushed long black strands of his hair back from his face as he lifted his head. Crouched in the centre of the room, he looked all the way around the space, even ducking his head down to peer beneath the bed.

Suddenly, Liam's heart and lungs were racing away at

full pelt, but he still couldn't control any muscles that required his conscious input. He simply sat and stared at Marcus as if he were a ghost rather than a vampire.

"Are you okay?"

Very slowly, Liam managed to nod, one jerky little motion, before he fell still again.

Marcus glared around the room once more. Liam half expected him to check for bogymen in the wardrobes too. As Marcus glanced at the doorway, Liam also turned his attention toward the splinters of wood where the door should have been.

"You screamed."

Liam's gaze snapped back to Marcus.

He'd screamed and Marcus had... What had he done exactly? Come to rescue him?

Sudden footsteps on the stairs sent tension flooding back into Liam's body. For once, he found himself stupidly reassured by the fact he didn't have a viable way to escape from a room. Marcus was positioned firmly between him and the door. Anyone who was stupid enough to launch themselves through that doorway now would have to go through Marcus before they could reach Liam. From the look in Marcus's eyes, that would be no easy task.

It was almost impossible to imagine the vampire lying peacefully in a hospital bed now. He was all bunched muscles and tightened nerves. Marcus turned toward the door, shifting his feet into a position that indicated he was ready to fight.

He looked as ready to kill as Liam had ever seen any man. Liam helplessly followed the vampire's gaze. A man appeared in the hallway in a flurry of paisley dressing gown and bedroom slippers, brass fire-poker in hand.

Liam stared. Very slowly, he caught hints of familiarity in the guy's face. It was hard to imagine that the wild grey hair or furious expression could belong to the same man who'd turned up at the hospital looking as if he'd just stepped

105

straight out of an old-fashioned guide to formal etiquette.

Jenson looked from Marcus to Liam and back again. "Good evening, sir," he said. Only the fact he was slightly out of breath betrayed that they weren't actually meeting under entirely normal circumstances. He lowered the poker to his side and corrected his stance.

"Good evening," Marcus replied. Straightening his spine, he once more pushed his hair back from his face. The glossy black strands were tossed and wild after his tumble through the door. All important considerations aside, Liam's fingers itched to reach out and stroke through Marcus's hair.

Gradually, Liam managed to take in other details about Marcus. The vampire's chest was bare. Black pyjama bottoms covered the lower half of his body, but the material appeared to be thinner and softer than any Liam had ever worn. It clung to far more than they concealed, clearly outlining Marcus's cock. He might as well have been as naked as he had been when he first woke up in the hospital.

Liam swallowed rapidly as he finally managed to tear his gaze away from Marcus. Being in a coma hadn't done the vampire's muscle definition any harm at all. He looked far more like he'd just stepped out of a gym, or perhaps off a runway, than as if he'd just left a hospital.

Liam risked another glance at Marcus's face just in time to see him raise one eyebrow at his butler. Marcus's lips twitched, but didn't quite give into any temptation to smile. "Nice poker."

"Thank you, sir. It is indeed a very fine example of its type," Jenson replied, not missing a beat. "Is there something you require my assistance with?"

Marcus shook his head. "Everything's fine."

Suddenly Liam found himself the subject of the butler's intense scrutiny. "Do you agree that is the case, Mr Bates?"

All Liam could do was peer at the butler in confusion.

"Liam had a nightmare," Marcus said. "I came crashing in here because I heard a scream. He didn't scream because I burst in on him, desperate for his blood."

Jenson's eyes never wavered from Liam's face. It was as if he really didn't care what Marcus had to say about it.

Finally, Liam managed to make his lips move. "I'm fine. I...I'm sorry, Mr Jenson. I didn't mean to disturb anyone."

"Very good, sir," Jenson said with a curt little half nod, half bow. He turned to Marcus. "Shall I show Mr Bates to another room for the remainder of the night, sir?"

Marcus shook his head. "No. Go back to bed. We're both fine."

"Just as you wish, sir." Jenson turned back to Liam. "If you require anything, just pull the bell, sir."

He spun on his slipper-clad heel and walked away with complete composure, poker swinging at his side like a high class walking stick.

Marcus seemed to listen to his butler's footsteps retreat all the way to the base of the stairs before he finally turned back to Liam. For just the briefest moment, he hesitated. "Was I right—are you okay?"

Liam nodded, pulling his knees up in front of him and wrapping his arms around his legs over the blankets.

Marcus stepped closer. "May I sit?" he waved a hand to the unoccupied side of the huge bed Liam lay in.

Liam managed another nod. Taking a deep breath, he tried very hard to look completely at ease. He was pretty sure he failed spectacularly.

"I didn't mean to scare you."

Liam blinked at Marcus. It took a long time for the words to sink in and make sense inside his head—as much sense as it was possible for those words to make at any rate.

"I should be the one apologising," Liam whispered, staring down at his entwined fingers.

"For having a nightmare?" Marcus asked. "I didn't realise you had it on purpose."

Liam managed a slight smile in response to Marcus's

teasing, but his heart wasn't in it.

Once more, Marcus hesitated, just for a second. "Do you want to tell me what it was about?"

The grip Liam's right hand had on his left turned white-knuckled. Marcus's gaze flicked down to his hands and Liam was left in no doubt that the vampire had noticed his moment of panic.

"You only need to talk about it if you want to," Marcus said, very gently.

Liam shook his head.

"That's fine."

Staring at the blanket between them, Liam tried to wait for Marcus to speak again, but it wasn't long before he had to break the silence. It was that, or lose his mind completely.

"Do you need to feed?" It hadn't been that long since the last time Marcus had fed from him—the effect of the bite was still making the pain from Liam's injuries tolerable. But it was the only thing he could think of to say.

Marcus didn't speak, he didn't move. He didn't even seem to breathe for what felt like a very long time. Finally, his chest began to rise and fall again. "I didn't bring you here because I wanted to turn you into a blood whore, Liam. I wouldn't have even suggested feeding from you since I woke up, if you weren't in so much pain."

Heat rushed to Liam's cheeks. He tightened his grip on his fingers until he was half sure the digits would break under his grip, just as they had last year, beneath Ralph's shoe. "I'm sorry. I mean, I know you've probably got better options now that you're out of the hospital. You don't have to settle for someone like me—"

Marcus leaned forward and put one fingertip gently against Liam's lips. Every muscle in Liam's body tensed.

Even after he'd silenced Liam, Marcus seemed to struggle to find any words he wanted to say himself. "In time, perhaps we will each want more from each other, but right now, all I wish you to do is stay safely in my house until you've healed." He met Liam's gaze. "Both physically, and in any other ways necessary."

Liam parted his lips.

Marcus didn't immediately take his finger away. Liam's tongue brushed against the tip of the digit as he tried to speak. Quickly shutting his mouth again, Liam turned his face away.

When he looked back, his attention went straight to Marcus's body, to his bare chest and the lines of his abs. Liam's hands once more begged for permission to touch, even as part of his mind screamed it's horror at the idea of ever touching anyone again.

"I'm fine," Liam whispered, praying that Marcus couldn't guess what he was thinking.

"Do you want to try going back to sleep?"

Liam shook his head so quickly, dizziness took over. The room threatened to start spinning uncontrollably around him. "You don't have to stay or anything," Liam said. "I'll just…" He looked around the room for inspiration but found none. Apparently, vampires weren't big readers. There wasn't even a book he could feign interest in.

"We've shared a bed before," Marcus reminded him, his voice strangely soft and intimate.

Liam met his eyes.

"You slept well on those nights," the vampire added.

Liam couldn't deny it.

"I can just as easily sleep here as anywhere else. Just sleep."

As relief rushed through Liam, words weren't an option. His throat had closed up so tightly, all he could do was nod his gratitude.

Marcus didn't say anything more; he simply pulled back the blankets and laid down next to Liam, adjusting his pillow to ensure a comfortable night's rest. The bed had to be at least twice the width of the one in the hospital. Somehow Liam found himself lying just as close to Marcus as he had the previous night. His head soon rested on Marcus's shoulder as Marcus wrapped an arm around him.

"Everything will be fine," Marcus whispered as he turned out the light and let darkness flood the room. "I'll see to it."

Liam closed his eyes and tried to believe him, but he knew it was a lie. He was curled up with a half-naked and completely stunning man, and the only thing Marcus meant to him was warmth and security. Despite being acutely aware of how beautiful Marcus was, Liam didn't feel even the slightest tingle of physical desire. Marcus might as well have been a teddy bear as an embodiment of every one of Liam's sexual fantasies.

In that moment, Liam had no doubt that Ralph's threats had been genuine. A wave of fresh pain tore through him at the idea of never wanting to do anything more than sleep next to Marcus.

Ralph had been right. That night had broken something inside him. Without a fresh bite sending pleasure racing around his body, there was nothing there at all, not even a flicker of lust. Liam's cock remained soft. His muscles remained tense.

Liam closed his eyes very tight and curled a little more closely into Marcus's side, begging sleep to claim him quickly, if only so he could escape his waking thoughts.

Chapter Eight

A fingertip brushed back and forth against Liam's lips, teasing him and tempting him, only to pull away every time he tried to lean forward and take it properly between his lips. The pale skin called to him, so did the restrained strength he sensed beneath the touch.

Whimpering his frustration, Liam tried to reach up and catch hold of the hand hovering before his face, but his fingers found nothing but empty air. The darkness hid everything except that hand, but that didn't matter. Liam was still sure everything about the man it belonged to would be just as perfect as the long, graceful fingers were.

Suddenly, Liam felt another hand wrap around his wrist. It held him still, pinning him down and preventing any attempt to make another grab for the teasing fingers.

Panic spiking inside Liam, he tried to pull away but something wrapped itself around his shoulders. Liam lurched forward and gasped as his squirming caused his cock to rub against something warm and hard in front of him. So much pleasure rushed through his veins, he forgot to be frightened. He forgot why he was trying to get away. Rocking his hips, Liam pushed his crotch forward instead.

Very slowly, different senses nudged at Liam's brain, begging him to respond. Piece by piece, his body came alive, making him writhe and press his skin against the form in front of him.

Another wave of bliss rewarded his efforts. Purring his pleasure, Liam arched his back and thrust again. He tried to drop his hand down and wrap his fingers around his shaft. It had been so long since he'd come. He wasn't even sure he could remember the last time he really enjoyed feeling anyone's hand against his cock, even his own. But now, a few strokes would be all he needed.

Warmth surrounded Liam, cocooning him, letting him know that he was safe, and the whole world was perfect. Liam felt his breathing change as his movements sped up and he helplessly rubbed himself against the nameless, formless object before him.

He needed to come, needed it in a way that he couldn't remember needing anything in his life. His cock throbbed, aching for release in a way it never had before. His head spun, his heart raced, and still Liam's hips kept moving, maintaining a rhythm far steadier than his heartbeat.

Possibilities flashed through Liam's mind, but they were fleeting half-formed things that he couldn't catch hold of. Sensations overruled anything that might have been able to pass for a thought process.

One more thrust, and pleasure exploded through Liam. Shock waves rolled out from the epicentre of his cock, along his spine, and to every part of his body. Tightening his hold on whatever was within his reach, Liam tried to maintain some connection with reality but the ecstasy was so pure, so perfect, it was impossible and —

Liam's eyes snapped open. Quickly turning his head, he desperately tried to work out where the hell he was.

Ralph hated it when he curled up against him as they slept. Liam couldn't take it if his boyfriend was going to be pissed off with him again so soon. He hadn't had long enough to heal from their last argument and…

And he wasn't in the bedroom his sleep fogged mind expected him to wake up in. And it wasn't Ralph he was curled up next to. And there was cum slowly drying on the inside of his pyjama bottoms.

Liam stared at Marcus in horror as details lined up inside his head and patiently waited their turn to present themselves for his consideration. His left leg was hooked over

Marcus's lower body, his crotch pressed up against Marcus's hip. His hand had a white knuckle grip on the blankets. Marcus's left arm was wrapped around him while his other hand rested on Liam's wrist, just as it had in his dream. Liam sent silent thanks up to a deity he wasn't even sure he believed in, for the most important fact of all—Marcus was still asleep.

As if he heard that last item on the list and decided that, out of all of them, that was the one detail that needed to change as soon as possible, Marcus gently stirred. He opened his eyes.

"Good morning,"

Liam held his breath as Marcus stretched and his leg rubbed against Liam's still softening cock.

"Sleep well?" Marcus asked.

Liam nodded, trying not to let his groin come in contact with Marcus as he pulled away.

"So did I."

Liam nibbled at his bottom lip, looking everywhere in the room but at Marcus.

"I'd better go back to my room and get dressed," Marcus murmured, sitting up and rubbing at his eyes in an apparent effort to wake himself up properly. "Mrs Jenson is going to give me hell for making a mess of that door. No point putting off the inevitable."

He pushed back the blankets, levered himself up from the bed, and stretched again. Liam watched him, unable to make a single word come to his lips as he studied the way the muscles in Marcus's back moved around to let others stretch in their turn.

"I'll meet you downstairs for breakfast?" Marcus said, looking over his shoulder and smiling sleepily down at him.

Liam swallowed rapidly. He managed another nod. He was pretty sure if he hadn't just come, he'd have climaxed just from the look in Marcus's eyes.

Suddenly, the fact that he'd never want to have sex

with another man was the last thing Liam felt like he needed to worry about.

* * * * *

"Is there something I can do to help you, Mr Bates?"

Liam's trainers actually left the rough flagstone floor. Spinning around, he looked guiltily along the corridor at the bottom of the stairs that had led him down into Marcus's basement and what Liam guessed was some sort of servants' area. Mr Jenson stood at the other end of the corridor. He was once more dressed in his butlering suit. Any trace of the mad man with a poker was long gone.

"I, um…that's what I was coming to ask you," Liam stuttered out, all too well aware that his cheeks were flaming bright red at the memory of the previous night.

Marcus had told him not to worry about it, before disappearing into his study to make some phone calls, but it wasn't turning out to be an easy order to obey. Vampires might be used to their servants walking into their bedrooms at unexpected moments, but Liam was pretty sure he'd never be able to look the butler in the eye again without mentally cringing.

Mr Jenson said nothing.

Liam pushed his hands deep into his pockets and tried not to feel a complete fool. "I just…after everything you and Marcus have done for me, I thought, if there was anything I could do to help out around the house. Sort of pay for my keep a bit, or…"

Mr Jenson's expression didn't change as Liam's words trailed off, dying a slow and not entirely painless death. The butler's impassive gaze sucked the life out of the syllables one by one, just as easily as any vampire could drain the blood from a person.

"No repayment is required, Mr Bates. Mr Corrigan has made it clear that you are here as an honoured guest. It would hardly be appropriate for you to be put to work scrubbing the floors."

"I wouldn't mind." Liam forced himself to lift his eyes and hold Mr Jenson's gaze despite his embarrassment. "I'm not afraid of hard work. I know what you must think of me, that I'm just—"

"Harold? Don't keep the boy standing around out there all day." A small female form appeared behind Mr Jenson. "There's tea on, if you want some, love."

"I, um..." Liam looked from the white curls framing a face full of laughter lines, to Mr Jenson's sombre expression, and back again.

"Come along." The mildly chiding tone slipped straight past Liam's conscious brain and into that part that had been carefully moulded by his mother, his grandmothers and a succession of female school teachers, to respond to a voice of maternal authority. Liam made his way cautiously past the butler into the large old-fashioned kitchen set at the back of Marcus's house.

From there, he was led by the strings of a flowered apron into the room on the far side of the main kitchen. Peeking into what appeared to be a quaint if rather crowded little sitting room, Liam hesitated on the threshold.

"Take a seat, love. The tea won't be a minute."

Liam obediently sat down upon one end of an overstuffed chintz sofa. He wasn't sure what to do with his hands. He folded his arms, realised that looked far too defensive, and moved his palms to rest on his knees.

The woman had her back to him as she bustled about, china rattling as she worked. The silence may well have been easy and companionable, if Liam hadn't been so on edge. As it was, he couldn't stand it for more than a few moments.

"I'm sorry about my bedroom door," he blurted out.

"*You* weren't the one who broke it," Mrs Jenson pointed out as she turned to him, set the teapot down on the table and took a seat on the other end of the sofa.

"It was still my fault," Liam said, already feeling the heat rushing back to his cheeks at having to admit such a thing. "I—"

Mrs Jenson made a sceptical noise in the back of her throat, stopping Liam short. "Young Master Marcus would do well to learn some self-control. He always has been far too rough with his toys."

Liam's blush threatened to trigger spontaneous human combustion. He wasn't sure if it would be even more embarrassing to tell her he'd had a childish nightmare, or to leave her thinking Marcus had been that enthusiastic about screwing him.

He cleared his throat but, coward though it made him, said nothing.

"Take a cake, love." A plate filled with generously sized fairy cakes was proffered toward him. "You could do with feeding up."

Liam did as he was told.

"You enjoyed your breakfast?" she asked.

"Yes, thank you," Liam said, hurriedly covering his mouth in an effort not to spit cake crumbs everywhere. "Marcus, at breakfast this morning, and at dinner last night, he um..."

"Don't you worry about him. He's a typical vampire when it comes to his meals—he only ever picks at human food."

"Oh." Liam wasn't sure what else to say. "This cake is delicious," he hazarded.

"You're much better off without that bastard of an ex, you know."

"Martha!"

Liam looked across to the doorway leading back into the main kitchen. Mr Jenson stood just outside the little sitting room, glaring into the homely space, his frown so deep his thick grey eyebrows almost met in the middle.

"Well, he *is* better off without him," Mrs Jenson said,

once more busying herself with the tea things. "In my day, there were names for a man who hit those he was supposed to care for—and they weren't polite ones. If I had my way, your ex would be—"

"It's none of our business, Martha," Mr Jenson said, as he came in and sat down in the armchair opposite them.

Keeping all his attention on the large section of cake still on his plate, Liam silently wished that a hole would open up in the well-scrubbed floor and swallow him whole. It didn't.

There was nothing he could do but attempt some sort of distraction. "You both worked for Marcus before his...his accident?"

"Ever since the day he was born," Mrs Jenson said. "Vampires don't raise their own children as a rule. Although how anyone could walk away from such a sweet little bundle as the young Master Marcus was, is beyond me. You know, I don't think he's set eyes on his parents more than half a dozen times in his whole life."

She added milk and sugar to Liam's mug without bothering to ask if he wanted any. He could only suppose that was part of her plan to feed him up.

"Are your parents still around, love?"

"Martha..."

Apparently, Marcus's housekeeper outranked his butler—in the servants' quarters, if nowhere else. Mrs Jenson handed her husband a cup of tea and cheerfully ignored the note of warning in his voice.

"We're just having a cosy chat, aren't we, love?" she said to Liam, reaching out and gently squeezing his knee.

Liam managed a small smile, but it quickly faded. "We've sort of lost touch," he whispered, quickly lifting his cup and taking a sip of the warm, sweet brew.

"When you came out?" she asked, as if it were the type of thing little old ladies were quite entitled to ask a gay man the first time they met.

Liam shook his head, and dropped his gaze. "They didn't really get on with Ralph," he mumbled.

And when he'd been forced to choose between them, fear of Ralph's temper had made the decision for him. Liam mentally cursed himself, but he straightened his spine as best he could. There was no going back now.

A disapproving sound emerged from the back of the housekeeper's throat. Liam had the distinct impression that, had Ralph been there, he might well have been sent to bed without his supper.

By the time Liam was finally ushered back up the stairs to the main house, having been ordered to either relax in the morning room or explore the rest of the house, he couldn't help but feel relieved that he'd escaped without having told a sweet little old lady his entire life story in minute and embarrassing detail.

Even the soft sound of his trainers against the floorboards sounded loud as he walked along the upstairs halls. It was one thing to be told that nowhere was off limits to him. It was quite another to hear the old house creak under the force of the rising wind outside and not believe that someone was going to throw open one of the multitude of doors as he strolled past and demand to know who the hell he thought he was, poking around where he had no right.

An uneasy shiver ran down his spine an hour or two after he left the Jensons, as he wandered silently down one of the maze of corridors on the upper floor, making his way toward the western edge of Marcus's house.

Liam took a deep breath in an effort to control his nerves. His ribs reminded him why that was a stupid thing to do now that the effect of Marcus's bite was wearing off again. The bruises may have faded and the worst of his pain had eased, but the all too familiar twinges were still there. Lifting one hand to his chest, Liam let the heat from his palm soak through his T-shirt and into his skin.

Marcus's body heat was much better at soothing aches

and pains than Liam's own was. It had been like sleeping next to his own personal hot water bottle. A living, breathing bed warmer that had held him close and went out of its way to encourage snuggling.

Liam shook his head at himself. Much better to think of Marcus as a man he'd come dangerously close to humiliating himself in front of while he'd humped him in his sleep. Liam's hands shook at the memory. His cock stiffened slightly.

Marcus didn't know about that, Liam reminded himself for what had to be at least the hundredth time. And Marcus was never going to know about it. All Liam had to do was pretend it had never happened, and everything would be fine.

Reaching out to a random door, Liam pushed it open and peeked inside. Just like every other room in the house, it was elegant and expensively furnished — probably by someone who'd lived and died several generations ago. The Jensons had obviously been hard at work the entire time Marcus had been in the hospital, keeping every single inch of the place spic-and-span in their employer's absence.

Liam looked up at the huge chandelier hanging in the centre of the room. Each drop of crystal sparkled and gleamed. Below it stood a beautifully polished grand piano. Crossing the room, Liam couldn't help but give in to temptation and lift the lid. His fingertips caressed the ivory keys — and the instrument did look old enough to be furnished with actual ivory.

The notes sang out, light, delicate and perfectly pitched. It had been kept tuned, as if the Jensons had expected their employer to walk in and sit down at the piano at any time.

Liam's fingers made their way a little further along the row of keys as he pulled out the piano stool with his other hand and sat down on the plush gold seat. Old piano lessons quickly came flooding back to the forefront of his mind.

He smiled slightly to himself as half-remembered tunes and lessons slowly re-established themselves inside his head. Closing his eyes, it was almost possible for Liam to believe he was nine years old, in his piano teacher's house, and his biggest care in the world was that week's lesson.

The knuckles along his left hand were still ever so faintly discoloured where he'd tried to fend off one of Ralph's kicks, but even the trace of pain that had lingered despite Marcus's feedings, faded away when he lost himself in the music. Liam only opened his eyes again when he reached the end of the piece. Staring down at the keys, it was hard to see anything except the echo of the injury to his knuckles.

His hands looked out of place on such a beautiful instrument. He was out of place in that room, in that house. Liam slowly closed the lid of the piano. Rising, he put the stool back neatly in its place and retreated from the room.

Closing the door behind him, Liam shook his head at himself. He was not going to feel sorry for himself. He wasn't going to be the kind of person who was lucky enough to end up in this house rather than on the street, yet still found something to complain about.

Crossing the hall, Liam approached another door at random, eager to take his mind off melancholy thoughts. There was no distraction to be found in a room shrouded with complete darkness, but that didn't matter because Liam was going to heal and get back on his feet, and once he'd done that...

Liam's fingertips, working without any conscious direction from his brain, found the switch on the wall just inside the door. Light flooded the room. Every thought in Liam's head slowly slipped away. The only parts of his body that retained the ability to move were his eyes. They scanned the room very slowly, taking in every detail visible from that particular vantage point.

The important thing, Liam told himself, was not to panic.

* * * * *

120

"No, I don't know what his current address is," Marcus snapped. "If I knew that, I would hardly need to engage the services of a private investigator, would I?"

The man on the other end of the phone began to stutter out his apologies. Marcus barely let him get a few words in before he cut him off.

"Theo Wallace. He's a vampire. Five foot ten, slight build, thirty years old. Blond hair and blue eyes—last time I saw him he was considered remarkably pretty. Check out the clubs that are popular on the vampires' feeding scene, then those around the edges of it. Look in the places no respectable vampire would stoop to feed, too. Do I need to do your job for you?"

The private investigator began to mumble something.

Marcus wasn't interested in hearing it. "Call me as soon as you know anything. If you can find him, you can name your price."

"What if I can't find him?" the guy asked.

"Then we can have a little competition and see if my investigative skills are better than yours," Marcus said. He made a point of letting his tone become far more polite than it had been at any other point during the call. "What do you think, Mr Grant—will a vampire who's been starved of blood for three years be able to find you?"

All Marcus heard from the other end of the phone was a little gulp. He smiled slightly as he hung up and leaned back in his chair.

As he glanced across the room, he noticed Jenson's expression. "As and when I need your approval, I'll let you know."

"Very good, sir," Jenson said, obviously not the slightest bit unnerved.

Marcus stretched his arms out and back behind his head. His body still felt strange, as if it didn't entirely belong to him. He needed to reclaim it, to feel his muscles move and know that he controlled every one of them. He needed to get the adrenaline pumping through his body again.

Killing Theo Wallace would be the perfect way to do that. All he'd have to do was wrap his hands around the little prick's throat and lift him from the floor. But maybe he'd just let him get a little toe hold on the ground beneath him every now and again — tease the guy with a little bit of hope before snatching it away.

He needed to know that Theo wasn't behind every pillar and post he passed. Maybe then he'd be able to step outside the house without feeling that the world was a far larger and more frightening place than he ever remembered it being before his last encounter with Theo. He needed to...

Dropping his gaze, Marcus carefully ran a fingertip across the scar on his index finger. Maybe even more than that, he needed a feeding that didn't involve either an IV bag, or a boy who was crammed full of pain and fear.

"Perhaps now would be a good time for you to seek out Mr Bates's company, sir," Jenson said, mildly.

Marcus jerked up his head. The butler stood directly in front of his desk.

"I'm not using him as a blood whore," Marcus snapped, not entirely sure who he was trying to convince anymore. He slammed both his hands down on the desk as he launched himself to his feet. "I never paid for a human's blood before my accident. What makes you think I'd take it off him in return for a roof over his head now? Damn it — I wouldn't have fed from him at all if he hadn't been in so much pain!"

"I am aware of that, sir. However, it would be difficult for any observer not to realise that Mr Bates does have a somewhat calming effect on you."

Marcus found his lips twitching in spite of everything. "Are you suggesting that I go and find the boy so he can cheer me up and talk me out of my temper tantrum?"

"I wouldn't dream of suggesting any such thing, sir." Jenson's face remained completely expressionless.

Marcus looked down at the desktop for a few moments.

"He's going to pay," he said, making sure each syllable hit the air, clear and unmistakable. "Wallace is going to hang."

Jenson said nothing. He was a smart man. There was nothing he could say that would convince Marcus to set aside three years of plotting and dreaming about his revenge, and he didn't waste his time trying.

By the time he got his strength back, Marcus was determined that he was going to have every detail of Theo's current location, and be ready to set everything in motion. He was going to be ready for Theo this time.

However, in the meantime…

Pushing his chair back, Marcus stepped out from behind the desk. "Did you buy the magazines?"

"Certainly, sir. I placed them in the morning room, as you directed."

Marcus nodded. That solved the problem of where to find Liam very nicely. If there was one thing the boy really couldn't resist it was a sensationalised story about some Z-list celebrity who was falling in or out of love with some other talentless cretin and —

"However, I believe Mr Bates is currently enjoying a tour of the house," Jenson said, just as Marcus reached the door.

"What?"

"His doctor suggested that once he feels capable, he should take some gentle exercise. Since you made it quite clear that he wasn't to leave the house unless you were free to accompany him, I suggested he take you up on your invitation to explore the building further."

Marcus's hand clenched tightly around the door handle. There were dozens of rooms on each floor of the sprawling old house. There was no reason for Marcus to believe he could successfully predict which one Liam would be in. But, in that moment, Marcus harboured no doubts regarding the boy's location.

He strode out of his study without another word,

letting the door swing idly closed in his wake. Taking the stairs two at a time, he quickly turned several corners and strode along the hall toward the western edge of the house.

Just as he expected, there was only one door open along that corridor, and it led into the one room he'd been quietly determined to introduce Liam to in person.

It was an introduction that should have occurred several weeks or months in the future, and it would have been conducted so very carefully and... And it was pointless to regret that now.

Slowing his steps, treading lightly to ensure no floorboards creaked and betrayed his presence, Marcus crept closer to the open doorway. The light was on. Liam was clearly illuminated — standing in the middle of the stark black and white surroundings, his attention completely ensnared by a large object on the far side of the room.

Marcus realised then that there had been no reason to creep. Liam was mesmerised; he wouldn't have heard even the heaviest stomping step.

"It's called a St. Andrew's cross," Marcus said, as softly as he knew how.

Liam spun around. His face was paler than Marcus had ever seen it — highlighting the injuries that still lingered on his face and making the leather that filled the room appear all the darker and more sinister.

Stepping forward, Marcus forced himself to come to a halt in the doorway, leaving several feet of empty space between them.

"I'm sorry, I..."

Marcus shook his head. "I told you that you had free rein in the house. I meant it. If I'd wanted to keep the room a secret from you, I could easily have locked it."

Leaning one shoulder against the doorframe, Marcus looked around his playroom. A substantial film of dust lay over every item. The Jensons had obviously respected his preference that they didn't enter the room — even to clean it.

The last people in there had been Marcus and…if he'd remembered rightly, it had been a rather bratty little Italian submissive in his early twenties. Marcus didn't bother to try to recall the boy's name; he doubted he had even inquired what it was to begin with. The boy had been pretty enough, and his masochism had made him a reasonably interesting human to feed from, but he couldn't compare with the man standing before him now.

Turning his gaze back to Liam, Marcus smiled slightly, desperately trying to appear relaxed and at ease when he felt anything but. Liam didn't smile back. Marcus's expression slowly turned more sombre too.

He'd brought more than enough men and women back to that room to learn that an instinctive talent for submission wasn't the same as a taste for leather or the games that a dominant might like to play. The sheer weight of disappointment that raced through him surprised Marcus, but he made damn sure that no trace of it appeared in his expression. That particular precaution turned out to be entirely unnecessary.

Liam's gaze rested somewhere around Marcus's feet and it stayed there. He folded his arms across his chest in a move all about self-defence. A second passed, and he shuffled his feet on the dusty floor, as if getting ready to run.

"Liam," Marcus said, stepping forward.

The boy jerked away from him, retreating rapidly until his back hit the St. Andrew's cross. He spun around, as if the dark wooden beams might wrap around him and trap him there if he stayed within their reach.

His shoulder connected heavily with a rack of paddles, sending them tumbling to the floor. Liam twisted around again. Marcus saw the panic in Liam's eyes as fight and flight collided inside him.

Marcus's own instincts took over. Two strides had him within arm's reach of the boy. Wrapping Liam in a strong embrace, Marcus pulled him close, thinking of nothing but keeping Liam still and preventing him from hurting himself in his panic.

Frantic hands pushed against his chest, scrabbling at his shirt, as Liam desperately tried to free himself from Marcus's hold. Even the strength inspired by human panic was no match for a vampire, even one as malnourished as Marcus.

Planting his feet firmly on the floor in the centre of the room, Marcus became a statue, just waiting Liam out. Finally, the hands that had been trying to push Marcus away relaxed against his shirt. Liam's head dropped forward to rest against Marcus's shoulder.

"What's wrong with me?" The words would have been inaudible to a human's ear.

"Nothing at all," Marcus whispered back, moving one hand up to rest on the back of Liam's head and welcome him close, while he smoothed what he hoped were reassuring circles on the boy's back with his other palm.

"Then why is it that I only ever fall for men who are completely screwed up?" Liam asked.

Frowning over the top of Liam's head, Marcus tried to follow the boy's line of thought and failed completely.

"Even Ralph wasn't into *this* kind of —"

"What?" Pulling back a little, Marcus dipped his head, determined to catch Liam's gaze.

"Why do I only ever fall for guys who want to hurt me?" Liam seemed to be talking to himself far more than to Marcus now. His eyes held a far-off quality, as if he were staring far back into the past, or maybe way out into the future. All Marcus could be sure of was that Liam really didn't like the view.

Holding him at arm's length, Marcus frowned down at him. "What the hell makes you think I want to hurt you?"

A burst of laughter, verging on the hysterical, escaped from Liam's lips. Covering his mouth with one hand, he stared up at Marcus, wide-eyed for several seconds before turning his head to look in every direction around the room.

Marcus didn't follow his gaze, he didn't need to. He knew every inch of that space. He knew how it all looked through his own eyes. It only then occurred to him that it would look very different to Liam.

"This has nothing to do with the way Ralph hurt you," he said, putting all the strength and certainty he could into the words.

Liam swallowed. His hand was still over his mouth. He looked as if he was only just managing to keep his breakfast down.

"It has nothing to do with anyone wanting to hurt you," Marcus said again.

"Don't lie to me!" Liam pushed against him. The sudden move caught Marcus by surprise. Slipping from his grasp, Liam headed straight for the door.

Shoe prints lingered in his wake, the stumbling steps scuffing the dust as he rushed away. Liam's fingers caught hold of the doorframe and propelled him forward. He threw himself through the doorway so hard, he tumbled against the wall opposite it.

"I won't chase you."

Liam stopped trying to get his feet back under him, the words seemed to have shocked all movement out of him. He looked over his shoulder at Marcus.

"I have no interest in keeping you in this room unless it's where you want to be. The same goes for any other room in this house."

Liam turned to face Marcus, leaning against the wall directly opposite the door as if he wasn't capable of supporting himself on his own.

Marcus didn't move. He didn't step forward. He didn't reach out to try and catch hold of Liam again. He stood perfectly still, his empty hands hanging idly at his sides. "You don't need an escape route anymore, Liam," he said, very carefully. "And you don't have to worry about me being between you and the door. If you want to leave somewhere and I'm in your way, all you have to do is ask me to step aside and I will. And I won't chase you if you run."

One detail suddenly became apparent as Marcus studied both Liam's body language and his body in general. It wasn't just the room that was freaking Liam out. It wasn't merely the realisation that Marcus liked the kind of games that were played in there that was making him panic.

Unless Marcus was very much mistaken, Liam was far more worried by his own reaction to the leather he'd stumbled upon. Marcus ran his gaze over the way Liam's erection tented his jeans. The room hadn't only made him scared. It had also made him hard. His breaths weren't just uneven from fear.

He seemed even more freaked out by his reaction to the room than he had been by his wet dream that morning, but still for much the same reason. It would take time for him to realise that he was safe and that no one would expect him to do anything, no matter how many erections he might have.

Marcus dragged his attention back to Liam's face. He saw the blush on Liam's cheeks and knew it was too late to hide the fact he'd noticed Liam's hard-on the way he'd managed to hide the fact he'd been wide awake that morning and had thoroughly enjoyed feeling Liam rub against him that way.

"Was this why Ralph…?" Liam began, in a voice so full of pain, it was all Marcus could do to keep himself those few yards away.

"No!" It was impossible to keep the word calm and gentle. It snapped across the room like a whip.

Liam instantly dropped his gaze, his blush fading as the blood drained from his face.

"Ralph hurt you because he is a complete bastard, and he knew he could get away with it," Marcus expanded.

Liam didn't look up. He slowly slid down the wall to sit on the hallway floor.

"Do you really think he hit you because he thought you *liked* it?" Marcus asked, stepping forward just one pace.

Liam shrugged. "Maybe he sensed that I'm wired wrong and..."

"You're not wired wrong," Marcus corrected.

Liam glanced up for a moment, not at Marcus, but past him into the room.

"Even if you were, that wouldn't give him the right to hurt you."

"But you like hurting —?" Liam began.

"No!"

Liam blinked, meeting Marcus's eyes just for the briefest fraction of a second before looking away again.

"Not in the way you mean," Marcus said. Taking a step to his left he leaned back against the edge of the spanking bench.

Liam said nothing, he just stared at his own hands as if they might hold the answers to every question he had.

"I may not be the most moral of men by human standards," Marcus admitted. "But that doesn't change the fact that pain tastes vile."

If nothing else, the words shocked Liam into looking up at him properly.

"Whenever I've brought men, or women, to this room, I've always intended to feed from them as well as play with them or screw them."

Liam's hand went to his neck, but it was impossible to tell if that was because he wanted to protect the jugular from attack or if he was imagining how good it might feel when a vampire's teeth broke the skin there.

"You can taste..." Liam whispered.

"Yes."

The boy's hand moved to his wrist, to where Marcus had taken his first brief feedings from him.

"In the hospital, you..."

"That wasn't about sex," Marcus said, even more softly

than he intended. "It wasn't about getting off on tasting your pleasure. It wasn't erotic, it was medicinal."

Liam's fingers caressed the little patch of skin, over and over, back and forth as a frown built on his forehead.

"You needed me." Marcus was sure he hadn't intended to say any such thing, but the words were out before he could stop them. "You needed the help the bite could offer you."

"This would taste different?" Liam asked, turning his attention to the room once more. He'd pulled his legs up in front of him; there was no way for Marcus to tell if the sight of the leather and chains was still turning him on.

Marcus looked around the room too, trying to see it through the eyes of an inexperienced submissive. "When everything comes together perfectly, it's the most sublime taste in the world," he said.

Memories rushed to the front of Marcus's brain. Men chained to the diagonal cross. Women too, before he'd discovered that he generally liked a man's flavour better.

Dozens of humans had been locked into the cage in the corner of the room over the years—enthusiastic masochists each and every one of them.

"Adrenaline, endorphins, trust, pleasure, desire, submission," Marcus said. "When they're mixed together, nothing tastes better. The pain a certain kind of man feels then...it doesn't feel like pain—and it doesn't taste like pain either. It's..." He frowned, pushing his hand through his hair as he struggled for the right words. "I couldn't have enjoyed the games I played in here if the men I was with didn't get genuine pleasure from them."

Liam lifted his eyes and met Marcus's gaze for a moment. "Do you want me to—?"

"I want you," Marcus cut in. "To stay in my house and to give yourself time to heal. Anything else that happens will be because it's what we both want, not because you think you owe me for room and board."

Liam frowned too. "You...you can feed from me, if you

130

want—properly I mean, not just what it takes to help me heal. I guess you probably have some kind of better arrangement with other people... I know there are people who do things like this professionally—blood whores and stuff, but if I'm here, and convenient and everything... Maybe..."

Marcus stared across at him, unable to make real sense of the jumbled scraps of sentences.

Every cell in his body screamed at him to take what Liam was offering. He needed blood, from a human, not from the IV bags he'd been making do with since he woke up. His teeth ached for it, every nerve and sinew he possessed clambered for even the briefest taste. His cock wanted anything Liam was willing to offer him, too.

"I don't mind," Liam whispered.

Marcus took a deep breath. The scent of leather hanging in the air did nothing to help him control his baser desires. "I mind." The words sounded far too rough, far too harsh for someone like Liam.

"Because I won't taste right unless we..." Liam waved a hand toward the playroom.

"Because when I feed from you, I want to taste your pleasure, not your fear," Marcus corrected. "I want you to taste safe and protected and completely at ease with me. I want to drink your blood and know I'm the man who makes you feel that way."

Liam held his gaze for several long moments, his eyes full of confusion.

"I know how that bastard made you feel. I can't allow you to feel the same way when you're with me," Marcus blurted out. It was a stupid thing to say. God knew that Liam needed strength from him, not weakness.

Liam swallowed rapidly. "I..." He looked down. "Am I allowed to go?" The words were rushed out so quickly, they almost tripped over themselves in their haste to be spoken.

"You don't need my permission to go wherever you want within the house," Marcus said, mentally cursing himself for making the worst possible mess of the whole conversation.

Liam nodded. He was obviously trying his best to appear calm and collected. He was failing miserably, but he was trying. Marcus watched Liam drag himself to his feet only to see Liam hesitate as if he was unsure where he belonged.

"The sun should be flooding into the morning room now. There are some magazines you might enjoy on the coffee table," Marcus offered.

He listened to Liam's footsteps as Liam turned and walked away. Marcus's senses allowed him to track Liam all the way to the morning room.

Finally, Marcus pulled himself to his feet, too. Standing in the middle of the room, he looked at the toys and the furniture around him.

It was so easy for him to imagine Liam bound down against the examination table on the far side of the room, to picture the boy looking out at him from between the bars of the cage, or glancing over his shoulder at him while his limbs remained bound to the cross.

Marcus closed his eyes for a moment. It was also all too easy to imagine Liam allowing all those things to happen just because he was too scared to admit that he didn't want anything like that—because Ralph had beaten the idea that he had no option into him so hard, Liam had forgotten that there were people in the world who weren't like that.

Stepping out of the playroom, Marcus closed the door very quietly behind him. The latch caught with a gentle click. Humans didn't have to be like that unless they chose to be. Neither did vampires.

Chapter Nine

Marcus slammed the phone down so hard it was only luck the plastic didn't crack.

He was quickly becoming convinced that fast, efficient private investigators were a Hollywood myth. All the ones that existed in the real world seemed to be singularly incompetent. And Theo was still out there somewhere, wandering around as if he somehow deserved be free and happy and at peace, when the only thing he truly deserved was a very slow, very painful death.

As the door to the study swung open, Marcus pinned a friendly smile to his lips and pushed all thought of Theo as far out of his mind as possible, just in case it was Liam.

Jenson stepped into the room, carrying a silver serving tray.

Marcus slumped back in his chair, not bothering to keep up the cheerful façade a moment longer. "When I'm done with Theo, I might turn my attention to ridding the world of every incompetent man who dares to call himself a private investigator."

"Very good, sir," Jenson said, calmly. He set the tray, which was covered with a domed silver lid, on Marcus's desk. "Dinner will he served in the dining room in a few minutes."

Marcus nodded his understanding.

As Jenson stepped back and left the room, Marcus picked up one of the IV bags of blood that had been concealed under the silver dome. Biting into it was nothing like piercing a vein, but it didn't feel quite so bizarre now as it had a few weeks before. God help him, but a tiny part of him was actually getting used to it.

Marcus closed his eyes as he drained the bag dry. His

fangs might be getting used to it, but his stomach still turned over, just as it always did.

As he set the empty bag aside, Marcus sighed and pushed his hand through his hair. Closing his eyes, he reminded himself once more that it would be worth it. One day, Liam would be ready, and it would be worth having waited, worth having survived on bagged blood for however many weeks or months it took. They would both know he hadn't rushed Liam, or taken refuge in feeding from another man, and in that moment it would be all worth it.

Marcus pulled himself out of the chair behind his desk and made his way towards the dining room. He smiled when he saw Liam approaching the room from the opposite direction.

Liam smiled shyly up at him in return as they took their seats.

The routine had become as oddly familiar as the bagged blood had. As Jenson brought in the food, then left them alone in the room, Marcus took careful stock of Liam. It wasn't so much about tracking how well the last of Liam's physical injuries were healing now. As far as Marcus could tell, Liam was as healed as anyone could be—physically at least.

Now, it was Liam's mood that Marcus found himself assessing as he absentmindedly copied Liam's actions— selecting a similar size portion of whatever Liam took from the platters in the centre of the table, and putting it on his own plate.

"Has there been any news today?" Marcus asked, when Liam had finished filling his plate with whatever he wanted.

Liam shook his head slightly.

"That makes the baby five days overdue, doesn't it?" Marcus prompted.

"Yes." Liam only hesitated for a moment. "One of the magazines had a new article about a baby shower some of the other football players' wives and girlfriends threw for her."

Marcus nodded his encouragement.

By the time he was a few bites into his meal, Liam had relaxed a little. He was soon recounting every detail of the magazine article on Sandra Smithson's baby shower.

His tone was just as excited as it had been when he told Marcus about her wedding, her honeymoon and every other major, and minor thing that had occurred in Sandra Smithson's life while Marcus had been in his coma. But now Marcus didn't have to imagine how Liam's eyes lit up at each new snippet of X-listed celebrity gossip—he could see just how stunning he was in his enthusiasm.

Marcus smiled across at Liam as he dutifully pushed some food around his plate to make it look like he was there to eat rather than just admire his dining companion.

He'd never been so well informed regarding the personal lives of boring strangers. He'd never spent so much time at a human dining table either. Who could have guessed something that involved both could have become one of his favourite portions of the day?

Liam glanced up as he came to the end of the story.

"If she doesn't go into labour tomorrow, perhaps her husband will be able to be there for the birth after all. He finishes his international commitments at the end of the week, doesn't he?"

Liam nodded, blushing slightly, obviously pleased that Marcus had remembered.

Marcus felt a rush of success.

This was the vital part of the process that had been missing while he'd been in his coma. Back then, he hadn't been able to tell Liam that he was listening, he hadn't been able to prove it by asking the kind of questions that made it clear he was paying attention. Being able to do it now made all the difference.

Marcus had the pleasure of hearing about two other magazine articles focused on the lives of two other very silly celebrities before Liam pushed his empty plate away.

Marcus copied the motion. His own food was barely touched, but as he stood up he felt the benefit of sharing the meal with Liam in every part of his body. He would never have believed that gossip could soothe the soul, until he met Liam.

Usually, Liam stood up then, but that day he remained in his chair. Marcus waited for a few seconds, but Liam didn't say anything.

"Liam?"

Liam jerked his gaze up. "Yes?" He looked anxious all of a sudden. It wasn't quite the first time he'd suddenly become wary at the end of the meal, but it was no more understandable this time than it had been the other times.

"Is everything okay?" Marcus asked.

Liam nodded, but his Adam's apple bobbed rapidly as if he was desperately trying to swallow down his nerves.

"If there is something wrong, you can tell me," Marcus said, carefully. "There's nothing that you could ever say, or ever do, that would make me angry with you." It was as close as he could risk coming to saying what he really wanted Liam to know — *I'll never treat you the way Ralph did.*

"No, everything's fine," Liam promised.

"Do you have any plans for this evening?" Marcus asked, trying to think of something, anything, unthreatening to say.

Liam paused for a second before shaking his head. "Unless there's something I can do for you?" His voice was still slightly off.

It wasn't obvious, but Marcus was nothing if not an expert at listening to Liam's voice. Liam was deeply worried about something. Perhaps about what kind of thing Marcus might ask him to do? Was that why he kept getting anxious at the end of meals lately, because he thought that might be the time Marcus was most likely to make demands on him?

Marcus shook his head. "You're free to do whatever you want. I have a little more work to get done."

Liam nodded again, the motion just a fraction too jerky, as if his muscles were all tensed up.

"You'll let me or Jenson know if there's anything you want?" Marcus checked.

Another jerky nod.

Marcus watched Liam head up the stairs and, presumably, back to the magazines in the morning room. As Liam turned out of sight, Marcus felt sure there was something he was missing. There had definitely been something Liam wished to say to him at the end of the meal, something Liam was holding back.

Marcus retreated to his study and his work on tracking down Theo, but even as he resumed his seat behind his desk, he know that he wasn't at that moment as interested in his revenge as he was used to. Perhaps it wouldn't be a bad idea if he didn't leave Liam to his own devices for too long that evening before he checked in with him.

He could wait a little longer for revenge if he needed to.

* * * * *

"Liam."

The word was said very gently, as if the person saying it was doing his damnedest not to startle him. All that person's hard work was for nothing. Liam almost tripped over his own feet in his haste to turn around.

Marcus stood in the playroom doorway, his shoulders seeming to fill the space completely. He hadn't tied his hair back at the nape of his neck the way he sometimes did. Liam's palms ached with the desire to reach out and stroke the glossy black strands, just as they always did when Marcus's hair was loose, but his palms were the least of his troubles right then.

As Liam watched, frozen in place, Marcus looked slowly around the playroom, taking in every detail of each leather clad piece of furniture and each carefully arranged toy.

"I thought," Liam began, but he quickly stopped

himself short.

What had he thought exactly? That his complete inability to speak to Marcus about anything other than celebrity gossip gave him the right to give up on words entirely? That being unable to find the right terms to express his willingness, damn it—his *desperation*, to have sex with Marcus, gave him the right to venture into the man's playroom without an invitation, or even permission?

Now, as he faced Marcus across the freshly cleaned room, it was obvious to Liam that he had no right to think, no right, in fact, to do anything that he hadn't been told to do. He had no business being in that room at all. All at once, it was clear that he should have just stayed in the morning room reading his magazines.

It was equally clear to Liam that he completely deserved whatever happened next. It was all he could do not to flinch away from Marcus in anticipation of the first blow. It was going to be just like it had been with Ralph, except perhaps, if he was lucky, Marcus would be hungry afterward.

Marcus hadn't even suggested feeding from him since the last of Liam's injuries had healed. But if Marcus wanted to feed today, then at least Liam would be able to get some of the healing properties of his bite and—

"Thank you."

Liam blinked. Against all logic, Marcus hadn't sounded the least bit sarcastic as he said it.

Marcus stepped forward and skirted around the edge of the room to sit on the… Liam wasn't exactly sure. It looked like it was designed to enable one man to tie another guy in place with his head down, his arse up and his legs spread wide apart. It might have been designed for spanking or screwing—it could just as easily have been intended for both.

Liam took a deep breath and lifted a hand to push his fingers through his hair. He saw the dust smeared across his hand, but it was too late. His arm had too much momentum. Swallowing down his nerves as best he could, Liam told himself it didn't matter. He probably looked like a fool anyway, a bit of dust on his face wouldn't make that much difference.

Shoving both of his grubby hands into his pockets, Liam looked briefly at the open door. There was a clear path from him to the hallway. If he needed to run, he could. Knowing that eased a little of his panic. He turned his attention back to Marcus.

"You've been working hard," the vampire observed.

Liam followed Marcus's gaze as it swept the room again. There was no longer a single speck of dust to be found there, his own more practical kind of sweeping had taken care of that.

"Take care that you don't do too much too soon," Marcus warned, as he had so many times. "Humans take time to heal."

"I'm fine. It's been weeks now and I...the bite...when you..." Liam took one hand out of his pocket and waved it around vaguely. "It helped a lot." He'd never recovered from a beating that quickly—and few of them had been as bad as that night's had been. Liam shook his head, trying to clear the memory from his mind before it took hold there.

"I'm glad," Marcus said.

Liam shuffled his feet as he focused back in on the here and now.

"Is this what you wanted to try to speak to me about at the end of dinner?"

Liam nodded.

"Do my toys seem less scary now that you've realised what a huge dust trap they are?" Marcus asked, one leg idly swinging as he settled himself more comfortably on the edge of the...the thing.

Liam was surprised at just how easy he found it to smile at Marcus's teasing. For a few moments he was just as relaxed as he had been back at the dining table, when they had been talking about a celebrity's relationships rather than their own, but he soon found himself growing more serious again.

"I...if we did, would it just be because you need to feed and I'm convenient, or would it be because you actually want...well...*me*?" Even though he knew it was a stupid question to ask, Liam couldn't keep it back. "I don't mind either way," he rushed to add. "I'd just prefer to know."

"If all I wanted was convenience, I could get a take-away — pick up an overly enthusiastic vampire-fetishist in a bad part of town and receive everything I wanted from him in the back of my car."

Liam was shocked into looking up and meeting Marcus's eyes. God help him, but even being that take-away sounded hot to him. Half-hard the entire time he'd been cleaning, Liam suddenly found himself as stiff as a damn telegraph pole. There was no way he could take his hands back out of his pockets a third time. It wasn't only his nerves he had to hide now.

"My interest in you has nothing to do with convenience," Marcus said.

Liam nodded his understanding. Unable to hold Marcus's gaze for more than a minute, he looked around the room again and took a deep breath. He nodded again. He could do this. "Where do you want us to start?"

"You want to try playing with me?"

Liam nodded. He was reasonably sure that was the only way he was going to save his sanity or manage to get a whole night's sleep without all this stuff creeping into his dreams.

"Then we'll start in the red drawing room," Marcus announced.

Marcus extended one hand toward the door, inviting Liam to exit the playroom before him. Frowning slightly, and not in the least sure what was going on, Liam still didn't see that he had much option but to walk out of the freshly cleaned playroom. Glancing over his shoulder, he was just in time to see Marcus closing the door behind them.

As they stood in one of the drawing rooms a few minutes later, Liam had no idea what to expect. Marcus walked straight past him, and drew the full length curtains over all the windows, until they effectively covered one wall of the room. Liam hadn't spent more than a few minutes in that room before, but it was obviously called the red drawing room for a reason. The curtains, the walls, the sofas, everything was some shade of the same colour.

The same colour as blood. A shiver ran down Liam's spine — half fear, half anticipation.

"There are DVDs in that cabinet," Marcus said, with a wave of his hand. "Pick one out and put it in the machine."

Liam knew exactly what kind of DVDs would be in there before he even opened the door. He had no doubt that every title on a case would include the word dominance, or submission, or leather — if not other words that were even further outside his experience. Opening the cabinet, Liam crouched down in front of it and steeled himself for the worst.

A frown flittered across his brow as he saw what kind of titles were actually there. Each one was brand new, not even removed from the cellophane, and they were all his secret favourites — the kind of movies he'd never dream of admitting he liked out loud — at least, not to anyone who he knew was able to hear him.

Liam closed his eyes for a moment. Marcus really had heard every word...

Aware that he was keeping Marcus waiting, Liam forced himself to open his eyes and face reality head on. Selecting a DVD at random, he slipped it into the machine, just as Marcus had ordered. Marcus was already sitting on the sofa waiting for him. Liam turned toward him just in time to see Marcus lift one hand and push his hair back off his face.

It should have looked like a feminine gesture, cute and flirtatious. Somehow, on Marcus, it looked as strong and as dominant as a senior matador posturing in the middle of a bullring.

Marcus lowered his hand and tapped the seat next to him as he caught Liam's eye.

"I thought we were going to—" Liam began, perching on the very edge of the sofa cushion.

"We are."

Marcus held out his other hand. A set of leather cuffs hung from his fingertips.

Liam swallowed rapidly as he watched them swing back and forth, like a hypnotist's watch, only far more mesmerising.

"I'm going to tell you exactly what I intend to do. You're going to tell me if you like the sound of it. Understand?"

Liam nodded.

"I'm going to put these around your wrists, and we're going to sit here and watch a movie together."

Liam managed another jerky nod.

"After the movie has finished, if it's what you still want, I'm going to feed from you."

One more nod.

Marcus smiled encouragingly. It didn't seem to be an expression that came entirely naturally to him, but he was certainly trying hard.

Liam clung to that encouragement as he held out his wrists to be bound, his movements as jerky as a puppet whose strings had been cut. The leather was wrapped around his skin in seconds, the shining silver buckles neatly fastened in place. Staring down at the thickly padded restraints, Liam took another deep breath and tried not to panic. There was no way anything around his wrists could restrict his ability to breathe.

They were just strips of leather, just toys. Just things that would make it even harder for him to get away when everything hit the fan.

Hands came to rest on Liam's cheeks and tilted back his

face until he had no choice but to meet Marcus's eyes.

"I'm—"

"Don't apologise." Marcus stroked his thumb across Liam's cheekbone. "You're doing fine. It's only natural that it should feel a little strange at first."

Liam tried to look away, but his eyes kept swinging back to Marcus's lips and there was nothing he could do to stop them.

"The important thing for you to remember is that these cuffs aren't about me forcing you to stay anywhere you don't wish to be. They're about you knowing that you don't need your hands free if you ever want to get away from me—all you will ever have to do in that scenario is tell me to stop."

Liam blinked. Unable to turn his head, it was the only thing he could do.

"Every time you look at the cuffs, I want you to try to repeat to yourself that they're a symbol of how safe you are with me. Can you do that?"

Liam nodded, pressing his cheeks more firmly against Marcus's hands in the process.

Marcus gently released his face. "That's good."

He picked up the remote and pressed the button to begin the film without any further ado. Leaning comfortably against the highly cushioned sofa back, Marcus turned his attention to the screen and seemed to immediately become absorbed in it.

Liam took another deep breath, as if the third one just might be the charm that let him not make a complete pillock of himself. Looking down at the leather around his wrists, he did his best to remember what Marcus had told him.

He was safe, and nothing was going to happen unless he wanted it to. Liam repeated the words one more time for good measure and, gathering up every piece of courage he had at his disposal, shuffled back until he sat properly on the sofa next to Marcus.

The movie played across the huge screen mounted on

the wall above the fireplace. Liam stared intently at the image, making a point of never once looking to his right.

"I only bite if you want me to."

The words made a mockery of Liam's determination to keep his eyes facing forward. He turned his head so quickly, the muscles in his neck hurt.

Marcus smiled slightly as their gazes met. "You can come closer." He held up one arm, inviting Liam to curl into his side and snuggle against him as if they were just a normal couple who'd decided their date would be conducted at home rather than the cinema that night.

Without thinking about it, Liam reached out to brace his hand against the back of the sofa as he moved closer to Marcus. The leather around his wrists stopped him short.

An unexpected wave of pleasure rolled through Liam's body in response. Was that because he was remembering what Marcus said about being safe, or was it something else? The fact his cock was already screaming for release didn't help Liam feel that he was thinking clearly. His movements became clumsier than ever as he finally closed the gap between them.

Eventually, he was close enough to rest his head on Marcus's chest. The vampire's heartbeat was slow and steady, just like the beep of the monitor that had stood next to his bed in the hospital. The rhythm seeped into Liam's body, telling him that he was as safe there as he had been when Marcus was still asleep.

Marcus's arm settled comfortably around Liam's shoulders. His skin was warmer than a human man's, his touch was gentler, too.

The film continued to play in front of Liam, but for once the fairy tale romance that filled the characters' lives couldn't hold his attention. He closed his eyes, all the better to savour his closeness with Marcus.

It was only a sudden burst of music that alerted him to the fact that the credits were rolling. Liam blinked open his eyes, trying desperately to make his pupils adjust to the light more quickly so Marcus wouldn't realise he hadn't been watching the actors.

Liam looked up. He was wide awake, but he wouldn't have blamed Marcus for believing otherwise. Hell, he might as well have fallen asleep for all he had seen of the show.

Marcus softly stroked his fingers over the leather covering Liam's wrists. "How do they feel?"

"Good." Liam had no idea the word was going to leave his lips until it was out there, hanging in the air between them.

Marcus ran his fingers down Liam's cheek just as tenderly as he'd caressed the bondage. "I've wanted to kiss you for months."

Liam swallowed. His tongue slipped out to moisten his lips in what had to look like a calculated flirtation. He dipped his head, blushing at the idea he'd ever be confident enough to try something like that on any man, let alone one like Marcus.

Marcus smiled. He slipped a knuckle under Liam's chin, and he gently tilted his head back.

The first touch of his lips was so light Liam barely felt it. His eyes drifted closed. He leaned forward, blindly searching for more. Marcus's mouth was impossibly soft as it moulded against his. As soon as Marcus's tongue caressed his bottom lip, Liam opened his mouth in acceptance.

Marcus kissed as if that was all he ever wanted to do, as if there really was no rush to move on to the more exciting parts of the evening. In some stupid way, Liam actually felt as if the simple little kiss would be enough to completely satisfy Marcus.

He could pull away without pissing Marcus off. That knowledge just made him lean all the more enthusiastically into Marcus's embrace.

Marcus stroked across Liam's neck with his other hand. His thumb rubbed back and forth on the skin just above his jugular. Liam whimpered into the kiss. His body remembered how good Marcus's bite made him feel before. Pure instinct made Liam tilt his head back and offer his veins to him.

Marcus groaned into the kiss as he deepened it. He moved his hand to the back of Liam's head, simultaneously supporting him at just the right angle for kissing and preventing any further attempt at offering his blood.

Barely able to catch his breath, Liam brought his bound hands up to rest on Marcus's chest. He pushed at him slightly, his head spinning from lack of oxygen as much as from desire. Marcus immediately pulled back. Liam's hands tightened into fists, grabbing Marcus's shirt before he could retreat out of reach. The chain between the cuffs rattled.

"Don't go!" The words were breathless, but Liam had to get them out.

Marcus smiled slightly, his eyes heavy-lidded with desire. "I'm not going anywhere."

Liam managed to smile back. He couldn't look away from Marcus's lips. He desperately needed to taste them again, but at the same time, he had to feel the vampire's teeth break through his skin. His bite represented both pleasure and the one kind of penetration Liam thought he might be able to cope with, but the kiss was so sweet. Caught between the two desires, he had no idea what to actually ask for.

"Please?" That was all Liam could say. All he could do was beg and hope that Marcus would make the right decision for them both.

"Here." Marcus ran his fingers over Liam's jugular once more.

The word was half question and half statement. That was where Marcus wanted to bite him, but he wasn't demanding to get what he wanted.

Liam nodded, willing to agree to anything.

Marcus moved his hands to Liam's shoulders and turned him around, so Liam's back was to Marcus's chest. Liam glanced over his shoulder at Marcus before tentatively tilting his head to the side to give him better access.

His cock was so hard, Liam had a terrible suspicion that

he was going to come in his jeans the moment Marcus bit, but he couldn't bring himself to care about that right then. Nothing was too embarrassing if it meant getting what he wanted — if it meant giving Marcus what he wanted, too.

Marcus dipped his head. The kiss he placed against Liam's neck was impossibly delicate. He paused for a moment, as if testing Liam's reaction.

Tilting his head even farther to the side, Liam squirmed against Marcus's body in an attempt to encourage him on. Marcus's erection pressed against the back of Liam's jeans. Liam hesitated, but relaxed when he realised that Marcus seemed to be entirely oblivious to any part of him but his throat. Marcus brushed his lips against Liam's neck once more. His tongue caressed the skin just above his pulse and, just when Liam was starting to feel sure it was never going to happen, Marcus bit.

Every muscle in Liam's body tensed. He bucked against Marcus's larger frame as pure pleasure shot through him. He whimpered, a high keening noise unlike anything he ever remembered making before.

Without any warning, Marcus pulled back, extracting his teeth from the vein.

"Don't! You can't stop." Liam tried to reach behind him, to catch hold of Marcus's head and pull it back, but the cuffs were in his way. "I'm not scared, I swear."

"I know," Marcus whispered into his ear, as he reached around Liam's body and caught hold of the links between the cuffs, stilling Liam's hands. "I know exactly how you feel." He lowered his head and lapped against the wounds he'd left on Liam's neck. The sensation went straight to Liam's cock, making him swell further behind his fly.

"You're not in pain this time," Marcus murmured, his approval obvious.

Liam didn't even try to respond.

"That makes it feel very different, doesn't it?" Marcus whispered his words against the bite. The vibrations flooded through Liam's body, making him whimper his agreement with anything and everything Marcus ever wanted to say to him.

"Much more intense..." Marcus suggested.

Yes. Intense. That was a very good word for it. Intense, and wonderful, and oh so very, very frustrating...

Liam shrugged his shoulder, trying to convince Marcus to bite deeper, suck harder.

"I know what I'm doing, Liam."

Liam swallowed very rapidly, as if he were the one who needed to feed, not Marcus.

"I've been looking forward to this since the first time you stepped into that hospital room. You're not going to rush me now."

Helpless to get what he really wanted, Liam had little choice but to accept whatever Marcus was willing to offer him. Leaning back against Marcus's body, he stopped trying to change what would happen. Any control he might have had, he released.

"That's right," Marcus said. His tongue toyed against the wounds in Liam's neck, making him squirm.

As he pressed himself back against Marcus's body, Liam was once more reminded that Marcus was just as hard as he was. The wave of fear he expected, failed to roll through him. There was too much pleasure in his blood. There wasn't room for anything else.

Then, finally, just as Liam was on the verge of insanity, Marcus slid his teeth back into Liam's neck. Pleasure spiked inside him, and Marcus began to feed in earnest.

Every time the vampire sucked against the bite, another wave of bliss tore through Liam. Caught in a sudden storm, he was tossed and buffeted on the rolling swells of ecstasy like a tiny boat unable to drop anchor in uncharted waters. It was too much. Out of sight of all land, it was too dangerous to simply let the sea swallow him.

Something tugged at Liam's arms. He glanced down.

Marcus's fist was wrapped tightly around the metal links between the cuffs. Safe. The cuffs meant he was safe. They were his life raft in the storm. Liam clung to the sight of them as he struggled to keep his head above the water and remember how to breathe.

He was safe. There was nothing to fear. The storm was loud and dramatic, but it couldn't really hurt him. Safe.

Liam rocked back against Marcus, glorying in the way Marcus wrapped around him and the way Marcus's hard shaft pressed against his arse through their clothes. There was no room for memories inside Liam's mind now—nothing could intrude and remind him why he should be scared. The feeding filled the whole world.

Adrenaline hastened through him, faster and faster, as Marcus took more of Liam's blood and replaced it with pure rapture. Pleasure built up inside Liam. His cock throbbed with it. He was riding the highest wave of all, on the verge of coming harder than he ever had in his life and—

Nothing.

Liam gasped for breath. He turned his head toward Marcus, unable to hide his horror.

"No more," Marcus said. His voice was rougher now, his gaze brighter. "It wouldn't be safe."

"But—"

A finger came to rest on Liam's lips. "I said no." There was no arguing with that tone of voice.

Liam looked down.

"I wouldn't be looking after you if I let you talk me into taking more," Marcus whispered, his tone quickly gentling.

Facing forward, Liam nodded again. None of that changed the fact that he really wanted to come. He squirmed a little uncomfortably, not sure what to do with himself now that Marcus was finished feeding from him.

And he wasn't the only one who still needed to get off. Marcus was just as hard as he was. Liam froze as the feeding ceased to fill his universe and uncertainty crept into his mind, like a thief determined to steal away his pleasure.

Last time, there'd been a reason for Liam to say no. He'd been so badly beaten and Ralph was so fresh in his mind. Marcus had understood then. But this time...

"When a vampire feeds from a man, he has certain rights afterward," Marcus suddenly informed Liam in that same incontrovertible tone.

"I understand—"

"The first is to politely excuse himself to another room and take matters into his own hand by himself," Marcus continued.

Frowning with confusion, Liam pulled away to turn and look up at him.

Marcus appeared to be completely serious. "I'm not some teenage boy who thinks a little bit of frustration gives him the right to jump on anyone he wants, Liam."

Still struggling to make his brain work or get enough air into his lungs, Liam could only stare at Marcus for several long seconds. It took him a ridiculous length of time to work out what that strange bubbling of emotion inside him was.

Disappointment. He was disappointed that they weren't going to have sex.

"We can," he blurted out.

Marcus stroked across the skin he'd just fed from. "Someday, yes. But not today. You're not ready."

Liam didn't open his mouth to argue, he knew that would only result in a fingertip being placed gently across his lips.

Marcus glanced toward the door.

"Don't go."

Marcus frowned slightly, obviously irritated by the request, but he still turned his attention away from the door. His smile only appeared slightly forced. "Okay."

Liam dropped his gaze. It wasn't entirely a coincidence that his gaze fell on the vampire's crotch. "The bit where you move into another room before you jack off, is that part

150

essential?" he rushed out.

*

Marcus studied Liam very carefully. He could see how nervous asking the question had made him, how much determination it had taken for him to be so bold.

Marcus had been very clear with himself during several mental lectures. He was going to be careful with Liam. He was going to take things slowly — very slowly. But he was also quite willing to be damned before he threw such a request back in the boy's face.

"I could just as easily stay here," Marcus said, trying to sound confident rather than cautious.

Liam swallowed rapidly.

"We can both stay right where we are, if you like."

Liam gave a jerky nod.

Reaching out, concentrating very hard on not spooking Liam with any sudden movements, Marcus guided him forward to be kissed.

Liam liked being kissed. That was one thing Marcus was already very sure about. Liam seemed to feed on the kisses just like a vampire fed on a bite, gaining strength and confidence from each moment their lips lingered together.

Just as Marcus hoped, Liam leaned into him as if it were the most natural thing in the world. The taste of both Liam's pleasure and his frustration still danced in Marcus's veins. It was quickly joined by a supreme sense of satisfaction that he was the one who made Liam feel that way.

Breaking the kiss, Marcus slowly pulled back. Wary that every movement he made could be the one that meant they were moving too far too fast, he cautiously reached for his fly.

Liam watched him as if mesmerised. Zip down, Marcus pushed the fabric aside and freed his cock. With hands still bound by leather, Liam half reached out toward Marcus, then

151

hesitated.

"You don't have to," Marcus reminded him.

Liam paused for a moment before shuffling a little closer so their legs were pressed firmly together, thigh against thigh. He wrapped his right hand around Marcus's shaft and it was easily the most perfect sensation Marcus had ever felt. After so long without any sort of contact between another person and his cock, he was willing to swear that just that mild touch was better than any sex he'd ever had.

Marcus dropped his head back to rest against the high back of the sofa as delight swept through him and mingled with what he'd tasted of Liam's bliss. His hips rocked forward, thrusting his erection against Liam's palm. Prying open his eyes, Marcus studied Liam carefully.

The boy appeared to be just as enthralled as Marcus was. Very slowly, Liam began to move his hand. They were bound together so closely it was only seconds before Liam's other hand joined its friend around Marcus's cock.

Moaning his approval, Marcus forced his own hands to remain at his sides. Whether Liam knew it or not, it was his show. The man wearing the bondage was the one in control.

It took Marcus's joy-addled brain too long to work out what was going on when Liam started to slide down toward the floor at his feet.

He quickly reached out to stop him. "You don't have —"

"I know I don't have to." Liam dropped his gaze for a moment. "But let me anyway?" He'd never sounded surer of his own desires, more eager for a request to be granted. "I want to."

And Marcus couldn't say no to him. He nodded his acceptance. Liam slid down to kneel properly between Marcus's legs. For a few seconds, all Marcus received from him was a hand job provided at a different angle. Then, as if in slow motion, Liam leaned in and wrapped his lips around the tip of Marcus's cock.

Slick, wet heat surrounded the glans. It was all Marcus could do to keep his hips still as Liam carefully leaned forward and took more of the shaft into his mouth. Pulling back, he lapped softly at the head, swirling his tongue around it as if it were the tastiest treat he had ever been offered.

Marcus knew he should say something. He should offer encouragement, make sure that Liam knew he wasn't going to be pissed off with him if he needed to stop, and...

And all he was actually capable of doing was listening to the pretty fizzle and crackle of disappearing brain cells as Liam made his brain melt. Liam kept his bound hands wrapped around the base of Marcus's cock, steadying the shaft as his lips worshiped the head.

Perfection danced through Marcus's body, pirouetting and leaping with joy. There was no way to hold back and remain cool, brooding on the edge of the dance floor. There was magic in the music born of Liam's enthusiastic whimpering. It had to be followed.

"Liam!" Marcus barely got the warning out before he came.

Forcing himself to keep his eyes open, Marcus stared down at Liam as his semen spilled into the boy's mouth for the first time. There was no shock in Liam's eyes, no panic. He swallowed rapidly, apparently eager to take it all.

Reassured that there was nothing to worry about, Marcus helplessly gave himself over to a deeper kind of satisfaction. He let pleasure rule him, just for a little while. His eyes fell closed, all the better for him to savour the sensations that couldn't be seen or heard, but only felt.

He didn't even try to open his eyes until he felt Liam begin to pull away. Blinking down at him, Marcus watched Liam wipe his fingers across his mouth, cleaning up the cum that he hadn't been quite able to swallow down with the rest.

"I believe I owe you an apology," Marcus said, as he stroked Liam's cheek with the back of his fingers.

Liam blinked up at him, uncertainty quick to make its

way back into his gaze.

"All that time I spent in the hospital, imagining what it would feel like the first time you went down on me, and I completely underestimated how bloody brilliant you'd be at it."

Heat flamed in Liam's cheeks, but more than pleased with the praise, he looked confused by it, as if he couldn't believe it was really true.

"You have no idea how amazing you are, do you?" Marcus asked.

Liam shrugged. "Ralph didn't really enjoy the way I liked to...I mean, he always preferred to..." Liam moved his hands as if to put one on the back of his scalp and push his head down.

"Then he's not just a bastard, he's an idiot as well," Marcus said, yawning as lethargy born from satisfaction made its way deep into his bones. "Didn't recognise perfection when it was wrapped around his own damn cock."

Liam smiled again, a more certain expression now.

"What about you?" Marcus asked, gently.

Liam looked up for a second. His teeth crept out and nibbled at his bottom lip. He looked down.

Marcus knew the answer long before Liam gave it. While he waited, he found himself praying that the boy would have enough confidence to be honest.

Liam shook his head.

Marcus tried not to grin in relief. "That's fine."

Liam looked quickly up at him.

"Nothing's compulsory," Marcus said. Standing up, he offered Liam his hand.

Liam put both his bound hands into Marcus's grip and allowed him to help him to his feet. Acutely aware that the strength from Liam's blood was pounding through his veins, Marcus made a conscious effort not to accidentally pull Liam right off his feet.

He didn't want to take the cuffs away. Marcus stared

down at the strips of black leather for a long time before he was finally able to convince himself to undo the restraints. Liam said nothing as the buckles were undone.

"It's time for bed," Marcus said.

Liam nodded. He didn't pull away.

"I'm going to go up. Go to your room and get changed. If you'd like to join me and sleep in my room after that, you'd be very welcome."

They went their separate ways at the bedroom door. Marcus was pretty sure he didn't inhale another breath for the entire ten minutes he waited for Liam to take him up on his offer and join him.

He made sure Liam didn't see his relief, or see his smile when he glanced down at Liam's crotch and saw that Liam, sensible boy that he was, had obviously taken advantage of a few minutes in a room on his own to make himself more comfortable before joining him.

Chapter Ten

"Marcus?"

Marcus looked over his shoulder, to where the grand staircase rose up the other side of the entrance hall. For some reason, Liam had stopped halfway down the stairs. Marcus smiled as soon as he saw him.

The reaction was quickly becoming second nature, but this time, he knew the expression probably appeared somewhat strained. He didn't linger in his admiration of the boy the way he usually would.

"Are you going out?" Liam asked as he reached the bottom of the stairs.

I'm the vampire, you're the prey. You're answerable to me, not the other way around.

Marcus took a deep breath and kept the words back through sheer strength of will. It wasn't Liam's fault the thought of stepping out of the house still made Marcus's stomach clench and his insides knot.

"Just for a little while. I have business in town that I can't put off any longer."

"Oh." Liam's footsteps came to a halt partway across the hall as his confidence seemed to fail him.

Marcus mentally cursed himself. Pulling on his coat with the air of a man readying himself for battle, he turned back to Liam. "Everything is fine." He held out a hand, inviting Liam closer.

Liam was quick to accept the invitation and step into Marcus's space. Then, unsure what Liam needed him to say in order to feel safe and at ease, Marcus took the easy option.

A tug on Liam's hand brought him closer, well within

kissing range, and words became irrelevant. By the time they parted, Marcus wasn't entirely sure who had taken more reassurance from the way their mouths had lingered together.

"I won't be long," he said. "And when I come home..."

Liam smiled. His eyes sparkled with anticipation. He nodded, not needing Marcus to finish the sentence to know that they would both enjoy it a great deal.

It took far more willpower than it should have for Marcus to release Liam and turn toward the door. He jerked it open harder than was strictly necessary, determined not to show any weakness in front of his... No, not his prey. His... and that was the problem, none of the words in Marcus's head seemed to fit what Liam was to him. All he knew was that Liam was his, and he wouldn't give a man he owned any reason to believe him incapable of protecting what was his.

The gentle breeze hit Marcus's face like a sandblaster. The pale blue sky loomed over him, dotted with irritating fluffy white clouds, and far larger than anything had a right to be.

Four walls, a space the size of a hospital room—that was what was natural. The rooms in his house were quite a bit larger, but Marcus could accept them easily enough. But, the proportions of the world outside the house...

Marcus's breath rushed out of his body. His head spun. His knees turned weak. And Liam was still watching. Somehow, Marcus forced himself to walk down the two deep steps leading onto the gravel driveway.

"Take care."

Marcus looked over his shoulder. Liam stood in the doorway, his hand holding on to the door handle as he peeked out past the heavy woodwork.

Nodding, just once, Marcus made sure he kept his steps calm and controlled as he approached the limo. But, he didn't actually breathe easily until he slammed the car door behind him and reduced the world around him back into a more manageable size.

He was going to kill Theo for this.

Marcus closed his eyes and dropped his head back against the headrest. The limo's engine started up, and he felt the car begin to roll forward, but Marcus didn't open his eyes.

He was going to kill Theo for putting him in that damn hospital, then he was going to go and find someone to save Theo's life and patch him up, just so he could kill the little prick all over again for screwing his mind over this way.

A simple hanging would be far too good for him. So would being drawn and quartered. Something more inventive would have to be planned. Theo needed to suffer just as much as Marcus had. No, more than that—as much as Liam had suffered at Ralph's hands while Marcus was unable to wake up and put a stop to it.

As his new chauffeur drove him into one of the less reputable parts of town, Marcus glowered angrily through the window, but he didn't really see the rundown houses and abandoned buildings they passed.

He ran his thumb over the scar on his finger in what was quickly becoming a hard habit to shake. The real world wasn't as interesting as conjuring up mental images of Theo Wallace howling in pain.

The car came to a smooth stop. Marcus frowned as he forced himself to focus on the world beyond the car window. The low brick building looked like exactly what it was—a whorehouse for those who wanted to buy access to someone's blood along with their body.

One glance at the peeling paint and crumbling stonework and Marcus wrinkled his nose at the prospect of entering such a slum. The chauffeur, who Jenson had hired and no doubt mentioned the name of at some point, appeared and blocked Marcus's view as he opened the door for him.

It was only a few paces across the narrow pavement before Marcus was once more surrounded by walls that cut the world into manageable portions. Just one step inside the safety of the building, he stopped.

The stench of blood struck him like a physical blow. The whole place reeked of it, and desperation was mixed in with every drop. Marcus's stomach turned over, but he couldn't deny it was just the kind of place in which he could easily imagine Theo thriving.

Marcus wasn't going to get his revenge in one of the genteel establishments on the other side of town. There was no more avoiding that fact than avoiding the building. Snarling his annoyance under his breath, Marcus strode further into the space, his pace so fast, his hair whipped out behind him.

At the end of the narrow corridor was a small room. A man sat behind a desk. Further back, a dozen blood whores of various ages and appearances lounged on grubby sofas. Their pale skin, the dark shadows under their eyes and the messy scars along their veins proclaimed that far too much blood had been taken from them, and far too carelessly.

The man at the desk straightened up at the sight of Marcus, smiling as he no doubt planned how he'd spend the kind of money a client like Marcus could throw around if he had a mind to.

"Are you looking for something special today, sir?" he asked. "We have a fantastic—"

Marcus took several large notes from his pocket and dropped them on the desk. Before the man had a chance to snatch them up, Marcus leaned forward and placed his knuckles on them.

"I'm not interested in a feeding—or in anything else you or your...associates might be able to offer me," Marcus snapped. "I want information."

The man hesitated. He looked over his shoulder.

"Consider this a down payment. The real money will be given to whoever can provide me with the location of a vampire called Theo Wallace."

Within a few minutes Marcus was content that he'd made a suitably deep impression. Anyone who was desperate enough to sell themselves in a place like that now had all the incentive they could need to give up Theo's whereabouts.

Turning on his heel, Marcus strode out of the hovel, not bothering to hide his distaste for the place. Ducking into the car as quickly as possible, he wiped his hands on his trousers, as if that would help him feel less polluted by the place.

The chauffeur needed no additional orders. The car was soon on its way to the next whorehouse on the list. Marcus leaned back against his seat. If the private investigator couldn't do his job, there really was no other option than to do it himself.

* * * * *

"Mr Bates?"

Liam looked up quickly from the magazine he'd been reading. Relief rushed through him as he met Mr Jenson's eyes. For some reason, the stories he usually loved so much weren't holding his attention that day. The prospect of being of some use was infinitely more appealing. "Can I help you and Mrs Jenson with — ?"

"You have a visitor."

Ralph.

The magazine tumbled to the floor at Liam's feet, gossip columns crumpling under the weight of problem pages.

"A lady by the name of Miss Trent," Mr Jenson said, calmly stepping forward and picking up the magazine, as if he hadn't noticed that every drop of blood had drained out of Liam's face. "If you don't wish to see her — "

"No, it's fine," Liam said, jerking himself to his feet. "For a moment I thought..." He shook his head at himself, knowing he was acting like an idiot. Jenny wasn't anyone to be scared of. Nurses were on the good guys' side — it was practically part of the definition. Still, he didn't rush to meet her.

160

A glance at the butler and Liam became aware that Mr Jenson was studying him very carefully. It was possible that he had noticed how pale he was after all.

"Is, um…is Marcus back?" Liam asked, as casually as he could manage.

"No, sir. He's still engaged in town on business."

"That's okay." Liam straightened his T-shirt. Jenny was a nurse, not a psychopath, he reminded himself one more time. He didn't need Marcus to hold his hand when he spoke to her.

"I'll show her into the blue sitting room downstairs," Mr Jenson said.

"Yes, thank you. I'll be straight down." Liam watched Mr Jenson walk out of the room. Frowning slightly, he nibbled at one of his fingertips as he tried to work out what the hell Jenny could be doing there, what her visit might mean.

Mr Jenson had said she was there to visit him, not Marcus. If it had been a message taken by anyone else, Liam might have assumed they simply got it wrong, but Mr Jenson wasn't the type to relay a message incorrectly.

Minutes ticked by, Liam still stood in the middle of the morning room trying to work up the will to move, and failing.

Marcus had done so much for him. He shouldn't have to deal with his visitors too. If Marcus came home and stumbled upon Jenny before Liam even managed to leave the morning room, that would be yet another burden he'd placed on him. It was only that realisation that finally convinced Liam to step forward.

He didn't stop until he stood outside the door leading into the blue sitting room. Even then, he couldn't let go of his momentum for fear he'd never regain it.

Pushing open the door, Liam stepped inside and kept walking determinedly forward until he stood directly in front of Jenny.

She rose gracefully from her seat on the sofa. It was the first time Liam had seen her wearing anything other than her nurse's uniform.

"Hello, Liam."

"Hi."

She ran her gaze over him very slowly, as if checking him for injuries. Liam was pretty sure he'd had x-rays that would have been more likely to miss things. "I..." He swallowed down a bitter taste in the back of his throat as he remembered how he'd looked when Jenny last saw him. "Why are you here? I mean, how did you find...?" Liam closed his eyes. Pushing a hand through his hair, he tried to calm his racing pulse and make sense of it all.

"Shall we sit down?" Jenny suggested.

Liam opened his eyes. "Of course, sorry. I'm just..." Liam forced a smile as he dropped heavily down onto a chair opposite the sofa where Jenny had been sitting.

"Marcus's address was on his hospital records. Tony from security saw you getting into his limo when you were both discharged," Jenny said.

Liam nodded slowly, well aware that she was still assessing his every movement. Everything she said made sense. There was no reason to panic; it was all very straightforward once it was broken down into manageable chunks. Paperwork. Gossip. Nothing scary about that.

"How is he treating you?"

Liam lifted his gaze and met Jenny's eyes. "Marcus has never hurt me."

Jenny sat back in her seat. She looked different in her jeans and checked shirt, but her eyes were as quick as ever.

"He wouldn't do that," Liam said, putting every bit of strength he had into the words.

"Vampires are..." Jenny seemed to consider her next words carefully. "I met quite a few of them during the years I worked at the blood bank. They aren't the same as humans."

Liam felt his spine stiffen. His grip on the arm of his chair turned white-knuckled.

"Even if he doesn't want to harm you, he could easily

162

hurt you by accident," Jenny went on.

Liam shook his head. "You don't know him."

"I know that just because he treats you better than Ralph did, that doesn't mean he treats you well enough," Jenny said.

Liam stared down at the back of his hand. There wasn't the slightest mark lingering there anymore. "Marcus has been nothing but kind to me," he whispered. "And believe me, I'd have tried the patience of a saint these last few weeks."

"Oh?" Jenny said.

Liam said nothing; he just continued to glare at his fingers as if they were to blame for all his troubles.

"He's feeding from you?" Jenny asked.

Liam shrugged. "Sometimes. I wouldn't mind if he did it more, but he says he shouldn't."

"And you two are...?" she hinted, more delicately.

Heat rushed to Liam's cheeks. He stopped worrying about appearing too pale.

"Sweetheart, I'm not trying to embarrass you," Jenny said, leaning forward and taking hold of his hands. Her palms were warm against his skin, her touch comforting without demanding anything in return. "But I know vampires, and I know what kind of bastards you're used to. You need someone looking out for you."

"Liam already has someone looking out for him."

Liam jerked his head up.

Marcus stood in the doorway leading in from the hall. He was still wearing his coat.

"Marcus!" Liam snatched his hands away from Jenny's and scrambled to his feet, only to hesitate before stepping forward. Part of him wanted nothing more than to race across the room and throw his arms around Marcus as if he hadn't seen him for years, but he didn't dare. Marcus's expression didn't invite anyone to come within five yards of him.

Liam looked from Marcus to Jenny and back again. "I..."

I'm not bi.

He couldn't force the words out. He wasn't even sure if he should be trying to get them out or not. If Marcus thought that he and Jenny were sneaking around behind his back the moment he stepped out of the door, then which way Liam swung was really the least of his troubles and—

"Liam."

He met Marcus's eyes at the sound of his name.

"You're not in trouble."

Liam let out a breath he hadn't been aware of holding.

"Everything's fine," Marcus told him. "Go down and see Mrs Jenson—I'm sure she'd appreciate some company for a few minutes."

Liam glanced toward Jenny.

"Liam," Marcus said again.

Liam found his feet carrying him across to Marcus without his brain having any further say in the matter, drawn to Marcus like the tiniest iron filing to the most powerful magnet in existence.

Marcus reached out to him as soon as Liam stepped within arm's reach. His hand slid across Liam's cheek in a gentle caress.

Liam's eyes dropped closed as he savoured it.

"Go on," Marcus ordered. "Jenny and I will be fine."

"He's right, Liam," Jenny piped up from behind him. "You really don't need to worry about me."

Not seeing what else he could do, only knowing that he suddenly felt more nervous than he had in weeks, Liam took refuge in obedience and slipped from the room without another word.

* * * * *

Spinning away from the door the moment Liam closed it behind him, Marcus glared across the room at the intruder. The woman stared back at him, evidently not the least bit intimidated by facing off against a vampire.

"Yes," she said. "I know the signs. I can tell you're not getting as much blood as you really need, not directly from a human—Liam or anyone else. And yes, I know that any vampire will feed from either sex at a push. But no, I'm not scared of you. Do you have any other questions?"

"What the hell are you doing in my house?" Marcus demanded, striding forward to loom over his undesired guest.

"Liam isn't allowed to have visitors?" Jenny asked.

Marcus's frown deepened. "That's not what I said."

Jenny leaned back in her seat and rested one of her hands calmly on the arm of the sofa, as relaxed as it was possible for a human to be. Marcus's muscles knotted tighter and tighter by the moment.

"Liam knows full well that he may do exactly as he pleases! You are the one who has no business here," Marcus snapped. He strode across to the other side of the room, not willing to sit as if they were having a perfectly agreeable conversation, but not quite able to stand still either.

Even though he was back in the security of his home, the unease of being out in the wider world hadn't disappeared the moment he stepped inside. Finding an interloper there wasn't helping. The last thing he needed was someone questioning his ability to look after what was his. He barely kept back a snarl as he glared over his shoulder at her.

"And what exactly is Liam to you?" Jenny asked, turning her head to track his progress around the room. Apparently, the process somehow made it easier for her to read his mind.

Marcus swung back to face her properly. "What?"

"Is he your whore?" Jenny asked. "Your toy, your prey?"

"No!" The very thought of anyone applying those terms to Liam made his knuckles itch.

"What then?" Jenny pushed. "I've never yet met a vampire who called any human their boyfriend? Is Liam your

165

property? Your pet?"

Marcus came to a stop barely a step away from Jenny. He blinked down at the nurse as if seeing her for the first time. "Pet...?" he said, very softly, considering the term very carefully. He wasn't even sure he'd said it aloud until he saw the woman's expression change.

Jenny's eyes narrowed as she studied his expression.

For once, Marcus wasn't entirely sure if he was capable of hiding his emotions effectively.

"You really care for him, don't you?" she said, as if the possibility had never occurred to her before.

Marcus said nothing. His feelings for Liam were none of her business. He turned his back on her as he marched to the window and looked out over the drive. Her car was still parked there, a horrible green little thing sitting in the middle of his property – as bold as brass and twice as ugly. At least the sight of it didn't send panic racing through his veins anymore. At least he knew it wasn't Ralph's car now.

"If you do care for him, then it's time you started taking proper care of him," Jenny announced.

Marcus slowly turned to face her. Anger unlike anything he'd ever known suddenly flooded through his veins. He stepped forward. He wasn't sure what he was going to do, or even what he'd say, as he closed the gap between them. Then, without him ever having been aware of making a decision, it had already been made.

* * * * *

Liam jumped as he heard a door slam on the ground floor. He stared up at the ceiling of the servants' area, as if he might suddenly develop the ability to see through the white paint on the ceiling, the heavy floorboards, and everything else between him and Marcus.

"Don't you worry about him, love. Vampires are a resilient lot," Mrs Jenson said, from the other side of the

166

kitchen table.

Liam forced a smile and tried to turn his attention back to the carrots he'd been given to peel for a stew.

"Young Master Marcus has been known to enjoy the occasional cup of coffee, you know," Mrs Jenson said. Her lips quirked into a truly infectious smile. She nodded toward a tray already set with coffee pot, mugs, and biscuits. "If you really think you need an excuse to go up and see him, that should do you well enough."

Liam quickly set aside the peeler and the carrot he'd been working on. "Thank you." The words didn't express anywhere near the amount of gratitude he felt, but they were all he had. It would take him far too long to come up with anything else.

Picking up the tray, Liam hurried out of the kitchen and up the stairs into the main part of the house as rapidly as his feet would carry him. He paused in the hallway, listening for any hint of where Marcus might be, but there wasn't a sound to be heard.

Liam cautiously approached the blue sitting room. The door was slightly ajar. Liam peeked inside. Jenny was gone. Only Marcus remained. He stood at the window, overlooking the empty drive.

"I..." Liam cleared his throat and tried again. "I thought you might like some coffee."

Marcus glanced toward him. His expression was very serious. He didn't say a single word as Liam stepped into the room and set the tray down on the coffee table.

Liam perched on the edge of the sofa, just where Jenny had sat a little while before. He struggled to keep his hands steady as he fussed with the coffee things. Marcus slowly crossed the room and sat down in the chair opposite him. Liam could feel the vampire's gaze on him, but he didn't have it in him to look up and meet Marcus's eyes yet.

The atmosphere in the room was somewhere between chilly and downright frigid. It was all Liam could do not to shiver.

Two coffees poured, Liam wrapped his hands around his cup and tried to force a little warmth into his body. It didn't help. He took one hand away, picked up a biscuit and nibbled on a corner.

"Did you—?" Liam finally began.

"It's time for you to start thinking about going back to work," Marcus cut in.

Liam's coffee didn't spill across the tray as he set down his cup. He didn't drop the biscuit either. Liam sat very still and very quiet for a few seconds without showing any outward reaction. He was quite proud of himself for that.

Closing his eyes for just a moment, he swallowed down the tiny bite he'd taken of the biscuit, but not before it completed its transformation into ash inside his mouth. "I think that's a good idea, too," he whispered.

His appetite was gone. Sure he wouldn't be able to swallow another bite, Liam focused on setting the remainder of the biscuit down on the saucer next to his cup and straightening up the various items on the tray—anything to avoid having to look up and meet Marcus's eyes.

He supposed that's what he got for letting himself daydream. If he'd had any sense at all, he'd have stuck to reading about other people's fairy tale endings in the magazines. Believing that he could really get something like that for himself had been asking for trouble.

"Liam?"

"Yes?" he managed to whisper.

"Are you going to look up at me at any point?" Marcus asked.

Liam hadn't actually planned to do anything of the sort, but he couldn't refuse, either. He dragged his gaze slowly up Marcus's shirt. Marcus had been very kind to him over the last few weeks, doing anything else would have been tantamount to throwing everything back in the vampire's face.

Marcus's frown was deeper than ever.

Somehow, Liam forced a smile to his own lips. "It's fine," he said.

Marcus seemed to be waiting for him to add something else. Liam scrambled for a few extra words.

"It's better this way. Quit while the going is good and all that."

Marcus's eyes narrowed. He put down the cup of coffee he'd been sipping from. "Quit?" he repeated.

Liam nodded. "I think maybe if Ralph and I had walked away from each other when things were still good, then—"

"I won't hit you if you stay," Marcus cut in.

"I know," Liam said, softly. "I...I've been thinking about that a lot. And I think... I think some men hit their lovers and some men don't. You're one of the ones that doesn't, not unless you're in the playroom with someone who likes it, anyway." He tried to smile at his own joke and failed completely.

Marcus's lips didn't even twitch. "So why are you talking about leaving?"

Liam blinked at him, not sure what was going on. "As soon I get a job, I can start saving up enough to—"

Marcus held up a hand. "Jenny pointed out that, as much as I would like to keep you in this house twenty-four hours a day, humans have some sort of need to interact with a variety of other humans," he said. "That doesn't mean I won't expect you to come back to this house the moment you finish work each day."

Liam nibbled at his bottom lip.

"Permission to go to work and be," Marcus waved a hand, obviously trying to remember a term Jenny had used, "*financially independent*, is not permission to wander off whenever the hell you feel like it. It's not permission to leave!"

By the time he finished, Marcus was sitting on the very edge of his seat, as if ready to jump up and tackle Liam to the ground if he tried to run toward the door.

For the first time Liam could remember, the idea of someone doing that didn't scare him. It gave him hope. "You want me to stay?"

"Yes." Marcus sounded so certain about everything.

"As your...?" Liam couldn't have sounded less like Marcus if he'd tried. He wasn't even sure how to finish a damn sentence.

Marcus seemed to think about the half-asked question very carefully. "Vampires have traditionally called the human companions they care about their submissives. Their pet might be another appropriate term."

Liam looked up and met Marcus's gaze. He had no doubt that those were the most polite words they used for them.

"But a human might call himself a vampire's lover, or his boyfriend," Marcus offered.

Liam swallowed rapidly as all sorts of different scenarios played through his mind. He tried to tell himself he was only interested in the human terms, but he knew it was a lie. His mind kept swinging back to Marcus's first terms, desperate to latch onto them and make them an intrinsic part of himself.

"A human definition of a submissive would be someone who wanted to commit himself to pleasing one person, to belonging to one man," Marcus said. "There's nothing wrong with that — with wanting to put your complete trust in someone the way you're just starting to learn to do when you're in bondage."

"Are all vampires mind-readers?" Liam asked.

"Dominants understand submissives," Marcus said. "Even if they are a different species."

"And what do dominants want?" Liam whispered.

"To take another man under their protection, to keep him safe, to provide for him, to help him feel safe and secure in his ownership, to teach him, to help him find his confidence again, to..." Marcus trailed off.

170

Liam frowned slightly, wondering why.

Marcus smiled, his expression more than a little rueful. "To do more things than I could possibly list."

Liam nodded. "Okay."

"And to give you back the right to take on a job after Ralph insisted you leave your last place of employment," Marcus added.

Liam looked down at the table for several long seconds. "I'd like that," he finally whispered. In that moment, even he wasn't sure if he was just talking about the idea of going back to work or the whole way of life Marcus seemed to be offering him.

"Jenny mentioned a suitable vacancy at an animal shelter run by one of her friends. She assures me that you would be perfectly safe there. Your main task will be to help socialise the animals before they are re-homed." Marcus nodded to himself. "It will be exactly the same as you did when you visited me at the hospital, but with animals. You can start tomorrow."

Liam bit back a smile. Apparently, it was all settled. The decisions had all been made. He glanced up at Marcus through his lashes.

He wanted him. Marcus wanted him. He wasn't going to be thrown out onto the street; he was just going to get to visit some streets now and again.

"Thank you." Marcus dutifully drained the last of the coffee from his cup. "That was good."

Liam smiled. Maybe it was just relief at being wanted, but he couldn't help but find Marcus's attempts to be polite made him even easier to fall in love with than ever.

* * * * *

Liam took a deep breath as he looked in the mirror above the dressing table. There wasn't a mark on him—no bruises to hide, no sore joints to disguise. He didn't have to

171

worry about that anymore. He was fine. And he was going to work. He nodded to himself. He could do this.

"Ready?"

Liam glanced at Marcus's reflection in the mirror. The vampire stood in the doorway leading into his bedroom, his image no different than any human's would be. He was dressed just as casually as Liam, in nothing more exciting than blue jeans and a plain white T-shirt. But that didn't change the fact he was stunning.

Hoping he didn't look even half as nervous as he felt, Liam wiped his damp palms on his jeans and walked across to Marcus.

"You know, you really don't need to give me a ride into work. I can—"

Marcus's fingertip came to rest on Liam's lips.

Liam couldn't help but smile in response. He was really falling in love with that gentle little gesture. There were no angry shouts or backhanders when Marcus wanted him to shut up.

Without thinking, Liam pressed a kiss against the vampire's finger. Marcus did nothing worse than smile at his silliness. Stepping forward, he even offered Liam a proper kiss, just as Liam had hoped he would.

Their lips fitted together so perfectly, Liam would have given almost anything in the world to be able to stay there all day, to curl up with Marcus in his huge bed and simply wile away the day with more and more kisses. Liam's cock grew heavy with increased blood flow. Perhaps it wouldn't be such a bad idea to mix a few other activities with those kisses…

Liam whimpered as Marcus pulled back, but his protest had no effect. "Come along," the vampire ordered. "It would hardly do for you to be late on your first day."

Early, late, or right on time, it took every ounce of courage Liam had just to step out of the house and onto the drive. Neither the limo, Mr Jenson, nor the chauffeur were there to greet them. Liam blinked at the sleek black sports car as Marcus folded his tall frame into the low slung driver's seat.

"I didn't know you could drive," Liam blurted out as he clumsily scrambled into the passenger seat. "I mean, I assumed with the limo and the chauffeur and everything..."

Marcus turned the key in the ignition. The engine purred into life. The sound of it rushed straight to Liam's cock. Marcus smiled, and it was impossible for Liam to believe that Marcus didn't like the noise just as much as his...as his submissive did.

Liam smiled back at him.

"If you have to go to work, we should at least be able to enjoy the journey there and back each day," Marcus said, as he pulled away.

The car was a wet dream on wheels. That just made the fact that the drive to the animal sanctuary only seemed to take seconds, crueller than ever. All too soon, Marcus was pulling into a parking space outside a low grey building complete with cartoon animals covering the brightly painted sign above the door.

"So, I guess I'll, um...see you when I get home?" Liam mumbled. He forced himself to reach for the car door, knowing he'd still be sitting there in an hour's time if he let himself linger any longer.

*

Marcus undid his seatbelt and calmly unfolded his long limbs from the cramped space behind the wheel. Liam looked over the car at him, surprise opening his eyes very wide, as if he'd really thought there was any way in hell Marcus was going to let his pet walk in there on his own. That would have been an even worse fate than having to get out of the car and walk into an unknown space himself.

Marcus raised an eyebrow at Liam, desperately trying to resist the temptation to grab the boy and hurry him out of the open and into the building. Liam blushed, but it seemed to be more about pleasure at someone making a fuss over him than any sort of real embarrassment. Still, Marcus kept a careful eye on him as they went inside, watching for any sign of distress.

The expression of the woman standing behind the counter morphed into a huge grin the moment she caught sight of them. Short blonde curls, green eyes, freckles. She was obviously the woman Jenny spoke to him about—Diana something-or-other.

She hurried around the counter and immediately enveloped Liam in a huge hug, standing on her tiptoes to wrap her arms around his neck. Marcus's hand clenched into a fist at his side.

She wasn't hitting on Liam. She wasn't copping a feel either. For God's sake, she was a damn lesbian. Liam wasn't her type—Jenny was. It was still far harder than it should have been for Marcus to accept the spontaneous show of affection with complete composure.

He did his best not to glower at Diana when she finally released Liam, and turned to him. Marcus didn't have time to say a word, polite or otherwise, before she had her arms wrapped around him in an equally intense gesture.

Marcus met Liam's eyes over the girl's shoulder. Even if his pet hadn't relaxed when Diana threw herself at him, his amusement over Marcus's plight seemed to be doing the trick perfectly.

"Come on, I'll give you the tour!" Diana grinned up at Marcus as if he was her new best friend.

He'd been so sure Jenny would have had better taste in women. Marcus found himself more than a little disappointed by the nurse.

"No." Marcus only just stopped her catching hold of his hand.

Diana blinked up at him. Liam's smile faltered.
Damn!

"Thank you, but I think we can all do without hearing every animal in the place screeching at the top of its lungs," Marcus rephrased.

Diana was instantly all smiles again. "Of course! Jenny told me you were a vampire." She turned to Liam. "The animals tend to get a little nervous around top predators."

"Oh." Liam hesitated.

"Go and enjoy your tour," Marcus said. "I'm going to stay here for a while." He waved toward the tables and chairs where people could fill in whatever forms were considered necessary when someone wanted to adopt a non-human pet. "I've got a few calls to make. I'll make the most of the good reception while I can." Marcus held up his mobile phone as proof.

If Liam thought it was a very transparent excuse to stick around and keep an eye on him while he settled in to the job, he didn't mention it. He smiled briefly across at Marcus before he allowed Diana to drag him off to see whatever was to be seen.

Taking a seat at one of the tables, Marcus unlocked his phone and scrolled through the menu. He hadn't been convinced that phones could have become any more complicated and fiddly than they had been the last time he'd seen one, but they had. So many baffling new icons and applications. For once, he wished Jenson hadn't been quite so efficient.

Fashion and the latest technologies be damned, he'd have much preferred that Jenson simply provide him with the same model he'd had before he'd lost the last three years of his life.

Marcus pressed his thumb and forefinger against the bridge of his nose and took a deep breath. It was stupid which details brought it all rushing back. The image of his phone flying through the air and the casing smashing open as it landed. Marcus scratched irritably at the scar on his finger, trying to rub away the sensation of an impossibly sharp point breaking his skin.

Just the memory of it made his stomach twist into knots. Turning his attention back to his phone, Marcus found the appropriate number and waited impatiently for the man on the other end of the line to pick up. As the phone rang, Marcus's gaze wandered toward a glass panel in the far wall. In the room beyond it, he could see Diana enthusiastically pointing into a cage.

Liam grinned as she extracted something small and furry and placed it in his arms.

"Hello, Hansford and Associates."

"Have you tracked him down?" Marcus demanded. The man had better know who he was talking about without needing to hear a name. If Hansford was taking time off his case to work on anyone else's behalf, he was about to find out that at least one of his clients could be just as dangerous as any of the men he tracked down for a living.

"Mr Corrigan, I'm so glad you called! One of my associates just this second came back into the office and it seems they've found several very promising leads that we hope will—"

"A simple 'no, we still don't have a damn clue where he is', is quite sufficient," Marcus cut in.

Hansford fell silent.

"The other matter I asked you about," Marcus prompted, with another glance in Liam's direction. The furry ball was climbing up the boy's chest and trying to lick his face. Liam's attempts to push it away were half-hearted at best; he was too busy laughing to really stop the thing attacking him with its tiny pink tongue.

"I have some definite addresses for you there," the man said with obvious relief. He sounded like the kind of man who found vampires to be intimidating by definition. Marcus smiled. He rather liked dealing with people like that.

"Do you have pen and paper?" Hansford asked.

"I'm a vampire," Marcus reminded him, only partly

because screwing with the man's mind was mildly amusing. "A steady diet of human blood is very good for the memory. Get on with it."

Hansford rattled off two sets of contact details. Never taking his eyes off Liam, Marcus easily filed them away in his brain for future reference before hanging up without another word. What to do with himself now...

Marcus tapped his fingertips on the table and picked up the phone once more. Yes, it was about time everyone in the vampire community found out that reports of his demise had been very much premature.

Jenson, gem that he was, had already programmed in all the numbers Marcus could possibly need, as well as quite a few numbers that hell would need to freeze over before he'd deign to call. Ben Probert was only just on the side of the angels in that particular equation, but Marcus pressed the appropriate bit of the screen anyway.

There were apparently occasions where the font of all vampire gossip could be useful after all.

The phone only rang once before it was picked up. "Ben speaking! Spill the beans, darling!"

Marcus's lips twisted into something that probably looked like a complete mockery of a smile. "Ben. It's been a long time."

Static buzzed over the line for several long seconds. "Bloody hell! Marcus! You woke up! No one's going to believe it! Does Theo know? Stupid question. Of course he knows! That's why no one's seen him for weeks, isn't it?"

Marcus settled back a little more comfortably in the rickety lobby chair, for once content to let the other vampire babble on until he ran out of steam.

On the other side of the glass panel, Liam grinned at something the fur ball did. Marcus's smile became far less forced at the sight.

Chapter Eleven

"What do you think — should we name him Marcus?"

Liam peered down at the rabbit in his arms — its fur was pure white except for its ears which were completely black, just like the vampire's hair. Its two front teeth even looked a little like fangs.

Liam lifted his gaze to meet Diana's smiling eyes. He had to bite his lip to keep from laughing out loud. "I don't think Marcus would be all that impressed with his namesake."

Diana leaned toward Liam, and whispered in his ear. "That's the idea." She didn't even try to hold back her amusement. Her laughter was light and joyous. It was also completely infectious. "It would do him good to learn to laugh at himself a little."

Liam shook his head at her antics as he absentmindedly stroked the rabbit's ears. "How about we call the little guy Mark instead?" he offered in compromise. He didn't say the rest out loud, but the words were very clear inside his head. *And never tell Marcus what it's short for.*

Diana grinned as she wrote the name on the label above the hutch. "Done!" She looked down at her clipboard. "Only three more overnight arrivals for us to assess. Two dogs and a kitten."

Liam carefully placed the newly christened Mark in his hutch and checked the level in his food bowl before fastening the door. "I still don't get how people can just throw them away as if they're nothing," he said. Even after working there for over a month, he still didn't get it.

"Spoken like a true stray."

Liam spun around. Taking several rapid paces back, he

stumbled against one of the trolleys containing the supplies for the rabbit hutches, but he never once looked away from the man standing before him.

He'd recognised the voice the moment he heard it. It hadn't been his fear playing tricks on him. His paranoia was well-founded.

Ralph.

And he'd been drinking. Ralph wasn't slurring his words or staggering around in circles, but Liam knew the signs. Ralph had obviously popped his first can of beer the moment he woke up that morning.

"Pathetic," Ralph spat. He looked Liam up and down in disgust as he stepped forward.

Liam shook his head. This wasn't right. It couldn't be happening. Ralph didn't know he was there. He couldn't...

"What?" Ralph demanded. "Did you really think you could hide away here, that someone wouldn't spot you and tell me where you'd crawled off to?"

Liam pressed his spine back against the trolley. The wheels rolled back until it hit the hutches. Then, there was nowhere for him to go. Ralph was between Liam and the door. He was as trapped as the animals in the cages.

Liam's pulse raced faster and faster. His head spun as his breath lodged in his throat, making it impossible for him to draw enough oxygen into his lungs. Somewhere in the distance, a dog barked. Another joined in. Soon all the animals were in full voice, as if screaming their warnings at Liam. They were all too late.

Ralph didn't seem to notice the commotion. His eyes didn't leave Liam until, out of the corner of his eye, Liam saw Diana step forward. Ralph's attention was all on her then.

"Get out. You're not welcome here," Diana tilted up her chin. "If you don't leave immediately, I'll call security." She was far better at bluffing than Liam had ever been.

Ralph's face contorted into a deep sneer as he laughed. There was no humour in the sound, no invitation to join in. He stepped forward again. Diana didn't retreat. Her hands came to rest on her hips as she narrowed her eyes.

Liam didn't think. Before he knew what was happening, he was already standing between Ralph and Diana. There were men who would never dream of hitting a woman, but Liam knew damn well that Ralph wasn't one of them. Anyone weaker than him was a fair target and —

Ralph pushed against Liam's shoulder, almost sending him crashing backward. The only thing that kept Liam upright was the knowledge that, if he lost his balance, he'd take Diana down with him.

Ralph's expression distorted into something even more vile. "If you think I'm going to take you back after you've —"

"I don't want you to take me back."

"What?" Ralph glared down at Liam, making the most of his height advantage as he loomed over him.

"I don't want you to take me back," Liam repeated. It was impossible for him to keep the nervous tremor out of his voice, but he forced the words out.

"You ungrateful little shit," Ralph began. He was almost nose to nose with Liam now. The stench of stale beer overpowered all the various scents that filled the animal shelter.

"I thought I was in love with you," Liam rushed out, scrambling for anything he could say that might distract Ralph and buy him a little extra time before the first blow.

"What did you say?" Ralph demanded.

"I thought I was in love with you. If you'd treated me with even the tiniest hint of kindness, I'd have stayed and put up with your bull forever." Liam couldn't stop the words now, they were spilling out faster than he could control. "If you wanted me, you should have kept me then, because there's no way in hell I'm going to go back with you now."

Ralph didn't say anything. His hand rose. All Liam could do was brace himself for the blow.

He'd pleaded so often. Familiar words rushed to his

throat, but he swallowed them down. Not again. He'd rather take the beating than beg to be spared it.

Liam closed his eyes and Ralph's hand…

Liam frowned as the back of Ralph's hand completely failed to connect with his skin. He blinked open his eyes and looked up at his ex in confusion.

Ralph's face was twisted with pain. His hand was still raised, but someone else's fingers were wrapped around his wrist, twisting the joint in a white-knuckled grip. Ralph's mouth opened and closed, but no sound emerged.

Liam gazed past him in something akin to awe. Marcus's expression was deadly calm. As Liam stared at the vampire across the cluttered room in the back of the animal shelter, he felt the world around him change. It stopped being a place that was all about Ralph, about fear or pain, and it morphed seamlessly back into the version of reality he'd discovered since Marcus woke up.

Letting go of Ralph's wrist, Marcus tossed the limb aside with complete disregard for the fact it was still attached to a man's body.

Ralph stumbled several paces before lurching to a halt, clutching his wrist with his other hand. "Who the hell are you?"

Marcus ignored the question. He stepped forward until there was barely a few inches of empty air between him and Ralph. They were almost the same height. Their builds were very similar. But that was where any likeness ended.

"You really think you scare me?" Ralph demanded, his arms swinging out from his sides as he seemed to try to make himself look bigger and more threatening. Marcus remained perfectly poised, making no attempt to match Ralph's posturing.

Liam saw another movement out of the corner of his eye. A quick glance and he realised that Diana had moved from behind him, apparently trying to get a better view of whatever was about to happen next.

"So this is who you've been selling your arse to since I chucked you out?" Ralph spat toward Liam. "Is your new sugar daddy your bodyguard as well? Have you been whoring yourself out in the hope of finding a real man to stand up for you because you're too bloody cowardly to—?"

"Liam is quite capable of standing up for himself," Marcus cut in, each word clipped and razor sharp. "He just proved that quite beautifully. However, since you're not only annoying Liam, but also me and everyone else in the building with this silly little temper tantrum, it hardly seems appropriate for him to be left to deal with you on his own."

"You think I'm going to turn and run at the sight of some pretty little ponytail?" Ralph goaded.

Marcus raised one perfectly shaped eyebrow. Then, he smiled. In all the times Marcus had smiled at Liam, Liam had never seen the vampire's fangs catch the light that way before.

Ralph took a step back. "You're a damn bloodsucker!" His hand went to his neck as if to protect his jugular.

"Don't flatter yourself," Marcus snapped. "Even vampires have standards."

"You won't get away with this!"

Liam glanced from Marcus to Ralph and back again. It was very hard in that moment to understand why he had ever found Ralph intimidating. Faced with someone who was far closer to his size than Liam would ever be, Ralph seemed to shrink into himself.

Ralph retreated from Marcus faster than Liam had ever been able to scramble away from Ralph. He stormed out of the shelter as if there was a vampire hot on his tail, but Marcus wasn't chasing him. Marcus remained perfectly still, watching Ralph's retreat until he was completely out of sight.

He had no interest in chasing anyone who didn't want to be with him, no interest in keeping anyone in his playroom who didn't want to be there, no intention of hurting someone who didn't enjoy it.

Liam dropped his gaze. He'd known all those things for

a long time, but the facts of the matter had never lodged itself in his brain as deeply as they did in that moment. Seeing Ralph and Marcus standing side by side, the differences between the two men were obvious — and they had nothing to do with the ability to drink blood.

Eventually, Marcus turned toward Liam. He didn't reach out to lay a hand on him, but he didn't need to. Liam still felt Marcus's presence arc over him as if Marcus had wrapped him in a huge blanket and bundled him up in front of a huge roaring fire.

Their eyes met for a brief moment before Liam quickly lowered his gaze.

A touch to his cheek encouraged Liam to look up again. "I'm going to give you fair warning before you say a single word, Liam. You will not apologise for him. You're not his boyfriend. He's nothing to you, and you have nothing to apologise to anyone for."

Liam closed his eyes for a moment. When he opened them, he saw the concern shining in Marcus's expression. He stroked his thumb across Liam's cheekbone, very gently, as if his touch might really be able to wipe away every backhander Ralph had ever layered onto the skin there.

Somehow, it didn't take as much effort as Liam had thought it would to drag a smile to his lips. Stopping his whole body from trembling, however, was a very different matter.

Dear God, had he actually said all those things to Ralph? Had he really stepped in front of Diana? Liam's knees decided that they had been brave enough for one day. He swayed where he stood, not sure if he was going to throw up or fall over first.

"W-would you like a cup of coffee?" Liam whispered. "There's a staff room." He couldn't wave his hand toward it, couldn't let Marcus see how badly he was shaking. He folded his arms across his chest instead.

Marcus smiled. This time there was no hint of fang

visible. "Good boy."

It took all the strength Liam had in him to turn away from Marcus and glance toward Diana. It was only then that he really thought about her presence.

A wave of panic rolled through him. She'd seen... She knew about —

"I'm looking forward to that coffee," Marcus announced.

"So am I!" Diana chipped in, sliding her arm through Liam's and walking him purposefully toward the staff room. "I love coffee. Actually, I think it's my favourite thing on the entire earth!"

The animals all became very vocal in their cages as Marcus strode past them, but within a minute, the worst of the noise had died down and the three of them were sitting around the tiny round table in the corner of the broom cupboard of a staff room.

Marcus leaned back in his seat, so calm, so composed, it was almost impossible to believe that anything out of the ordinary had just happened. He smiled encouragingly at Liam as he added coffee to his cup.

Liam managed to turn his lips upward in return.

"So," Diana said, her usual good humour only a tiny bit brittle as she added three times her usual spoonful of sugar to her coffee. "Have you told Marcus what we named our new rabbit?"

* * * * *

So beautiful, and yet so fragile.

Marcus stared down the hallway, taking in every detail of Liam's profile. Whatever had caught the boy's attention in the playroom, it appeared to have him completely fascinated.

The minutes ticked by. Liam didn't move a muscle. Marcus remained as motionless as possible, too. It would have been too big a risk. Breaking the moment could have far too many consequences.

Marcus's hand slowly curled into a fist at his side. Perhaps he'd been wrong to simply let Ralph run away. If Liam had known the bastard was dead then perhaps…

Marcus glanced down at his fist before quickly turning his attention back to Liam. Then, perhaps, Liam wouldn't have wanted to be within miles of the playroom rather than having been willing to approach the doorway without any prompting from his master. Could he have trusted a murderer the same way?

Liam rocked slightly on his heels. His arms were still wrapped tightly around his torso, as if he thought he needed to protect himself from low blows—as if he still didn't trust Marcus to be able to protect him adequately. Was that worse than Liam thinking him a murderer?

As Marcus watched, Liam nibbled at his bottom lip. Marcus's teeth ached at the sight, but it was the way the nervous gesture tugged at his heart that finally made him step forward.

"I was starting to think you might have been abducted by aliens. Have you been standing there ever since you left the dining table?"

*

Tearing his gaze away from the playroom, Liam blinked rapidly, refocusing his eyes as he turned and looked down the hallway. Marcus stood just a few yards away from him, his approach hadn't made a single sound to alert Liam to his presence.

A moment passed. Liam turned his attention back to the view through the doorway. The playroom was still relatively dust free, even though they had hardly ventured in there since he cleaned it that first time.

"Tie me up?" Liam whispered, not even glancing toward Marcus as he made the request. "Not just what we've done a few times with the cuffs. I mean properly — tie me up in there, like you've done with other men. Feed from me at the same time?"

He sensed Marcus move forward until the vampire stood directly beside him. "Do you think you need any more excitement today?"

Liam swallowed and pushed the image of Ralph raising his hand to strike him earlier that day out of his mind. His gaze moved slowly over the cage and the cross, determined not to waste another moment on thoughts of Ralph. "I'm not looking for excitement."

"What are you looking for?" Marcus asked.

Liam took a deep breath as he studied the rack of paddles and whips. "You. I'm looking for you."

"And that's where you think you'll find me?" Marcus's voice was softer than ever. "I'm out here, too."

"I mean the…the part of you that's the least like him," Liam whispered. He waved a hand toward the playroom. "That's where that part of you lives."

Marcus moved carefully around Liam to stand in front of him. His chest completely blocked the view into the playroom. Liam stared at Marcus's shirt for a full minute, knowing he wasn't making any sense. The idea was so clear inside his head, but the words to express it weren't there. Finally, he convinced himself to lift his gaze and look Marcus in the eye.

"If he had… When he had the power to do anything he wanted with me, Ralph…" Liam looked down for a moment, before determinedly dragging his gaze back up. Marcus knew full well what Ralph had done with that power. He didn't need to hear it repeated. "But now I want to know what you'll do with me when I'm helpless in that room. I need to know."

Marcus seemed to study him very carefully for a very long time. "You're scared."

There seemed little point in denying it. "Yes."

Marcus paused and took a deep breath. Liam pulled air

into his lungs in perfect synchronisation with him.

"For the record, if you'd lied to me about that, there was no way in hell I'd have ever allowed you to step over the threshold." Marcus took a pace back, then another and another, until he'd backed through the open doorway and stood in the centre of the playroom.

For each step Marcus moved back, Liam took one forward. Closing the door behind him, he sealed them both in there. In some strange way, when the door clicked closed, Ralph, and the rest of the world, ceased to exist. Nothing on the other side of the door was important.

"I want to see more of you," Marcus said.

Liam nodded his understanding. He looked down at his clothes, but for all the response the sight of them prompted inside him, he might as well have never set eyes on them before.

A hand appeared within Liam's field of view. It took hold of the edge of his T-shirt and very slowly pulled it up.

Marcus was giving him time to realise that he didn't want this, he was giving him time to say no—that much was clear. Liam looked up. "I don't want to say no," he whispered.

Marcus tugged the material further up, and Liam lifted his arms so Marcus could guide it over his head. The garment was set aside upon what Marcus had informed Liam was called a spanking bench.

Liam stared intently at his T-shirt, wondering if his bare skin was going to make the acquaintance of the leather covered bench that evening as well. His attention was brought firmly back to Marcus as Marcus stroked a knuckle gently down the centre of his chest. He looked up to meet Marcus's eyes, but Marcus's attention was all on his body.

Not a single mark remained from Ralph's last beating. In some stupid way, that let Liam feel clean in a way he hadn't since that first black eye. Lifting his arms from his sides, Liam looked down at the pale unmarked skin covering his forearms, as if he'd never really seen himself before.

Marcus drew another line over Liam's chest with his fingertip, brushing against his right nipple in the process. Every other bit of skin on Liam's body was forgotten about as he gasped at the sudden rush of pleasure.

"Sensitive?" Marcus asked, circling the nipple.

It was impossible to tell if he was teasing or really asking. Liam nodded regardless.

"Good." Marcus bent his finger a little more, his nail scraped at the bundle of nerve endings.

Liam jerked as a jolt of pure electricity shot down his spine. He was so on edge; every sensation seemed to be magnified a hundredfold. Or maybe it had nothing to do with his nerves and everything to do with the man standing before him. A shiver of anticipation rolled through Liam with the idea.

"Do you remember how good it felt last time I fed from you?" Marcus asked, his fingers still toying with Liam's nipple.

Somehow Liam managed another nod.

"Even when I'm not trying to feed, I still have teeth—I can still bite, even in places where I know there are no veins."

Liam closed his eyes as possibilities careered wildly through his mind. He opened them again, just in time to see Marcus bend down and bring his mouth level with his chest.

Lips caressed, an agile tongue swirled around Liam's nipple, making the skin tingle. He waited impatiently for the sharp scrape of teeth, but Marcus pulled back.

Liam frowned.

"But just because I *can* do something, that doesn't mean I *will*."

That statement shouldn't have sent a rush of pleasure to Liam's cock, but it did. The sheer confidence Marcus had in his control of the situation made him harden.

"Do you like the idea of knowing that all you can do is tell me if you don't want me to do something to you—that you want me to stop?" Marcus asked, dipping his head and blowing gently against Liam's damp nipple, making it peak. "Whenever we're in this room, everything else is up to me. I'll be the one to decide if I want to put you in bondage, or if I want to let you come."

Their eyes met as Marcus straightened up. Liam blinked. "Yes." The word was barely a whisper, it was also a lie. He didn't just *like* knowing that, he loved it.

There were no mistakes to be made now, no decisions to worry about. Liam smiled slightly. Giddy with bliss, he stared down his body and watched as Marcus took away his shoes, his socks, his trousers, and last of all, his boxers.

The panic he expected to race through him when standing naked and vulnerable before Marcus for the first time failed to materialise. Liam could never remember being calmer in his life. He couldn't recall ever feeling so right inside his own skin either.

Marcus took Liam's hand and guided him toward the diagonal cross that occupied the far side of the room. As Marcus stepped into the small gap between the cross and the wall, Liam met his eyes past the upper sections of woodwork.

"Reach up, take hold of the rings," Marcus ordered.

Liam somehow pulled his gaze away from Marcus's eyes. A large ring hung from the top of each support, forming inviting hand holds. He wrapped his fingers around them, willingly arranging himself in the way that would make it easiest for Marcus to tie him in place.

"I want you to keep hold of them. Don't let go unless you want us to stop. Understand?"

"But, I thought…"

"I fully intend to tie you up in the future, but today — today, I want you to know that you're making a choice, that you're choosing to stay where I put you just because it feels so good to be there."

Liam nodded, even if he would have been willing to sell his soul for the pleasure of feeling leather wrapped tightly around his wrists. He looked up at the rings again. There were leather cuffs hanging from eye-bolts next to them. It wouldn't have taken Marcus more than a moment to fasten them in place.

Liam twisted his neck, following Marcus's progress as he walked away. It soon became impossible to keep track of him as Liam's hold on the restraints stopped him turning any farther.

"Spread your legs, and line your feet up with the bottom supports," Marcus ordered.

Liam shuffled his bare soles into position.

"Perfect."

Strong hands came to rest on Liam's shoulders and stroked slowly down his back. Pure instinct demanded that Liam arch into Marcus's touch. The mental image of one of the stray kittens at the shelter rushed to the forefront of his mind. Suddenly, he understood how it felt to be that desperate to be petted.

Marcus's palms slid down farther, until they settled on Liam's arse. Long fingers kneaded the layers of muscle there, examining his buttocks, parting his cheeks slightly as they played with him.

Liam's head dropped forward as he closed his eyes, all the better to concentrate on the feel of Marcus's hands. His cock was so hard, he was sure he could come just from Marcus palming his arse. When Marcus's touch suddenly disappeared, he was almost ready to cry out in protest.

The skin Marcus had cupped felt cold, until a new warmth covered it. Marcus pressed his body against Liam's back, from shoulder to thigh. The vampire's clothes prevented Liam from enjoying real skin to skin contact, but at least he could be sure that Marcus was enjoying himself now—his erection pressed firmly against Liam's arse through his jeans. A wave of relief mingled with the pleasure already bubbling inside Liam.

Marcus wanted him.

Liam pressed back, blatantly rubbing his arse against

the vampire's crotch in invitation. Marcus slid his hands around Liam's body in response. He stroked over Liam's sides as he went, always letting him know exactly where his hands were.

With his every movement slow and deliberate, Marcus caressed his way down to Liam's cock. His fingers wrapped around the swollen shaft for the first time. His thumb rubbed against the head.

Gasping, Liam dropped his head back until it rested on Marcus's shoulder.

"So much blood pumping through you," Marcus whispered in his ear. "So much pleasure..."

Liam whimpered. If Marcus took some of his blood, he knew that would just make room for more pleasure to dance through his veins.

"I want to make you blush for me."

Liam frowned slightly, not sure what Marcus was asking for, not sure how to best please him — and his need to please his lover was stronger than ever now that it came from desire rather than fear.

Marcus wanted him to be embarrassed about something?

Marcus released Liam's cock and slid one hand between their bodies to palm his arse again. It left his skin for a moment, only to come quickly back and tap very gently against his right buttock.

"You're talking about spanking me," Liam realised.

"Yes."

Liam nodded. "Yes," he echoed.

Marcus dipped his head and kissed his neck. "I'll know if you lie to me about what you want. Blood doesn't lie — I don't want your lips to lie either."

Liam tilted his head to one side, inviting Marcus to check that he was telling the truth any time he wanted. Marcus chuckled slightly, but he did nothing more than press a kiss to Liam's throat before pulling away and separating their bodies.

A shiver ran down Liam's spine. For the first time since his clothes had been removed, he felt naked, exposed. Marcus's hand soon came back to caress his arse, but it wasn't the same as the pleasure of full body contact. When Marcus's palm left him once more, it returned swiftly, tapping lightly against his left buttock this time. Liam twisted his neck, trying to look past his own arm and meet Marcus's gaze.

Moving his hand back to Liam's right buttock, Marcus tapped his skin again, very lightly.

"You can..."

He trailed off as Marcus's lips twisted into a very self-satisfied little smile. "I can do whatever I want with you?" he suggested. "Yes, I realise that." He stroked his fingers over the skin he'd just struck. "I've given you the right to say stop, because I want you to be able to say it if you need to. As and when I want you to be able to say hurry the hell up and spank me properly, I'll give you leave to say that too."

Liam couldn't help but smile as he bowed his head. He really was Marcus's now. It wasn't just a vague mental concept. He felt the truth of it right down in his bones.

Once more, Marcus's slightly cupped hand made contact, but it was no more painful than a polite tap on the shoulder. Closing his eyes, Liam concentrated hard, determined to extract every sensation he could from the mild touch if that was all he'd be allowed.

The taps gradually came quicker, heat slowly building beneath them as they were layered over his skin. Liam instinctively pushed his backside out, looking for more. Marcus's touch was still too mild. Liam needed much more from him.

Rising up onto his tip toes, Liam balanced himself with his grip on the rings as he tried to coax Marcus into offering him what he suddenly wanted more than anything in the world. He needed to hear a slap as flesh met flesh, needed to feel Marcus's touch deep beneath his skin and not just on the surface.

"Please…" It was impossible for Liam to keep the word back.

"Go ahead," Marcus invited, his voice as calm and composed as ever. "Speak up. Say whatever you want. But remember — there's only one word that will change anything that happens between us in here. Anything other than a 'no' is only going to make me enjoy having my own way all the more."

A noise escaped from the back of Liam's throat, as close to a growl of frustration as he had ever made, but he couldn't deny that the reminder went straight to his cock, too.

His complete lack of control coiled and writhed around the intense feeling of safety already firmly knotted inside him, until the two were almost indistinguishable.

Maybe Marcus's almost-spanks grew a little harder, maybe it was only that Liam's skin grew more sensitive under the repeated contacts, but, gradually, the sensations became more powerful. They still didn't come close to sating the desire Liam felt, but they at least sent stronger waves of pleasure singing through his veins. He whimpered his approval as his breaths turned more ragged and his cock became more and more desperate for its release.

Each time Marcus's hand fell, Liam's hips rocked, rubbing his shaft against the centre portion of the cross. The wood was smooth. It teased him without offering him any actual chance of coming.

Liam muttered curses under his breath, relying on the sound of the spanks to shield the words from Marcus's ears. Without any warning, the steady rhythm of hand falls disappeared. Liam's shaky syllables trailed off. Silence descended upon the room.

Licking his lips, Liam cautiously tried to utter something he actually wanted the vampire to be able to hear. "Marcus?" The word was so hoarse it was almost unrecognisable.

"Liam?" Marcus responded.

Liam dropped his head forward, pure relief at not being left all alone in the world rushing through him like a runaway stagecoach from an old black and white movie.

Marcus's hand returned to Liam's world. It stroked over his buttocks and slipped between them to caress his hole. Liam quickly pushed back against the digits. He wanted Marcus inside him. He needed Marcus's cock buried deep in his arse just as much as he needed oxygen in his lungs.

"Please?" He squirmed against Marcus's hand and pulled against the rings on the cross, but he didn't dare let go of the rings in order to direct Marcus's touch himself.

Don't let go unless you want us to stop.

Liam shook his head. He didn't want that — wasn't even sure he'd survive that.

"Hush," Marcus ordered.

Liam heard tiny metal teeth scrape against each other as Marcus undid his fly. All Liam could think about then was Marcus's cock. He didn't have a thought to spare for anything else. It wasn't until the tip of Marcus's erection pressed against his hole that Liam managed to bring together enough brain cells to remember what the word lube meant — and what the word essential meant.

He opened his mouth, but no words emerged as Marcus reached around Liam's body and took Liam's cock back into his hand. His touch was even more perfect now that it was slicked with pre-cum. Liam's own desperate need to come demanded he stay silent as Marcus rocked his hips and rubbed against Liam's unprepared arse.

"That feels good, doesn't it?" Marcus whispered to him.

Liam managed to nod. He gasped for breath, waiting for the stab of pain as the vampire thrust inside him, desperate to please Marcus by holding his composure when that happened. But, the pain didn't come.

Marcus's cock slid firmly back and forth across Liam hole, but he didn't even seem to be trying to enter him. He seemed to be far more intent on working his hand rapidly around Liam's shaft, dragging him closer and closer to his orgasm.

Liam bit down on his bottom lip. He couldn't come too soon, he couldn't. Disappointing Marcus would be unbearable. Liam's teeth sank deeper into the sensitive skin inside his lip, threatening to split it, but it did little good.

He wasn't sure there was any way he could cling to his control much longer. Marcus seemed to know exactly how to drive him to the point of no return. Standing on the cliff's edge, Liam looked down into a sea of bliss, desperately trying to keep his balance as storm clouds gathered and howling winds swirled around him, threatening to toss him over the edge at any second.

Marcus brushed his lips against Liam's neck. "I want you to come while I feed from you."

Before Liam even had a chance to panic at his inability to hold back for another second, Marcus's teeth were cutting cleanly through his jugular and pure bliss was racing through his veins.

Any control Liam might have had over his own body evaporated. Marcus's hand moved faster and faster around Liam's cock. His hips made fierce contact with Liam's freshly spanked arse as he rubbed his shaft between Liam's buttocks again and again.

So many sensations collided inside Liam's body, he could barely breathe. His mind spun and ecstasy burst through him in a flash of brilliant white light as he came. Barely a moment later, he felt cum splash against his arse and up onto the small of his back as Marcus reached his own climax.

Marcus bit down harder, pushing his teeth deeper into Liam's neck. Tossing his head back, Liam screamed. His grip on the rings failed him. He started to tumble, but Marcus's arms were instantly wrapped around him, guiding him safely down toward the floor at the base of the cross.

Marcus descended with Liam, holding him close, never breaking the bite. Time passed, Liam had no idea how long, but he sensed the way the vampire moved against his neck was changing now.

As Marcus lapped at the wounds more slowly, Liam tightened his grip on the arm of Marcus's shirt, unwilling to let him go. A lifetime seemed to pass while Marcus spooned behind him on the floor, encouraging the wounds on Liam's neck to close and heal, but when Marcus began to pull away, it was still far too soon. *Any* end to it would have been too soon.

Liam made no protest. He didn't have the energy to complain, no matter how much he hated any distance existing between them. Marcus slowly extracted his arm from Liam's hold, but when he parted their bodies it was only to turn Liam around so he could snuggle against Marcus's side more easily.

Marcus slid one hand down Liam's back to caress his freshly spanked buttocks, encouraging Liam to murmur his pleasure into Marcus's shoulder. The skin tingled under Marcus's fingertips, not with pain, but in a way that made him feel alive for the first time in so long.

It took a full minute for Liam's brain to put together certain facts. Marcus was rubbing his cum into the sensitised skin, marking him in the most basic way any man ever could.

Liam smiled into the crook of Marcus's shoulder until he realised that being marked on the outside was only possible because he wasn't marked deep inside.

A frown creased his forehead. "Why didn't you...?" he whispered.

"Because if you were ready this time, you'll still be ready next time. But, if you weren't ready now," Marcus whispered to him. "Then you might never have wanted there to be a next time. That would be unacceptable."

Liam glanced up at Marcus as he realised just how important it was to Marcus that there be a next time. For the first time, he really believed he wasn't the only one who didn't ever want things to end between them.

Liam curled in closer to Marcus as an extra layer of reassurance wrapped around him. "This is what I want," Liam swallowed rapidly as his emotions threatened to get the better of him. "I want this—to be your submissive." He always wanted to feel this safe, this right in his own skin. He always wanted to know his master was watching over him, that his master was pleased with him and maybe even, someday, that his master loved him.

Marcus nodded, very slowly. "You're mine." He smiled.

A little of his fangs showed, but Liam couldn't see why anyone in the world would find them frightening. "Yours," he whispered.

Liam closed his eyes as satisfaction and contentment combined to make him sleepy. Part of him expected the image of Ralph from earlier that day to rush forward and fill his mind, but the only thing he saw against the inside of his eyelids was Marcus.

He didn't wake up when Marcus picked him up and carried him to their bed.

* * * * *

"Ready?"

Liam stopped staring at his trainers and looked up at Marcus—at his master. Sitting on the edge of Marcus's bed, he had to tilt his head right back to meet the vampire's gaze.

No, he wasn't ready to go back to work. He was pretty sure he never wanted to set foot outside the house again.

"Do you have any calls you need to make today?" he blurted out.

The mattress dipped as Marcus took a seat on the bed next to Liam. "You mean, will I be staying at the shelter with you all day?"

Liam swallowed down his embarrassment and nodded.

"No," Marcus said. "I'll stay for a few minutes, but not all day. I'll be leaving after a little while to run some errands."

"Oh..." Liam stared down at his hands. There was no reason why he should feel shocked. Marcus hadn't hung around all day every day for weeks now. It had been silly to think that what they'd shared in the playroom the previous night would change that. It wasn't even as if they'd had sex.

"You'll be fine," Marcus promised. His hand came to rest on Liam's back—a strong comforting presence, but one that he'd already admitted would be fleeting.

Liam shrugged, but the silence stretched out until he got the distinct impression that Marcus wasn't going to say anything until he received a proper response to his last statement. "I would have left yesterday if you hadn't been there," he whispered.

"With Ralph?" Marcus asked.

Liam glanced across at Marcus from the corner of his eye. "No. I wouldn't do that."

Marcus's arm slipped more firmly around him. Of all the things Liam expected the vampire to do, placing a gentle kiss on his temple wasn't one of them. He leaned into Marcus's embrace and rested his head on his shoulder, making the most of the unexpected gesture.

"Are you afraid he'll come back?"

Liam considered the possibility very carefully and from a variety of angles. "No. He won't come back." There was no way Ralph would risk running into Marcus again. Liam had seen the fear in Ralph's eyes. He'd run for the hills before he got in the way of anyone who might actually beat the hell out of him for a change.

Marcus remained silent for a few moments. "Just because I'm not there, that doesn't mean you aren't still safe there. It doesn't mean that you don't belong to me or that I'm not watching over you." He spoke slowly, as if weighing each word on his tongue before uttering it.

Liam nodded. Theoretical knowledge was all very well,

but he had the distinct feeling that it wouldn't compete with being able to actually see Marcus on the other side of the window that looked out into the reception area.

"There's an old vampire tradition that some of the more established families still maintain."

Liam glanced up at Marcus, more than ready to welcome any sort of insight into the vampire world, but unsure why the topic had suddenly changed.

Marcus brought his fingers to rest against Liam's throat and stroked them back and forth across his neck. There was no mark left from the previous evening's feeding, but he still seemed to come back to that spot again and again, as if he could see it, even if no one else could.

"A tradition?" Liam repeated. He swallowed rapidly and felt Marcus's fingertips move as his Adam's apple bobbed.

"A collar."

Marcus's touch suddenly seemed to create a direct line from Liam's throat to his cock. Each stroke might as well have been applied directly to his rapidly hardening shaft.

Marcus's lips quirked into a small smile. "I've seen you putting collars on the animals when they're ready to go home with their new masters. The fur balls seem to like it."

Liam swallowed again, still unable to make words happen.

"Do you like that idea?" Marcus asked.

Liam nodded. It wasn't just his cock it appealed to — it called to a far deeper part of his psyche too.

"To any other vampire it will be a clear signal to stay the hell away from you," Marcus said. "To the kind of human who knows what it's like to own a willing man, it will mean the same — that I own you and that anyone who tries to lay a hand on you will have to answer to me."

Liam managed another nod.

"And, to you," Marcus said. "It will mean that you belong to me."

Liam looked up and met Marcus's eyes. Even when his instincts screamed that he should drop his gaze in the face of a more dominant man, he forced himself to hold Marcus's gaze.

"If you get nervous or you're not sure what to do, I want you to reach up and tuck your fingers into your collar. And I want you to think about what I'd want you to do."

"Yes," Liam whispered.

"Not what I'd do," Marcus stressed, brushing his fingers through Liam's hair. "What I'd want *you* to do. And I don't want you to do anything that will risk you getting hurt. Understand?"

Liam nodded, unable to attempt speaking again, unsure what he'd blurt out if he tried.

When Marcus pulled away, Liam automatically tilted his head back, offering his lips up to be kissed, but Marcus didn't even seem to notice. He walked away without a word. Liam watched, trying his damnedest not to feel abandoned as Marcus strode across to the dresser on the other side of the room without a backward glance.

The vampire took something out of a drawer before coming back to Liam's side. Liam's gaze fell on the jewellery box in Marcus's hand. He couldn't look away from it; the attraction was far stronger than magnetism.

A moment passed. Marcus lifted the lid.

A simple silver chain stared up at Liam. A small padlock connected the two ends, complete with a tiny little key. Liam gripped the edge of the mattress very tightly in an effort not to reach out and grab it.

It was Marcus's to give, something else that Marcus was in complete control of—and that was exactly how it should be. All Liam could do was hope, and maybe... He dragged his eyes up to Marcus's face. "Please?"

Marcus didn't say a word as he took the collar out of the box and undid the fastening. "Once I put this on, I'm the only one who is allowed to remove it, and I have no intention of doing that. Ever."

"Yes." Liam cleared his throat. "Good. I'm glad."

It only took Marcus a few seconds to fasten it in place around Liam's neck. It was heavier than it looked. Liam had no doubt it would be a noticeable weight around his neck all through the day, binding him to Marcus, letting him feel like it was Marcus's hands continually wrapped around his throat — in the best possible way.

Reaching up, Liam hooked his fingers into the chain. Marcus smiled when he saw the gesture. It took Liam a moment to realise he was doing exactly what Marcus said he should do whenever he needed to feel his master's reassurance.

"Ready to go to work now?" Marcus asked again.

Liam nodded. Sliding his hand into Marcus's palm he allowed Marcus to help him to his feet and guide him out of the house to the waiting sports car.

He managed to smile his goodbyes to Marcus as Marcus left the shelter after only a few minutes conversation with Diana in reception.

The moment he was out of sight, Liam reached up and wrapped his fingers around his collar. A glance around the room proved that no one was looking at him strangely. No one had guessed that it was anything more than a silver chain.

Somehow, that just made it all the better.

Chapter Twelve

Liam sped up, walking faster and faster, until he was almost running along the pavement. He reached up to check that his collar was still firmly in place. It was.

At first, the metal links that completely encircled his throat had been enough to remind him that he was safe, even while Marcus was out of sight. They should still be enough.

It was three weeks since Marcus had first wrapped the collar around his neck, and Liam knew he shouldn't need any more reassurance than it provided.

He couldn't expect Marcus to be at his side every moment of the day. He couldn't expect his master to put up with him following him around like a besotted little puppy forever, either. In spite of everything, Liam managed a small smile. He was pretty sure that a besotted puppy was far closer to the truth of how he felt about Marcus than he had ever admitted to anyone out loud.

The smile didn't last long. Liam glanced over his shoulder. He didn't see anyone he recognised. There was no sign of Ralph anywhere in the vicinity, but that didn't change the way the back of Liam's neck prickled. Someone was following him. Even knowing there was no logical reason on earth why anyone would want to do that, Liam couldn't shake off the feeling that he was being watched.

He was a grown man, and he was going to walk the short distance required to meet his master, rather than wait for Marcus to pick him up at the door to the animal shelter. He wasn't so pathetic he couldn't even do that, was he? Liam wasn't so sure anymore. But that didn't change the fact that, after asking Marcus for permission to do it, Liam couldn't bear to turn back.

Rounding a corner, Liam only just stopped himself breaking into a sprint as he spotted Marcus's sports car parked just a little way down the street. Marcus was right where he'd said he'd meet Liam. Everything was fine. A few more hurried steps and he'd be safe. Finally reaching the car, Liam scrabbled at the door in his haste.

A shrill alarm filled the air. Liam jumped, then cursed. He ducked his head and peered into the car. Empty. Marcus was gone. Looking over both his shoulders, Liam searched the surrounding area for his master. People were staring at him now, probably wondering what sort of car thief was stupid enough to try to steal a car in the middle of a busy high street.

Liam took a step back from the car, spinning around, trying to keep everyone who was staring at him within his field of vision. As suddenly as it started, the alarm cut out. Liam sagged with relief, only just stopping himself from reaching out and bracing himself against the low car roof before he set off the damn car alarm again.

"Liam?"

Jerking around, Liam spotted Marcus coming out of the building on the nearest corner. Marcus was frowning, but it was all Liam could do not to throw himself at him in relief.

"What happened?"

Liam shook his head. "Nothing. I'm fine. I just... I'm sorry about setting the alarm off. I didn't think before I tried to open the door."

Marcus's frown didn't soften. Liam pushed his hands into his pockets and turned his gaze to the ground between them. "Did your meeting go well?" Merely asking the question sent another spike of adrenaline rushing through his veins.

There was a line in the sand around the meetings Marcus went to without him. It was drawn so deeply it was more like a moat that a man might need a drawbridge to cross, and Liam had the distinct impression that even if he managed to do that, there would be a portcullis on the other side of it.

"Get in the car."

The vehicle beeped as Marcus undid the central locking — even that brief friendly sound made Liam jump. He felt the blush rising to his cheeks as he slipped into the passenger seat and did up his belt, but Marcus made no comment. He didn't say a word as he pulled away from the curb and drove them toward his house. He didn't speak as Liam followed him through the front door either.

Liam scurried after Marcus.

Marcus didn't slam the door in Liam's face as he strode confidently into his study, and Liam was more than willing to take that as an invitation to join him.

"I'm sorry," Liam said, gently closing the door in his wake. "I shouldn't have tried to pry —"

"Are you ready to tell me what happened yet?" Marcus cut in as he lowered himself into the chair behind his desk.

Liam glanced up at Marcus through his lashes as he sat down opposite him. "Nothing happened."

Marcus leaned back in his seat and folded his arms across his chest.

Liam tightened his hold on his collar until he came dangerously close to throttling himself with it. "Nothing happened," he repeated. It was fast becoming the only mantra he could think of that might convince Marcus that he wasn't a complete and utter failure as a submissive.

*

Liam is safe.

Marcus took a deep breath and repeated the fact to himself one more time. Liam was safe. The boy was right there in front of him. He was fine. Nothing and no one could hurt him. But none of those facts changed anything. Every sense Marcus possessed was still on high alert, demanding that he fix whatever was wrong in his pet's world.

Whatever lies Liam told, Marcus knew without the slightest trace of doubt, what he'd taste if he fed from Liam right then—pure terror. He didn't want Liam tasting that way. The very thought of it turned Marcus's stomach.

For a moment, the idea of feeding from someone else presented itself for Marcus's consideration. He pinched the bridge of his nose as he tried to separate his desperate need to feed after visiting yet another whorehouse and finding himself no closer to tracking down Theo, from his panic over Liam's obvious distress.

Feeding from anyone else wasn't to be considered. He couldn't walk away from this kind of problem the way he would have a few years before. He couldn't simply exchange Liam for another food source. Marcus had to fix this, and he had to do it while lightheaded from damn near deadly low blood pressure.

God, but he needed to feed so badly, not from a bag— from a real person, and far more often than he was allowing himself to feed from Liam during their mild little scenes.

Marcus took a deep breath as he looked up. Liam seemed to be watching him just as carefully as Marcus had ever studied him. In his own discreet way, Liam was obviously trying to get a read on him.

"Yes, I am angry," Marcus said, more than happy to save Liam the trouble. "I don't like being lied to."

Liam swallowed rapidly, pulling Marcus's attention to his neck. The pulse was pounding quickly through his jugular, just begging Marcus to bite.

Liam closed his eyes for a moment.

"This isn't something that you can hide from that way," Marcus told him as gently as he knew how. "It's not something that will change until your behaviour changes."

Liam stood up, but he made no attempt to round the desk and come closer, the way Marcus had hoped he might. Liam took a few paces away, coming to a stop alongside the fireplace. He rocked on his heels as he stared down into the empty grate, as if trying to find some way to comfort himself while Marcus refused to provide that service for him.

"You gave control of certain things to me when you agreed to wear that collar," Marcus said. "But there are still some things that you control. You're the only one who can bring this situation to an end. All you have to do is tell me what's wrong, what happened before you met me at the car."

Marcus leaned forward and rested his forearms on the desk in front of him. He should never have given Liam permission to wander around on his own in the first place.

Jenny, Diana and every other human on the planet could cheerfully go to hell. Liam didn't need freedom. He didn't need independence. And he didn't need a master who was willing to give him those things either. Liam needed protecting, and Marcus felt his failure in that task cut deep inside him, threatening to spill what little blood he had.

"Maybe...maybe we could go up to the playroom?" Liam said.

Location be damned. Marcus wanted the truth. If that was the only place Liam would utter it, fine.

Marcus marched up to the playroom, paying no heed to how fast Liam would have to run to keep up with his longer strides. He pushed the door open with such force, it slammed back against the wall.

That was a mistake. Marcus mentally cursed himself. He knew how jumpy loud noises made Liam. He was just making things worse.

Marcus pushed his hand through his hair and took another deep breath. Maybe Liam had been right to take the conversation up here. The scent of the leather, the memory of the trust Liam had already placed in him when they'd played their few mild little games, settled something in Marcus.

He was in control. He could do this. He understood enough about humans now. Everything would be fine.

The click of the door, followed by a rustle of clothing

behind him, let Marcus know that Liam had caught up and joined him in the room. Marcus looked over his shoulder just in time to see Liam pull his T-shirt over his head and set it aside.

As Marcus watched, Liam's hands went briskly to the waistband of his jeans. In moments, the denim was down around his ankles and he was kicking away the tangle of shoes and clothing with more determination than Marcus had ever seen in him.

Seconds later, Liam stood before him, naked bar his collar. Without ever looking up or meeting his gaze, Liam stepped around Marcus. He didn't stop until he reached the spanking bench.

Liam looked at it for a second, as if not entirely sure how to make his next move. Then, very slowly, taking more care with his movements than any submissive Marcus had ever known, Liam knelt on the widely spread supports.

It wasn't easy for a man to fasten the ankle restraints around his own limbs in that position. Marcus knew that. He'd seen enough men struggle to do it after he'd ordered them to make the attempt.

He didn't issue any orders to Liam, all he did was observe as Liam first struggled, and finally succeeded in doing them up. Leaning forward, Liam bent over the bench, offering his exposed arse up to be spanked or screwed however his master wished. Marcus clenched his jaw, unwilling to be distracted no matter how great the temptation.

Liam managed to fasten the buckle around his left hand, but there was no way he could do up the right one. After a moment spent waving his hand around as if he thought he might be able to cast a magic spell on the leather and command the buckle to tighten itself, Liam placed his wrist neatly in the cuff that had yet to be fastened and fell still. He closed his eyes, and that was it.

Stepping forward, Marcus walked carefully around the spanking bench, assessing the arrangement from every angle.

He'd imagined Liam there many times. There was only one real difference between his mental images and the reality.

Liam's cock was completely soft. Whatever Marcus might have previously imagined happening, in reality Liam clearly wasn't there because he wanted to be, not in that way at least. He wasn't arranged so prettily because he was turned on by the thought of being restrained or helpless, he wasn't there because he wanted to be spanked.

Out of Liam's line of sight, Marcus reached out to run his fingers down Liam's back, only to stop himself short. Snatching his hand back, Marcus pushed it through his own hair instead. The strands were getting more disordered by the moment, but he didn't have time to worry about that.

This was obviously an offering of some sort. Liam was trying to send him some sort of message that he wasn't able to put into words. Now, if Marcus could just work out what the hell that message was…

He walked around to face Liam. For the first time in all his visits to that room, Marcus knelt before another man. Lowering himself onto his knees in front of the spanking bench, he sat back on his heels and brought himself eye to eye with his pet. Placing a hand carefully on each side of Liam's face, Marcus gave him no choice but to meet his gaze.

Marcus studied every line of expression on Liam's face, but he still found himself no closer to being able to guess at the truth. Leaning forward, he brought his forehead to rest against Liam's.

No thoughts miraculously leaped from one brain to the other through the division of skin and skull. Marcus opened his eyes. Past the blur of Liam's face, he could just about see where Liam's wrists were fastened. No, not wrists, just one wrist was bound. One was still free.

Pulling back a little, Marcus took hold of Liam's right hand. The need to know what was troubling his pet overwhelmed everything else. Holding Liam's gaze he bowed his head and gently pressed his lips against his wrist, letting him know what he was about to do.

He didn't see any hint of fear flit across Liam's expression. Liam didn't try to pull his hand away from the impending bite. Permission granted. Marcus scraped his teeth gently across the skin over the vein. Blood immediately seeped onto his tongue.

It was all he could do not to flinch as the acrid taste of fear filled his senses. Quickly running his tongue over the wounds to heal them, Marcus remained on his knees in front of the spanking bench for several long minutes.

Fear and panic. Panic and fear. The emotions raced through Marcus veins, threatening to take over his mind. It was almost impossible to believe that such a little drop of blood had contained so much pain.

"You're safe," Marcus whispered. "I won't hurt you. And I won't let anyone else hurt you either. You understand that?" Marcus stroked his hand through Liam's hair, clumsily trying to gentle him down from his terror.

Liam tried to avoid his gaze, but Marcus moved his hands back to either side of Liam's jaw and once more made Liam look into his eyes.

"Tell me what's wrong," he ordered.

Liam closed his eyes.

"I won't be angry with you," Marcus hazarded.

"You should be," Liam blurted out.

Marcus frowned.

"You should," Liam waved his free hand, indicating the playroom.

"I should hurt you, punish you?" Marcus asked. His voice was surprisingly calm, all things considered.

Liam nodded.

"No."

Liam blinked.

"I'm not going to punish you. I wouldn't even do that if I knew what you thought you deserved to be punished for!" Marcus said, unable to keep a snap from his words. "That's not what this room is about. Haven't you listened to anything I've said to you about that?"

Liam nodded. "I just thought..."

That was all he said. Whatever Liam had thought, he didn't seem the least bit interested in sharing it with his master. Marcus tensed. The whole situation was completely unacceptable. He swayed away from Liam, as if studying him from a slightly different angle might somehow give him the insight he lacked.

Silently cursing himself, Marcus glared at Liam, willing his own brain to work faster and more efficiently as he battled against his confusion. Nothing. He couldn't even guess what was wrong unless Liam was willing to give him some kind of clue.

He was completely at his pet's mercy. Marcus's spine stiffened at the knowledge. Closing his eyes, he took yet another deep breath. What did Liam need from him...?

Marcus had no idea how long he knelt there before he opened his eyes, but when he did, he had a plan. Leaning forward, he pressed a kiss against Liam's temple in the way that Liam seemed to like so much. "You'll tell me when you're ready."

Liam closed his eyes again.

"And we'll stay here until you do."

Unable to kneel any longer, Marcus gave in to the temptation to check that Liam didn't have any physical injuries. "I'm not leaving," he promised, as he pulled himself to his feet.

Walking slowly around the spanking bench, Marcus ran his palms over each inch of Liam's skin, analysing, testing, reassuring himself that whatever was hurting Liam, it wasn't causing him any physical pain.

He wasn't trying to turn Liam on, but he didn't fail to notice when Liam's body slowly began to respond to his touch. Muscles relaxed under Marcus's hands. Liam's pulse sped up. His breathing turned ragged. He was hardening, even if he wasn't talking.

Between the supports of the spanking bench, Liam's cock began to swell and stiffen. A droplet of pre-cum gathered on the tip. Marcus resisted the urge to taste it—even if that meant living with the taste of Liam's fear on his tongue for even longer.

Completing his circuit around the bench, Marcus traced the line of Liam's collar, gently caressing his way around his pet's neck before checking that the padlock was still securely fastened.

"It should be enough," Liam whispered.

In one movement, Marcus was back on his knees in front of the bench. "What?"

"The collar," Liam whispered. "It should be enough. The way you... You've been so kind to me, so patient. It should be enough. It's been weeks since I even set eyes on him, and I still..."

Liam closed his eyes very tightly. Marcus could only kneel there and wait for more words to hit the air—for words which he prayed would make more sense.

"The collar should be enough. Belonging to you should be enough," Liam repeated.

"To stop you from being afraid of Ralph?" Marcus asked, frowning as he desperately tried to put the fractured sentences together and form them into one complete idea.

Liam nodded.

Poor little sod...

Leaning forward, Marcus rested their foreheads together again. Relief rushed through him as a dozen far more terrifying possibilities faded back into nightmares that would never actually happen. "It doesn't work like that," he said.

"But it should! I shouldn't be scared," Liam insisted, squirming and twisting his head away from Marcus's touch. "I promised I wouldn't be and—"

"I don't want you to be scared of *me*," Marcus corrected, pulling back and catching Liam's gaze.

Liam looked down.

Their positions were insane. Any sort of physical distance between them at that moment was insufferable. Within moments, Marcus had the restraints around Liam's limbs undone. In no mood to hold back and pretend that vampires weren't a damn sight stronger than any human would ever be, he picked Liam up.

Liam's eyes opened very wide. As Marcus pulled the naked boy down onto the floor with him, to sit on his lap, Liam stared at him in some cross between shock and awe, but Marcus dismissed that as unimportant.

"Did you really think I'd punish you for being afraid?" Marcus demanded, as he tried to cradle Liam closely against his body.

It wasn't as easy an endeavour as humans made it look. Liam's limbs didn't seem to be designed for it. They were too long to be folded up into a suitable shape. Giving up on that, Marcus turned his attention to smoothing his hands across Liam's skin, but he had no idea if he was doing it correctly — if his actions were something a human could really take some sort of comfort from.

"Would have deserved it," Liam mumbled into Marcus shirt as he snuggled in closer to him. "Let you down."

Marcus shook his head. Looking up at the ceiling, he rested his head on the cold bars of the cage behind him and cursed Ralph.

"Keep thinking that I can feel him following me."

Marcus jerked his head away from the bars. "What?"

"Ralph," Liam whispered. "I keep imagining that he's following me, that I can feel someone watching me whenever you're not there."

"Ralph, or just someone?" Marcus asked. No one could have been more amazed than he was that the question sounded perfectly calm.

Liam lifted his head from Marcus's shoulder and peered up at him. "What do you mean?"

"Do you feel like it's Ralph in particular that's following you, or do you just get the sense that you're being —" Marcus only just stopped himself from saying stalked — hunted by a vampire searching for prey. "Followed?" he finished awkwardly.

Liam frowned as if it had never occurred to him that it might be someone else that was tracking his movements, biding his time and waiting for the perfect moment to strike.

Marcus's heart raced faster and faster. He should have considered the possibility before, should have known what could happen if someone had spotted him with Liam. "Ralph hasn't been following you," he said.

Liam frowned slightly. "I know there's no reason why —"

"No," Marcus cut in. "I'm telling you that I know for a fact that he hasn't been within five hundred yards of you since that day at the animal shelter."

"How would you know?" Liam whispered.

"Because I'd know," Marcus said, very simply.

For several long seconds, Liam remained perfectly still. He didn't even blink. Marcus held his breath as he waited to find out if he'd have to start explaining about hiring extra private investigators to tail Ralph full time, along with a few other precautions that he'd much rather Liam remain oblivious to.

Finally, Liam gave one slow nod. "Okay."

Marcus stared down at him. There was so much trust in his expression, it damn near took his breath away all over again. "I told you I'd keep you safe, didn't I?"

Liam nodded.

"Did you really think I'd leave you alone at the shelter again, without knowing you'd be safe there, that that bastard wasn't coming anywhere near you?"

Liam looked down for a moment, snuggling a little closer into Marcus's side as if searching for warmth in a world he had learned through experience was often a cold and hostile place. "Thank you."

"Have you actually seen anyone following you?" Marcus asked, doing his best to keep his tone level.

Liam shook his head, rubbing his cheek against Marcus's shoulder in the process.

Marcus barely held back a curse. If the person following him was a vampire, that meant nothing.

"Marcus?" Liam whispered.

Pressing a kiss onto his temple, Marcus patted his pet vaguely on the shoulder. Liam didn't need anything else to worry about. No, far better that he didn't know there might be a psychotic vampire hot on his heels. "Everything's going to be fine."

He stroked his hand down Liam's back until it came to rest on his arse. Liam pushed back against his palm a little, as if in invitation. At the same time, he glanced up at Marcus through his lashes.

In spite of everything else, Marcus felt his lips quirk into a smile. Apparently, his pet was feeling a great deal more at ease now that he'd received a little bit of reassurance. Trailing his finger along Liam's jaw line, Marcus guided him to tilt his head back and make his lips available to be kissed.

The moment their mouths met, Liam parted his lips and invited Marcus in.

More than willing to accept, Marcus let their first kiss lead into another, then another, before trailing his lips down to Liam's neck. Pressing a kiss against his jugular, Marcus resisted temptation to rush into a feeding. He traced his way further down Liam's throat as he rearranged them both on the floor at the base of the spanking bench.

Liam's hand came to rest on the back of Marcus's head. His fingers threaded through Marcus's hair and tugged gently at the long strands in an apparent effort to bring Marcus's fangs back to his jugular. Marcus ignored that. He dipped his head further instead, kissing just below Liam's collarbone.

Liam whimpered. Marcus suddenly found a wrist

being shoved in front of his face. The vein danced before his eyes, offering him another location to feed from, but Marcus ignored that too.

The line of kisses he was tracing down Liam's body reached his right nipple. Marcus paused for a moment, sucking the tight little bud of nerve endings into his mouth and swirling his tongue around it. Liam's fingers scratched against the back of Marcus's head, pulling helplessly at his hair, as Liam arched his back in pleasure.

There was no attempt to guide Marcus's movements now. Liam was just reacting, too lost in the moment to want to control anything.

Keeping his teeth to himself, Marcus smiled as he gently teased his pet, drawing murmurs and sighs of pleasure from him. Several minutes passed before Marcus reluctantly let go of Liam's nipple in order to make his way farther down his body.

By the time Marcus reached Liam's cock, it was hard and flushed with increased blood flow. The pressure on Marcus's hair changed as he lapped a bead of pre-cum from the tip.

Liam was trying to tug him away from his shaft.

Marcus looked up.

Liam mutely shook his head.

Keeping careful control of his facial muscles, Marcus made sure he didn't frown, or do anything else that might make Liam think that his master wasn't prepared to accept his refusal with good grace. "Liam?"

"Let me," Liam gasped. "For you?"

"You don't want this?" Marcus asked, cautiously. He ran his thumbs back and forth over the smooth skin covering Liam's hipbones as he studied him. Everything but Liam's actual words screamed that Liam wanted exactly what he was offering.

"I...For you," Liam whispered again.

Marcus smiled as he finally realised what Liam was

trying to tell him. He trailed his knuckles up the underside of Liam's cock in a teasing caress. "Because I'm the master and you're the pet?" he asked.

Liam bit down hard on his bottom lip.

Jealousy flew through Marcus's veins. He was the only one who was allowed to bite Liam.

"I..." Liam murmured.

"You think I'm going to start feeling all submissive toward you, just because I've gone down on you?" Marcus suggested.

Liam shook his head, denying any such possibility could exist.

"So, you're afraid that I can't keep my teeth to myself?" Marcus teased, light-hearted with relief at the knowledge that a submissive's natural desire to please his master was the only reason Liam wanted anything between them to stop. He kept his knuckles trailing up and down the vein on the base of Liam's cock while he waited for an answer.

Liam shook his head again. A whimper left his lips as he no doubt imagined how much pleasure a vampire's bite could force into a human's cock if he were to feed from there and drink more than his lover's cum.

"I w-want to..." Liam stuttered out.

"You want to suck my cock?" Marcus asked, helpfully.

Liam nodded vehemently. "Please?"

"Because you want to please me?"

Another nod and Liam squirmed against the cold playroom floor.

"Is that the only reason?" Marcus pushed, moving his hand slightly so he could trace circles against the very tip of Liam's cock.

Liam moaned, dropping his head back, baring his neck to Marcus. Finally, he managed to shake his head. "I like it," he said, his voice raw with need. "You taste good."

Marcus smiled. There was no way any man could be expected to resist such a beautiful admission. Marcus's hand went to his fly. In moments, he'd freed himself from behind the material.

Liam immediately tried to squirm into a different position. Marcus didn't say a word; he just placed his hands on those parts of Liam's body that he didn't want Liam to move. There was no way Liam would ever be strong enough to get his own way in that situation.

As it was, Liam didn't even seem to realise that it was Marcus who chose how they should arrange themselves. Liam was soon lying on his side on the playroom floor, his head down by Marcus's open fly, and that was all that seemed to matter to him. Marcus turned his own body slightly, making sure his own mouth remained just where he wanted it to be, too.

Liam had come a long way since his first tentative attempt to go down on Marcus in the drawing room. Now, soft, pliant lips quickly wrapped themselves around the tip of Marcus's cock, and an eager tongue rushed to lap at the sensitive head. Vibrations surrounded Marcus's shaft as Liam took him deeper and moaned his pleasure at feeling his master's cock filling his mouth that way.

Dipping his head, Marcus willingly returned the favour, taking Liam's shaft into his mouth.

Liam bucked. His whole body jolted, as if a bolt of electricity had shot straight through him. His lips left Marcus's cock as Liam jerked himself into a half-sitting position.

Cheerfully pretending that he hadn't noticed any of that, Marcus bobbed his head again, letting Liam's cock slide further between his lips. Liam whimpered. His hips rocked forward again.

Rearranging his hands slightly, Marcus quickly put a stop to that. There was no need to let Liam think he had *that* much control over what his master did with him. Marcus was still a vampire. And a cherished pet, was still a pet—no matter how besotted with him his master might be.

Moments passed. Marcus became aware of Liam lying down once more. His breaths caressed Marcus's cock. They were already unsteady. Liam was obviously struggling to maintain any kind of control over his own body.

Good.

Marcus took Liam's shaft deeper inside him, until the tip touched the back of his throat. With no gag reflex to worry about, he kept on pushing forward until it slid into his throat. Swallowing around the head several times in quick succession, he massaged the glans, pulling whimpers and moans from Liam.

As much as he loved the velvety soft skin moving against his lips, Marcus wasn't so focused on what he was doing that he didn't notice Liam regaining enough control over himself to be able to dip his head back toward his master's cock. Liam's mouth was clumsy. There was no technique there. He simply suckled around Marcus's shaft as if it were a delicious treat.

Marcus worked his tongue harder against Liam's cock, moving his head more quickly. Whatever tiny bit of control Liam had possessed deserted him. His hips fought against Marcus's grip on him, desperate to thrust as he spilled into Marcus's mouth for the first time.

Easily keeping him still, Marcus swallowed down everything his pet could offer him. In spite of all temptation, somehow he resisted the urge to let his teeth scrape against the shaft so he could feed from him right there and then.

Marcus kept his fangs to himself as Liam lost himself in pleasure, squirming and writhing against Marcus until he finally fell still. Liam's lips remained wrapped around Marcus's cock as he gasped for breath. Swift rushes of air caressed the length of Marcus's shaft. The ache in his balls was almost as unbearable as the ache in his teeth. Almost.

Shuffling around on the hard floor, Marcus pulled himself forward a few inches. His cock slipped from between Liam's lips, but Marcus ignored the way Liam protested against losing his treat. The vein high on the inside of Liam's thigh called to Marcus so strongly, nothing else mattered.

He pressed as gentle a kiss as he was capable of against the skin there. Liam eagerly spread his legs farther apart, as if he knew what his master needed and was more than happy to provide it. Nothing short of an actual refusal on Liam's part could have stopped Marcus then.

His teeth sliced cleanly through the pale skin, straight into the vein. Liam's body shuddered. There was no way Liam would be able to get hard this time, no way he'd be able to enjoy the feeding the way he had been able to in the past. All he could do was give himself to his master and enjoy knowing that he was owned and protected and —

Marcus's eyes snapped open. Never breaking the bite, he managed to peer down his body to catch a glimpse of Liam. The boy's mouth was nothing more than a thin pink line wrapped around Marcus's cock.

Pleasure rushed through Marcus. His eyes dropped closed. Fireworks exploded behind his eyes as Liam suckled around his cock, following the same rhythm at which Marcus fed from his femoral artery.

Any hint of fear that might have once existed in Liam's blood was long gone. Marcus tasted nothing but Liam's bliss at pleasing his master, and he cherished every drop as he swallowed down the certain knowledge of how safe and content Liam felt in that moment.

Biting down harder, Marcus let his fangs slide deeper as he coaxed more and more blood out of Liam's veins. His head spun with Liam's endorphins. Liam's adrenaline made his heart race. Long before he was ready for it, Marcus came hard and sudden. For the first time, he wasn't able to warn Liam just before his climax.

Marcus felt Liam swallowing rapidly around his shaft, desperately trying to take everything his master offered him. Time ceased to have any sort of meaning. Moments might have felt like lifetimes, hours could have rushed past in seconds. Marcus had no idea how long it took before they both finally fell still.

Slowly withdrawing from the bite, Marcus licked at the wounds, encouraging them to heal, but Liam made no move to retreat, his lips remained wrapped around Marcus's softening cock.

The room seemed very still, very quiet then. Fumbling around, Marcus managed to catch hold of Liam's wrist and rearrange him so he lay neatly in his master's arms.

"Good boy," he whispered, as he pressed a kiss to his temple. Liam made a pleased little noise in the back of his throat almost like the purrs the fur balls made.

Marcus tightened his hold around his pet. Liam was his and he would be kept safe.

If there was someone stalking Liam, then Marcus's course of action was clear. Theo may have taken three years of Marcus life, but he wasn't going to take a single second of Liam's.

Chapter Thirteen

Marcus tapped his fingers impatiently against the steering wheel. Still bursting with energy from the previous night's feeding, it took all the self-control he had ever practiced, and more, to sit quietly in his car and simply watch the street in front of him. There was no sign of the man yet, but Marcus had no doubt that he would make his appearance any moment now.

The recent feeding, yes, that was the reason he couldn't quite stop himself fidgeting, Marcus told himself. After all, there was no other reason why he should be on edge. He wasn't nervous. He had no need to be. The world was no longer overly large. He was used to being in open spaces now.

Marcus took a deep breath, never letting his gaze stray above the height of the buildings that lined the street. No one was going to appear out of the large expanse of blue sky that stretched out toward infinity above him. There was no reason for Marcus to look at it.

And Theo wasn't going to catch him off-guard again.

Marcus turned his hand over and glanced down at the barely visible scar on his fingertip. Seeing it still made his stomach knot. The only reason he didn't close his eyes against the sight was because he knew full well the kind of pictures that would flash up behind his eyelids if he did.

He didn't have time for those sorts of memories. Marcus folded his arms across his chest and turned his attention back to his view down the street. It was busy. That was why the animal shelter chose to walk those of their canine residents who needed to get used to bustling towns, down it at that particular time of day.

And this was the only spot upon the route where any kind of attack was possible. Marcus glared into the alleyway that lead off from the opposite side of the street. If Theo was stalking Liam, that was where he'd make his move.

Marcus sighed as he ran his gaze over the various humans who filed along the street. Mothers pushing screaming infants in buggies. Teenagers trying to look cool and grown-up and generally failing. Men in business suits rushing around thinking they were far more important than they really were, and —

Marcus's mind shut down. Nameless, faceless humans ceased to exist. *Theo.* The other vampire was strolling along the pavement as if he didn't have a care in the world. Without anything like conscious thought taking place, Marcus was out of the car and striding across the street.

Theo.

Marcus's steps sped up as he wove his way through the lunchtime crowd, but there was no need to rush. The little prick had obviously been keeping careful note of Liam's routine. He knew just as well as Marcus did, that Liam wouldn't be walking past for another few minutes yet.

Head bowed and shoulders hunched, Theo stepped into a doorway just to the right of the entrance into the alley and fumbled with a lighter. The street created a funnel that intensified the breeze into something easily capable of blowing out a flame. Theo tried to shield it with his hands for long enough to light up, but failed.

Approaching from downwind, Marcus smelled the other vampire's presence. He heard him cursing his lighter, too. Theo didn't have the same advantages. He didn't look up, didn't even glance in Marcus's direction.

Theo didn't know Marcus was within a hundred miles of him until Marcus had him by his shirt collar. Lighter and cigarette tumbled to the ground. Louder curses filled the air.

Not here. It was too crowded in the street. There was far too much chance of collateral damage to the human population.

Theo squirmed and tried to scrabble away, but Marcus pushed him forward, sending him stumbling into the narrow alleyway leading down between two shops.

Theo swung around, his fangs bared. The blood drained out of his face as he saw who was actually standing before him. Stepping into the alley, Marcus blocked any chance of Theo escaping. A smile came to his lips. He didn't try to hide his own, rather more impressive set of fangs.

"Theo," he said. His polite tone only seemed to make Theo more nervous. He took a step back and reversed into one of the huge rubbish bins that lined the alleyway.

"It's been a long time," Marcus went on, stepping forward and gradually closing the gap between them. "Three very, very long years, in fact."

Theo looked over his shoulder. The alley was a dead end. It seemed a very appropriate term to Marcus.

"I've been looking for you."

"Really?" Theo muttered. "I had no idea, I..."

"Apparently, you were too busy stalking a human," Marcus said. His eyes narrowed. "Anyone I know?"

"Marcus, I can..." Theo's hands came up as if to fend him off, as if there was any chance he'd win that fight.

"You can what?" Marcus demanded. "You can explain? Do you really think there is anything that you can say that will stop me — ?"

"Marcus?"

Twisting around, Marcus saw Liam standing in the entrance to the alley. The sunlight behind him put his face in shadows, but it didn't completely disguise his expression.

The boy looked nigh on terrified. "Are you okay?" he asked, his gaze quickly flicking between Marcus and Theo.

A growl pulled Marcus's attention to a spot near Liam's feet. A dog tugged at its lead.

"I saw..." Liam hesitated, obviously trying to work out what the hell he had seen and failing.

"I'm fine," Marcus said. "Go back to work."

A barely audible sound made Marcus turn back to Theo. The other vampire quickly took a step back, his hands coming up in surrender.

"If you need to feed…" Liam said, with obvious care.

Marcus couldn't have kept the burst of laughter back if his life had depended on it. "Feed on that?" he asked, looking Theo up and down, making no attempt to hide his disgust.

"I…" Liam obviously didn't know what to say, but that didn't stop the boy taking a step forward, obviously determined to be part of whatever was going on in Marcus's life, no matter how petrified he was.

A pipe ran down the far corner of the wall toward a gutter. Liam carefully tied his end of the dog's lead to it. His hands were shaking, but he merely folded his arms across his chest in an effort to hide that as he dragged himself closer still.

"Vampires don't feed from other vampires," Marcus snapped, quickly turning all his attention back to Theo.

He saw the panic in the Theo's eyes, too, but that only encouraged him. He wanted Theo afraid of him, he wanted the pathetic little prick to feel every bit of pain that had flowed through his body for every day of the three years he'd been stuck in that hospital bed.

Marcus's hand clenched into a fist at his side, as the desire to knock Theo's teeth out and make it completely impossible for him to ever feed from a living thing again spiked inside him. Yes…

Let Theo have no choice but to live on blood from an intravenous injection, make him rely on what would merely prolong his existence rather than really let him live. Marcus smiled. He was more than willing to sell his soul, and more, for the pleasure of seeing that.

Marcus stepped forward.

"Marcus?" Liam said again. The words came from closer than before.

"I told you to go back to work," Marcus reminded him,

224

not even looking over his shoulder. "You don't need to see this."

"W-What are you going to do?"

Marcus hadn't truly decided yet. Kill Theo outright? Make his life a living hell? Or, perhaps, he could just leave him in hell for three years before coming back to finish him off? There would be real karma in that kind of punishment.

"Go back to work," Marcus ordered again.

"No."

A new wave of anger raced through Marcus's veins, but there was no room in his head for him to deal with it now. Liam would simply have to wait until later, when Theo was no longer a threat to either of them.

Two steps were all it took to bring Marcus close enough to grab Theo by his neck.

Theo dipped his head, trying to snap at Marcus's fingers. His hands came up and wrapped around Marcus's wrist, but he wasn't quick enough. His teeth came nowhere near Marcus's fingers this time.

"Too slow, Theo. You won't catch me off guard twice."

Theo made a gurgling noise. Marcus merely tightened his grip.

"Marcus." By the sound of his voice, Liam was now only a few steps away from them.

"You said you wanted to know what put me into a coma for three years?" Marcus reminded him, never looking away from Theo.

Liam didn't answer. He didn't need to.

"Theo—that's what. And the coma—that's what happens when a vampire bites another vampire but fails to finish the job." The words were barely more than a growl. Marcus studied each flash of fear that shone in Theo's eyes, relishing every one.

After all those years of imagining what it would be like—it was even better than he'd ever guessed it could be. Feeling Theo's pulse race beneath his fingers, knowing that it was his choice if Theo lived or died, pushed so much adrenaline into Marcus's veins, his eyes blurred with it.

The helplessness he'd felt in the hospital drained away. Power was just as delicious as he always remembered it being. But Marcus frowned slightly. Something was niggling at the back of his brain, telling him that there was something else he should be thinking about.

No matter how hard he tried to ignore it, it continued to tug at his attention until he finally allowed the thought into the front of his mind. Liam hadn't said anything for far too long.

Ignoring the way Theo clawed at his hand, Marcus held him easily in place as he looked over his shoulder.

Liam met his gaze. There was no disapproval in his expression, not even a hint of chiding. "He bit you?" he asked.

"Yes." There was something freeing about finally saying it aloud.

The only thing to be seen in his pet's expression was sympathy. No disgust at discovering his master's weakness, no desire to turn and walk away. There was no way Liam could know what it was like for a vampire to admit such a thing, but as their gazes remained locked, it was impossible to believe that Liam would hate him for it, even if he did.

Marcus glanced back toward Theo. Lowering him a little, he let his feet touch the ground and eased his grip just enough for Theo to draw a breath.

"I'm sorry," Theo rasped.

"No, you're not," Marcus growled. "You're just sorry that you got caught."

Pure hate shone in Theo's eyes.

"Are you going to bite him?" Liam asked.

"No!" Marcus snapped.

It was the wrong tone of voice. Marcus shook his head, trying to clear it. That was the way he spoke to Theo, but Liam deserved better than that. Closing his eyes for a moment, Marcus tried to arrange both the men he was with into something that would fit properly within one brain.

"No vampire worthy of the name would bite another vampire," he explained, shoving the caring master he wished he could be to the forefront of his mind, while he was still capable. "It's simply not done."

Theo's nails clawed at Marcus's arm again, tearing his sleeve as he squirmed against the wall.

"What...what are you going to do then?" Liam whispered.

"I'm going to..." Marcus glanced over his shoulder again. Their eyes met and Marcus's next words died on his lips. He was going to make Theo wish he had never been born. He was going to...

Marcus frowned, but he couldn't look away. Liam still wasn't acting as if he thought there was anything wrong with what he was doing. The protests Marcus had expected to fill the air didn't materialise. Liam didn't plead for Theo the way Marcus suddenly realised he'd expected that Liam would, if he ever saw something like this happening. In fact, Liam seemed to think it was perfectly normal for him to walk around the corner and find his lover throttling another man.

Marcus blinked. His eyes were only closed for a second, but that was more than long enough for him to realise what that scene had to remind Liam of. He'd seen a man act like that, day after day, for months.

How many times had Ralph forced Liam into a similar position? Liam's collar caught a stray ray of sunlight that somehow managed to penetrate the otherwise gloomy alleyway.

That was the only thing that should ever be around Liam's throat.

Some men hit their lovers, some men don't.

Liam had said that to him once. Ralph was one of the ones that did, and Marcus was one of the ones who...

Theo had never been Marcus's lover, but he was a man who was both smaller and weaker than Marcus — a man who would never be a match for Marcus in a fair fight.

Marcus pulled a deep breath into his lungs, oblivious to the dank stench of the alley. What kind of man did he really want Liam to think he was? What kind of man did Marcus want Liam's master to be?

"Wait for me at the end of the alley, Liam. I won't be long." Marcus's voice was very calm now.

For the first time since he'd run into the alley after them, Liam hesitated, as if Marcus might actually be someone whose orders he wanted to follow after all.

"I won't hurt him," Marcus promised, never glancing in Theo's direction.

He smiled in what he hoped was a reassuring way, determined that his pet shouldn't have anything to worry about, that he should never need to doubt, even for a single moment, that his master would do the right thing.

Liam slowly nodded his understanding. He took a step back. Marcus watched him walk to the end of the alley. He crouched down to pet the dog tied there, but his attention remained on Marcus and Theo.

Leaning in, Marcus brought his lips to Theo's ear, ensuring that there was no way anyone could possibly overhear them.

"There is only one reason why you're still upright and capable of feeding," he snarled. "His name is Liam."

Theo tried to swallow and failed. Marcus took no notice.

"See that boy at the end of the alley? His name is Liam Bates. I know you've been following him. I know why. You think he's my weak link, don't you?"

Theo remained completely incapable of answering.

"Right here, right now, I'm not going to hurt you. But only because my pet believes that he belongs to the kind of man who doesn't hit people unless they like it, and because I want him to go on believing that."

Theo gurgled. His eyes bulged. Marcus didn't relent in

the slightest.

"But, if anything ever happens to him, if anyone—not just you, Theo, if *anyone*—so much as looks at him in a way that makes him feel uneasy, I won't have any reason to keep being a nice guy. I will track you down and I will kill you, very slowly. I might even take three years, but I promise you that for every second of that time, every cell in your body will know that you're dying, and it will know it will have nothing to do with what you did to me, and everything to do with whatever has happened to Liam. Understand?"

Marcus forced himself to allow the other vampire to breathe, just enough to be able to push an answer through his voice box.

"Yes."

Marcus stepped back. Theo instantly doubled over, half-collapsing onto the alley floor as he fought for breath. Marcus didn't stay to watch the after-party show. He wasn't some silly little boy who could waste time relishing his victory. He had responsibilities now. He had others to think of apart from himself. Within seconds, he was at the end of the alley, staring down into Liam's eyes.

"You're hurt," Liam whispered, reaching out and gently touching the ripped sleeve on his shirt.

"I'm fine," Marcus said.

Liam looked up at him for a moment, before turning his attention back to the crumpled mess on the alley floor. "He was really the guy who...?"

"Yes."

Liam wrapped his arms around his chest and nodded his understanding.

"He won't bother you, again."

Liam's eyes snapped back up to Marcus's face. A moment later, the light dawned in his expression. "He was the one who was following me."

"Yes. But he won't be following you again," Marcus repeated. That was the important point—maybe even more important than the sensation of teeth slicing through his skin three years ago.

"Why?" Liam asked.

Because he's a coward. Because he knows that your safety is the only thing keeping him breathing. "Because I spoke to him about it and told him not to," Marcus suggested.

Liam nodded again, apparently willing to accept that answer, for now, at least.

Marcus ran his eyes over Liam, automatically checking him for any sign of injury. The dog at his feet growled when Marcus looked down at him.

Liam's fingers went to the mutt's head. "I saw you walk in here with him. I thought you might need help. I forgot that Fred was with me."

Fred growled at Marcus again, and then proceeded to put muddy paws all over his trouser legs.

"We'll take him back to the shelter together," Marcus said. There was no point in making it a question. He wouldn't have taken no for an answer.

Liam merely nodded again.

Very carefully, Marcus reached out and put his hand on Liam's shoulder. Liam didn't pull away, he didn't even flinch. If anything, he actually leaned into his touch.

Marcus relaxed slightly. "Maybe I'll stay for a little while, you can show me what you've been working on," Marcus suggested, pointedly ignoring the grumbling dog.

That time Liam's nod was far more definite. "Yes. I'd like that."

* * * * *

As Liam placed a kitten gently into its cage at the end of his shift, he had to give the task his complete concentration. The tabby was more than a little hyper. All the animals were, since Marcus had decided that he no longer wanted to remain on the other side of the glass partition between the reception area and where the animals lived.

Liam scratched the kitten on the top of its head and closed the cage door. He could feel Marcus's gaze on him, just as he had through the entire afternoon. It was a good feeling.

Liam closed his eyes for a moment, still facing the row of cages. He'd never been more grateful to anyone for simply staring at him. Without even thinking about it, Liam hooked his fingers into his collar.

"Ready to go?" Marcus asked.

Liam opened his eyes and peered over his shoulder. Marcus was right behind him, easily within touching distance, yet neither of them reached out to each other as they made their way out of the shelter and back to where Marcus had left his car. Neither of them said a word, not even when Liam shivered at the sight of the alleyway he'd ran into earlier that day. Through the drive home, the only sound was the purr of the engine.

Finally, they closed Marcus's front door behind them, and Liam let out the breath he'd been half-holding through most of the day.

Looking up, he met Marcus's eyes. "The playroom?" he suggested.

"No."

Liam hesitated. It had never actually occurred to him that they wouldn't head straight for the leather and chains as soon as they could. The possibility that Marcus didn't want that too had Liam quickly reaching for his collar.

Before he had a chance to wrap his fingers around the silver, Marcus caught hold of his hand and led him purposefully into one of the ground floor sitting rooms. It was the room decorated in blue stripes—the one Jenson had shown Jenny into when she visited them. Striding across the room in a few easy strides, Marcus guided Liam to sit on the sofa next to him.

Then, for what seemed like aeons, Marcus did nothing more than stare down at his own hands. "You've asked me before about how I ended up in a coma," Marcus finally said.

"You don't have to tell me," Liam rushed out.

"I know I don't have to. I intend to anyway." That said, Marcus fell silent for several long moments. "Humans have their leather clubs. Vampires, those who don't have a private arrangement with an individual human, have their own clubs where they can go to get what they need."

Completely out of his depth, Liam merely listened. Half-turned in his seat, he studied Marcus's profile, but Marcus made no attempt to turn toward him in return.

"Vampires aren't nice people, but even we have standards. Theo's behaviour fell below what could be tolerated and I blackballed him — had him banned from the reputable feeding clubs. I cut off his blood supply until he showed he could learn better manners. After that, nothing but the most disreputable of whorehouses would allow him past their threshold."

"You could do that?" Liam asked.

Marcus smiled slightly, but there was no warmth in his expression, no humour. "Believe it or not, once upon a time, I was a leading light in vampire society."

"You will be again," Liam quickly reassured him.

Marcus cleared his throat. "Anyway, I saw to it that he was no longer invited into any club worth attending."

"And he bit you?" Liam asked.

"A stupid mistake on my part," Marcus said. He folded his arms across his chest, obviously uncomfortable with the admission. "I should have known better than to turn my back on him."

Reaching out, Liam carefully slipped his hand into Marcus's and encouraged Marcus to unfurl his fingers. "Here?" he asked, tracing the slight scar on his fingertip.

Marcus's hand tensed within Liam's hold, but he didn't try to pull away. "Yes."

Liam's desire to see his master smile overrode his nerves. Dipping his head, he placed a gentle kiss on the scar.

Marcus chuckled. It was a good sound, but his eyes quickly became serious again. "Vampires don't bite other vampires. It isn't done." He took a deep breath. "The few times it has happened, the vampire who was bitten died. If Theo had managed to place a proper bite on me, I would have died too. And I assume that's what he would have done, except someone else walked into the room before he had the chance. As it was, the little prick just caught my fingertip. It wasn't enough to kill me, just enough to send my body into some sort of state of shock."

"In the hospital?" Liam asked, gently.

"They had no idea what caused the coma. Theo told everyone I just collapsed for no reason. Even if they had known the truth, they couldn't have known what would bring me out of it. I didn't know myself until you kissed me and I tasted blood — human blood against my lips rather than any kind of blood delivered straight into my veins."

Liam reached out and touched Marcus's mouth with his fingertips. His own lips tingled with the memory of that first kiss, but Marcus's attention remained on the scar from Theo's bite and Liam found himself turning his attention to Marcus's hand too.

"It doesn't look like much, but for a vampire, feeling another vampire's teeth break their skin..."

Liam glanced up at him. "I think I understand," he whispered.

Their eyes met. For the first time, Liam didn't try to push away the pain of that final beating from Ralph, or from what had happened after it. He let it all shine in his gaze for Marcus to see.

"Yes, I believe you do," Marcus said, his voice rougher than Liam had ever heard it.

There were no other words that could be said, but Liam was suddenly desperate to remind Marcus that it wasn't just pain that bound them together.

Parting his lips, Liam took the topmost joint of

Marcus's finger into his mouth and sucked gently around it. He could make out the slightly raised skin of the scar with his tongue. He traced the line of it over and over again before leaning forward and taking more of Marcus's finger between his lips.

He looked up at Marcus, saw both pleasure and humour dance in Marcus's eyes, and knew that his master had realised what he was trying to say without a single syllable being uttered.

Marcus moved his other hand to the back of Liam's head and simply rested it there while Liam went down on his finger. Very gradually, Liam became aware that Marcus was gently guiding him down toward his cock.

Marcus was already hard behind his fly, his erection straining against the fabric. Marcus wanted a blowjob.

Pulling back slightly, Liam let Marcus's finger slip from between his lips. Marcus didn't try to stop him.

It took all of Liam's courage to speak, all of his control to make his words come out calmly. "Do you mind if I don't?" he whispered.

Marcus frowned slightly.

It took everything Liam had in him not to pull away from an expected blow. Marcus didn't look angry, he looked concerned. That was different. It was important that Liam remember that it was different.

"It's never been compulsory," Marcus reminded him, his concern seeming to redouble by the moment.

"I just thought, perhaps, tonight we could..." Liam looked up and met Marcus's eyes, hoping that silent communication wouldn't let him down now, when he needed it most.

"Say it," Marcus ordered.

The raw desire audible in his voice gave Liam courage. "I want us to have sex," he said, very softly.

He saw the light in Marcus's eyes and knew how much he loved hearing the offer, but Liam still held his breath as he waited for his actual verdict on the idea.

"Tell me exactly what you want," Marcus said.

"I want you," Liam said.

Marcus said nothing. That particular admission obviously wasn't going to be enough. Liam felt the heat rush to his cheeks, but he knew there was no chance of Marcus believing that he was ready to have sex if he wasn't even able to talk about it.

"I want to feel your cock buried deep in my arse," Liam said, choosing each word with care. "I want to feel you come inside me while you're feeding from my neck. I want to feel your body pressing down on me, pinning me in place. I want to feel owned and possessed and know that I'm completely yours."

As he stared into Marcus's eyes, Liam found his words flowing more easily than he could ever imagine.

"I want to stop pretending that I'm not in love with my master, that I don't want to belong to you in every way any man ever could."

Liam's heart raced so fast, he wasn't even sure he was going to survive for long enough to hear Marcus's answer. Then, Marcus leaned forward. He brought their mouths together. Liam couldn't have felt more relief rushing through him if Marcus had shouted his acceptance at the top of his lungs.

The fact that Marcus hadn't mentioned feeling the same away about him didn't seem important. As the kiss ended, all Liam cared about was the fact that his hand was in Marcus's hand and that Marcus was guiding him off the sofa and on to his feet.

At the top of the stairs, Liam tried to head to the playroom, but Marcus turned them toward his bedroom instead.

"I thought…" Liam whispered.

"You've done enough thinking for now," Marcus said. "Just let me take you forward from here."

Liam allowed Marcus to lead him into the master bedroom. He stood in the middle of the room alone while Marcus closed the door.

"I've wanted you since the first time you visited the hospital," Marcus whispered in Liam's ear as he stepped up behind him and reached for the hem of Liam's T-shirt.

Liam closed his eyes, relishing his master's words. He lifted his arms as Marcus pulled his T-shirt over his head. Clothing disappeared—and not just his own. Liam was vaguely aware of helping Marcus out of his torn shirt and paw stained trousers, but his mind was elsewhere, rushing forward to anticipate what would happen next.

Every cell in Liam's body sang out with pleasure, overjoyed that his mind finally seemed to have caught up with what his body had known for so long. He wanted his master. He wanted Marcus in a way he had never wanted anyone else, and now, finally, it was going to happen.

There was a strange kind of purity about Marcus's touch as his hands roved over Liam's naked body, caressing and inspecting each inch of him in turn. There was no bondage, no blood, there wasn't even sex at that moment. There was just them.

Liam took a deep breath. There was no fear either, no ulterior motive that required him to submit to whatever another man wanted to do with him. It was just them and there was no reason at all to remember how things were with anyone else.

Sitting down on the bed between Marcus's legs when prompted to do so, Liam allowed Marcus to guide him into leaning back against his chest.

As positions went, it wasn't going to be an easy one, but Liam couldn't bring himself to be worried about that. He was simply going to follow Marcus's lead and trust that his master would look after him. Another wave of pleasure raced through him with the idea, with the very possibility that he was still capable of doing such a thing.

Smiling to himself, Liam arched his back, rubbing his skin against Marcus's body, relishing the way the vampire's erection pressed against him. Marcus slid his hand around Liam's body and took hold of Liam's cock. As he slowly stroked, Marcus seemed to have no intention other than to offer pleasure and to enjoy the way Liam's erection felt in his hand.

Liam murmured his encouragement as he slid his hands over Marcus's arms, relishing the strength he felt in his master's muscles, but not feeling the need to try to control Marcus's movements in the least.

When Marcus reached out to his left, Liam leaned forward slightly and looked over his shoulder. He was just in time to see Marcus take a set of padded leather cuffs from the drawer by the side of the bed.

"I thought..." Liam trailed off.

"If you needed them to have sex with me, we'd have a problem. But if you just like them, if they make something you want to do even better, that's different," Marcus said.

Liam met his gaze over his shoulder. "I like them," he whispered.

Marcus pressed a kiss against the back of Liam's neck as he fastened the leather around Liam's right wrist.

Liam focused a little more accurately. Marcus hadn't taken one pair of cuffs from the drawer, he'd taken two. Half of the other pair was soon in place around Liam's left wrist.

Marcus wrapped his arms around Liam. A second later, he'd rolled them both over and Liam was trapped underneath Marcus, pinned to the bed. Instinctive pleasure rushed through him, screaming that this was exactly what he needed. It was impossible for Liam to do anything other than push his arse back against Marcus's crotch in encouragement.

Marcus pulled back a fraction, just far enough to be able to reach up and attach the free ends of each pair of cuffs to the rails on the bed frame. Liam's cock rubbed against the bed sheet beneath him as he squirmed up the mattress a few inches to make it even easier for his master to bind him that way.

"Perfect," Marcus whispered as he moved away a little and left Liam laying there all on his own.

Liam swallowed, sure that he wasn't anything of the sort, but loving Marcus for saying it anyway. Another dip into that same drawer by the side of the bed, and Marcus smeared lube onto his fingers. Liam shuffled his legs farther apart in anticipation.

Marcus's touch was incredibly gentle as he stroked the slick fluid against Liam's hole, circling the tight ring of muscle with his fingertips. Liam rocked his hips trying to push back and let Marcus know there was no need to be *that* careful with him.

"Patience," Marcus chided, but there was only amusement in his voice. There was no anger there.

Liam smiled into the pillow and closed his eyes, concentrating on memorising each sensation Marcus offered him. As he relaxed, Marcus's finger pressed against his hole, slipping inside him, before withdrawing.

Again and again, Marcus worked one finger inside him, before finally letting a second digit join in the fun and stretch him open a little further. "That's right," Marcus murmured.

Liam made an approving noise in the back of his throat, but he couldn't manage words right then. His entire brain was focused on analysing more pleasure than he'd ever known was possible. Marcus added another finger. They crooked inside him, stroking against Liam's prostate.

Gasping into the pillow, Liam jerked, pulling at his cuffs, thriving on the way they kept him still and helpless.

"Do you like that, Liam?"

Liam managed to rub his face into the pillow in something like a nod and Marcus seemed to understand that Liam loved it, even if Liam still couldn't make words happen.

Without any warning, Marcus's fingers disappeared. Liam lifted his head, looking over his shoulder, desperately trying to work out what he had done wrong and how to fix it.

The bed shifted as Marcus moved closer, until he lowered his body so it completely covered Liam's smaller frame.

Liam whimpered with relief as he felt Marcus's slicked cock slide between his buttocks. At the same time, Marcus dipped his head and nuzzled at Liam's neck. Liam quickly tilted his head, offering easier access to for Marcus to feed, but Marcus only kissed the skin covering the vein as he rocked his hips and let the tip of his cock rub against Liam's hole.

Liam's whimpers soon turned frustrated. He was on the edge of insanity when Marcus finally gave him one half of what he wanted. His teeth scraped against Liam's neck. Liam felt his blood seep through the wound.

Marcus groaned as he seemed to taste every bit of Liam's desire. Finally, just as Liam was sure he was going to lose his mind completely, Marcus pushed forward, burying his cock deep inside Liam's body in one slow, steady motion.

A moment of intense panic flashed through Liam as the memory of another man and another time tried to push its way to the forefront of his mind. Liam automatically tried to reach for his collar. The cuffs stopped his hands short.

"All mine," Marcus murmured in his ear.

Liam opened his eyes. Yes, he was all Marcus's. That was right. His body relaxed with the knowledge. He didn't need to feel the collar when Marcus was right there, when his master was literally inside him. Liam arched his back, offering himself ever more blatantly to Marcus.

"That's right," Marcus coaxed, rocking his hips slightly, letting Liam feel his cock move inside him, stretching him open, filling him completely.

Marcus lapped at his neck again. It wasn't a real bite, there was hardly any blood there, Liam knew that. Marcus was just tasting him, checking he was okay while he was too lost in his emotions to speak.

Mewing his satisfaction as best he could, Liam tugged

at the cuffs again as he tried to move in a way that might please his master. Marcus rocked his hips once more, then again. Slowly, he established a rhythm, pushing deep into Liam's arse over and over, until that rhythm was the only thing that existed in the world, until it was impossible to remember a time when Marcus hadn't been lodged deep inside him.

Liam lost himself in the waves of ecstasy that radiated through his body. There was no beginning to it, no end. He was adrift in the middle of an ocean, out of sight of all land. And he still knew he was safe. In that moment, nothing else mattered. The cuffs around his wrists, the collar around his neck — there was nothing more he could ask for from life.

"Come for me," Marcus whispered against his neck.

Perhaps it was more good timing than anything else, but the words seemed to go straight to Liam's cock.

One more hard thrust against his prostate, and Liam obeyed. As pure bliss exploded inside him, he felt Marcus's teeth sink into his neck. Marcus began to feed in earnest.

Time passed, but it had no meaning for Liam. It was something that happened to other people, people who weren't as lucky as he was. As pleasure very slowly began to fade away, Liam gradually became aware of other sensations.

Marcus was pulling away from him, cleaning them both up and undoing the cuffs. Through it all, Liam's mind floated on wave after wave of perfection. He just bobbed on that ocean's currents, trusting Marcus to steer them right.

By the time anything like a real thought process re-established itself inside his mind, Liam was curled up against Marcus's side, with Marcus's arm around him. "I don't want you to go to sleep," Liam whispered.

Marcus tensed. Any trace of sleepiness fled from his body as if chased by some kind of predator that could even scare a vampire. "What's wrong?"

Liam shook his head, rubbing his cheek against Marcus's chest with the motion. "Nothing's wrong, I just…I don't want you to go to sleep."

Liam was aware of Marcus frowning down at the top of his head, but he didn't lift his gaze.

"Sometimes, with Ralph, when I knew he was in a bad mood. If we... I knew he'd go to sleep straight after we had sex, so I'd suggest we..."

"Oh." Marcus didn't seem sure what else to say.

"But with you, it will never be because I want you to go to sleep," Liam whispered.

Marcus pulled away a little. Tucking a knuckle under his chin he made Liam look up and meet his gaze. "That might be the most beautiful thing I've ever heard any man say."

A blush came to Liam's cheeks, but for once it was one of happiness, not embarrassment. "It's true," he said with a little shrug before snuggling back into Marcus's side. He closed his eyes. Sleep claimed him almost immediately.

Chapter Fourteen

"We won't be dining alone tonight."

Liam glanced across the car at Marcus's profile. After an entire day spent chasing an insane collie who could run a hell of a lot faster than he could, Liam had been looking forward to doing nothing more than snuggling up with his master in the big double bed that he was finally coming to think of theirs instead of merely Marcus's. But, now, the idea of relaxing flew from Liam's mind.

He straightened up in his seat, giving Marcus his full attention.

"There are a couple of people I'd like you to meet with," Marcus went on as he changed gears.

"Vampires?" Liam asked, hardly daring to hope. "The ones you've been speaking to."

"No, there'll be plenty of time for you to meet them later," Marcus said, his eyes still firmly fixed on the road in front of him. "The people you'll be meeting tonight are more important than that."

Liam shifted slightly, shuffling his feet against the mat on the car's floor. "Okay?" he hazarded.

Marcus's hand came to rest on Liam's knee. "There's nothing to worry about. They're going to be thrilled to see you."

"Is it your family?" Liam guessed. A hand clamped down around his stomach at the prospect of meeting his master's parents. A wave of panic raced through him. He had no idea what kind of person they might have imagined Marcus ending up with, but he was pretty sure he wouldn't fit the bill.

It was going to be like when his parents met Ralph all over again, only this time—

Marcus let out a strange half-laugh that cut straight through every thought in Liam's head. "Vampires really aren't a family-orientated species in the same way humans are."

"Oh…" Strangely enough, that didn't make Liam feel any better. His hand went to his collar as he sought for reassurance. He studied Marcus's profile, but his master seemed determined not to look towards him, no matter how quiet the road was.

Marcus squeezed Liam's knee as if he wanted to reassure him, but he still didn't look in his direction. When Marcus had to take his hand back in order to turn into the driveway leading up to the house, Liam's leg quickly turned cold. A shiver ran down his spine.

The idea of curling up in their bed came back. Only this time, he just wanted to hide under the covers.

There was a car in the drive that Liam didn't recognise. It looked far more sensible than something Liam could imagine any of Marcus's friends driving. He frowned at it as if the vehicle might speak up and tell him what the hell was going on, but the car remained silent.

"They're here already?" Liam blurted out. He looked down at his clothes. The bottom two thirds of the trousers were still covered in collie hair. He probably smelled like a wet dog after the way the little bugger had soaked him when he finally caught it to bathe it.

A shower and a change of clothes suddenly became essential. A little while to talk himself into appearing calm, even if he was sure no amount of time in the world would allow him to actually *be* calm, was even more vital.

Marcus pulled to a stop and got out of the car. Liam tried to make his own limbs move, but they didn't want to obey his brain. It wasn't until Marcus turned chauffeur and walked around to open Liam's door that he managed to react.

Liam might have been completely incapable of getting out of the car on his own. But, it turned out that he was fully capable of putting his hand in his master's grip and allowing Marcus to guide him out of the low slung space and into the house.

"I'll just go up and..." Liam whispered as they stepped across the threshold.

At that moment, a voice floated through to Liam from one of the formal sitting rooms on the ground floor. He knew that voice. Liam looked up at Marcus. "I...I don't understand," he whispered.

Marcus said nothing, he just looked down at Liam, his eyes very serious. Liam stared up at him in return, really looking at him.

Marcus's shoulders were tense, his jaw clenched. He hadn't relaxed as they arrived home. Liam wasn't the only one who was nervous about the people they were about to meet.

That same voice floated through the hallway again. Liam looked over his shoulder. Unable to resist its allure, he cautiously crept closer to the door. Whoever had entered the room last, hadn't shut it tight behind them. Keeping out of sight as best he could, Liam peeked through the gap.

For a moment, all he was able to see was the back of Mr Jenson's coat as the butler walked past the door. Then, the view cleared.

Mr Jenson handed Mrs Jenson a drink. At any other time, Liam would have been shocked to see them sitting in that room. They had their quarters, and any suggestion that they relax anywhere else in the house would have been met by stern disapproval—from both of them, if no one else. But, right then, Liam didn't have any room left in his brain for any extra shock.

His gaze moved slowly over Jenny and Diana, but Liam barely paused to wonder what the hell they were doing there. He knew that voice and—

The breath rushed from Liam's lungs as his gaze fell on

the final two occupants of the sitting room. His mother and father sat next to each other on a small sofa. They had to have been beamed down there from some sort of alien spaceship. There was no other explanation.

His mother's grip on his father's hand was white knuckled.

"Mr Corrigan and Mr Bates will be home soon," Mr Jenson said. Liam dragged his attention away from his parents for long enough to see the encouraging look Mrs Jenson gave her husband.

The butler cleared his throat. "In the meantime, if I may make an observation?"

Every occupant of the room seemed to nod in sync.

"I'm sure you've heard enough horror stories about vampires and the way they've treated humans over the years. My wife and I practically raised Mr Corrigan. We're under no illusions about vampires in general or about him in particular. He's been as guilty of unwitting cruelty as any of them have in the past."

"We..." Liam saw his mother look toward his father. A moment of silent communication passed between them. "We're not looking to come between Liam and, and Mr—"

"And Marcus," Mrs Jenson cut in. "There's no need for formality."

"Between Liam and Marcus," his mother finished with a nod toward the other woman.

"It's only natural that you have concerns," Mr Jenson said, with a glance down at the glass in his hand. "If they'd met under different circumstances, I might even agree that they could have been warranted."

There was no way Liam could look away from the scene in the sitting room. He hung onto every word as if it were a tabloid drama playing out right in front of him.

"In other circumstances, my employer may well have used and discarded your son like he would have any other human. But, while Mr Corrigan was in his coma he had no choice but to listen to Mr Bates—to get to know him the way he's never really known another human, and learn to see him as something other than a blood supply."

Liam swayed closer to the gap in the door.

"He might never have fallen in love with Mr Bates under other circumstances," Mr Jenson added.

Liam forgot how to breathe. Words continued to flow on the other side of the door, but he could only give them half his attention.

"That's all very well, but if you'll excuse me saying so, talk is cheap," Liam's father cut in. "If he's so besotted with our son, it seems to me that he'd be the one who turned up on our doorstep, not his butler."

Mr Jenson smiled slightly. "At this point, Mr Corrigan's main concern is that you and your son have the best possible chance to rekindle your relationship. And, since he's well aware that he may well not make the best first impression, it seemed best to us that you met those who have had the benefit of seeing how he treats your son before you are actually introduced to him."

"Oh?" Liam had almost forgotten how sceptical his father was capable of sounding. If every muscle in his body wasn't frozen into place, he might have smiled at the memories the reminder raised inside him.

"Vampires don't share well," Mrs Jenson said. "Young Master Marcus would be quite content to keep them both locked up in this house and for Liam to never lay eyes on another human being. He didn't agree to Liam working at the animal shelter or meeting with you, for his own benefit. And after the way Ralph treated him, it might have been years before Liam felt healed enough to suggest contacting you himself."

Mr Jenson nodded as he took up the story again. "I think we can perhaps all agree that Mr Corrigan is doing the right thing by trying to heal the rift that Mr Bates's former partner created between you. However, he is still a vampire. I can't guarantee he'll succeed in pretending that he's enjoying it…"

"Liam?"

Liam took a step back. Tearing his eyes away from the view through the doorway, he turned toward Marcus.

Liam tilted his head back. His master had been standing right behind him.
Their eyes met, and Liam knew he wasn't the only one who had heard every word.

Liam swallowed several times in quick succession. Marcus held out a hand to him, his expression just as guarded as it was when he encountered one of the animals at the shelter. He didn't look scared as such, just very aware that he was facing a creature that could react to him in very unexpected ways. Liam took one step forward and suddenly he was in his master's embrace.

"I… Thank you." Liam wrapped his arms around Marcus's neck, hiding his face in his shoulder.

Marcus said nothing. He merely patted Liam on the back in that slightly awkward way he had.

"You don't mind?" Liam asked after a few moments, his words suddenly tumbling out faster than he could control them. "You said vampires aren't family people and—"

"That doesn't mean I don't want you to be," Marcus cut in, his tone allowing no room for argument. "A good master takes care of his pet. He doesn't let him lose touch with his family just because he had bad taste in men before they met."

Liam smiled against Marcus's shirt. "I meant what I said before. I really do love you," he whispered, unable to keep the words back.

"Yes," Marcus said, very simply.

Liam glanced up at him.

"And Jenson was right," Marcus said, the words soft and obviously intended for Liam's ears only. "I fell in love with you long before I ever managed to open my eyes." His tone was still very calm, as if there wasn't anything at all wondrous or magical about that fact, as if he wasn't giving Liam something more precious than he'd ever expected to receive.

Liam closed his eyes for a moment, just letting the fact sink in. Love. Not the poor mockery of the word that he'd shared with Ralph. The real thing. His head spun with the knowledge. How the hell was he ever going to live up to being the kind of man Marcus deserved?

Opening his eyes, Liam tilted his head back, offering his lips to be kissed as a tiny moment of uncertainty took hold inside him. Marcus didn't hesitate to give him that kiss—he didn't pretend it was about anything other than reassurance either.

Liam's smile was rueful when Marcus pulled away. "How come you were the one who was asleep for three years, and all you've done since waking up is sort out *my* life?" he asked. "I mean, I kiss you, you wake up, and you just get on with everything as if it's the easiest thing in the world, and I..." Liam shook his head at himself.

"My problem was comparatively simple," Marcus said. "One kiss was enough to solve it. But that doesn't mean one kiss is enough to wake everyone up or end every nightmare."

Liam blinked at him.

"What else would you call the time you spent with Ralph?" Marcus asked. "I might have been the only one who was asleep, but you had your own nightmare to deal with."

Liam looked down for a moment.

"That's okay," Marcus whispered to him. "One kiss doesn't need to be enough."

Liam swallowed rapidly, the world around him becoming embarrassingly misty.

"I'm not going anywhere," Marcus promised. "There'll be as many kisses as you need."

Tilting Liam's head back, Marcus dipped his head and brought their mouths together again. Liam sighed softly into the kiss as he woke up just a little bit more.

About the Author

Kim is a bisexual submissive from Wales (UK). First published in 2008, she has since released over 100 BDSM erotic romance titles ranging from short stories to full length novels. Having worked with a host of fantastic e-publishers, she moved into self publishing in 2013.

While she occasionally enjoys writing other pairings, most of Kim's stories focus on Male/Male relationships. But, no matter what the pairing, from paranormal to contemporary, and from the sweet to the intense, everything she writes will always feature three things - Kink, Love and a Happy Ending.

You can find out more about Kim's books on her website kimdare.com.

Also by Kim Dare

Series

Werewolves & Dragons
The Avian Shifters
Kinky Cupid
FIT Guys
Hearts and Handcuffs
Thrown to the Lions
Rawlings Men
Sex Sells
Sun, Sea and Submission
The Whole A-Z
Pack Discipline
G-A-Y Lust Bites
Perfect Timing
Collared
Pushing the Envelope

Kim has also written several free short stories.
You can find links to them on her website.

www.ingramcontent.com/pod-product-compliance
Lightning Source LLC
Chambersburg PA
CBHW030131180626
46812CB00002B/646